Full Share

ALSO BY
ELIZA FREED

The Lost Souls Series
Forgive Me
Redeem Me
Save Me

The Faraway Novels
The Devil's Playground
The Lion's Den

Short Stories
The Best Man
Finding Faith
The Dark Horse (an erotic short)

a Shore House novel

ELIZA FREED

Brunswick House
New York

Full Share
Copyright © 2016 by Eliza Freed
Excerpt from *Forgive Me* © 2015 by Eliza Freed

Edited by:
Rhonda Helms

Copyediting by:
Ashley Williams, AW Editing

Proofreading by:
Nichole Strauss, Perfectly Publishable

Interior Design and Formatting by:
Christine Borgford, Perfectly Publishable

Cover Design by:
Regina Wamba of MaeIDesign.com
Cover Copyright © 2015 by MaeIDesign
Cover Photo
EpicStockMedia, *shutterstock.com*

Brunswick House Publishing
244 Madison Avenue
New York, NY 10016
First Brunswick House ebook and print on demand edition: June 2016
The Brunswick House name and logo are trademarks of Brunswick House Publishing, LLC.
The publisher is not responsible for websites (or their content) that are not owned by the publisher.
Manufactured in the United States of America
ISBN 978-1-943622-04-7 (ebook edition)
ISBN 978-1-943622-05-4 (print on demand edition)

To those who know more darkness than light.
May you find peace on earth.

One

That Time My Mother had Sex on My Bed

IT'S NOT REALLY lying if no one's listening.

I wasn't brought up to be a liar. Character was discussed endlessly. Mine, my father's, my mother's, the building of . . . the irrevocable impact on a reputation poor character can have.

"Without character, you have nothing, Nora," my mother would say. I bought into all of it. Now I lie about everything.

I'm *always* fine.

Sometimes I'm also okay.

I love my job.

This is the first time I've been pulled over, officer.

I'm seeing someone.

I only smoke once a year.

I'm fluent in all Microsoft products, including Excel.

Your dick is huge.

I don't mind.

I don't miss my parents.

Value systems don't just spontaneously combust. They're destroyed, eroded by selfish choices of those we respect. Mine imploded on a Wednesday night my senior year of high school. Play practice was cancelled because a church bus hit a utility pole. No one was injured, but it took out the pole and the power to the school. My perfecting of Abigail Williams from *The Crucible* would have to wait.

John Proctor drove me home. He was a grade younger and spoke nervously the entire ride about his mother's new boyfriend, who had a gun in his car's glove compartment. When he pulled in my driveway, I wasn't sure whether to hug him or wave goodbye.

The black Trailblazer parked at my parents' house was familiar. The 26.2 circle on the back windshield reminded me of warm weather. I'd walked by it before but wasn't sure where. The vehicle was less odd than the pop music blaring from my bedroom. The house wasn't waiting for me to return. It was rocking.

Without a word, I walked into my room and out of my life.

My mother was on her forearms and knees, her head pointed toward the ceiling with her eyes closed. Her long hair, which she'd recently grown out from a mom haircut, was pulled back and held in the fist of the naked man riding her doggy style on my bed. The diamond pendant that always hung from her neck swung back and forth, hitting her chest with every thrust. The shirtless man looked up and winced at the sight of me.

You're fucking my mother and still only giving me a B in French?

Every word my mother had ever said to me formed a grotesque lump at the back of my throat. It was a powerful lesson in character. Followed by my mother seeing Mr. Durane out and begging me to not tell my father. It was also the moment I decided to disappear.

The next day, I quit the play. My understudy was the only one who was supportive. I quit my boyfriend of a year, too. He kept calling and texting, but how could I tell him my mother was a whore? That I was so filled with rage and betrayal that the only way to handle it was not to process it at all?

When his pleas to call him back began to sound logical, I threw my phone in the manmade lake in front of our school. I couldn't face him or anyone else, and I couldn't stand the sight of my mother.

I studied and kept the smile plastered on my face, and no one realized I wasn't really there.

Two

Every Place is Sexual

Five years later

"I DON'T UNDERSTAND how you got the time off," he said. "It's Memorial Day weekend." He didn't annoy me. I tolerated Ricky because, for some reason I couldn't even explain to myself, I liked him. Plus, he was chained to the phone in the cubicle next to the one I was shackled to. There was little else to do but endure him. "I'll be here most of the weekend." He smelled good, although I'd die before I admitted that to him. He thought highly enough of himself already. "Aren't you going to miss me?"

Most of the guys I got close to these days I met late night, at a bar, when no one smelled particularly good. Ricky always made an effort. Whether it was to come into the office or to crash a bachelorette party, Ricky was prepared to attract the opposite sex.

I stared at him with the blank expression of a woman who either didn't comprehend the language he was speaking or was dead inside. At times, both were true.

"No," I finally said, and he only laughed. In the ten months we'd been imprisoned at neighboring desks, I'd shunned his advances a thousand times, and each time he'd returned with a new compliment or sexual suggestion. We could do it upside down, in a tree, on the lawn, next to the bees. He was the Dr. Seuss of sex. He was impossible to offend and, unbelievably, attractive to most of my coworkers. He was also my only friend.

"I was watching porn in my car before I came in this morning, and there was a girl who reminded me of you."

Dead stare.

"Don't worry. She was totally hot."

"I wasn't worried."

Ricky leaned in farther to my cubicle. His hair was styled better than mine. "We could make sweet love together."

"You watch porn in the SafeOne Auto Insurance parking lot?" This morning I'd sat in my driver's seat with my eyes closed, wishing a tree would fall on my car and give me the perfect excuse for not working my shift. I'd hoped for a power outage or non-deadly natural disaster. Even the stomach flu.

"Most days. If you see me with my headphones on in the lunchroom . . ." Ricky shrugged as if this was obvious.

"You cannot watch porn in here. This is the least sexual place in the entire world."

"Every place is sexual. You just have to open your mind to it." Ricky's voice trailed off. "You should let me take you to lunch and we can have sex."

"We have thirty minutes for lunch."

"Good point. Let's have dinner."

"Can you move away from my desk before Sharon comes over and fires us?"

"She won't fire us."

"Why? Are you having sex with her?"

"Hell no! Ricky has standards. She'd probably poke my eye out with those earrings of hers."

Sharon's manager station was an enlarged cubicle with low walls that was perched in the center of our team. She could view all of us with a slight tilt of her head. Every day she wore a different pair of themed earrings. Like, every single day, a new pair. I couldn't even fathom where she stored them all. Squirrels in the fall—actually, one squirrel in her left ear and a nut in her right.

"I think Sharon is damaged." Ricky leaned against my cubicle wall as if we weren't being watched and timed and evaluated.

"Why? Because of the five-inch American flags hanging from her ear lobes?"

"I'm surprised they're not military coffins."

My brows furrowed at the image of both Sharon's ears and the soldiers we've lost. "Where does she even buy them?"

"I blame the internet."

Ricky sat down just as Sharon made her morning rounds. Like a guard banging her billy club along the bars of our cells, she lumbered along the carpet next to our line of cubicles, listening to our conversations and peering over our shoulders to make sure our output matched her expectations. I'd expected my first job to be entry-level and mind numbing. That would have been a step up from my reality.

I didn't lift my head. We weren't allowed to. There was no time for looking around. We could raise our eyes from the computer screen at our assigned break time. Until then, I'd keep working through the estimates, rental bills, scene photographs, and letters that popped up in the queues.

Ricky slipped a note onto my desk while Sharon was reapplying her fire-red lipstick in a small compact mirror. The note read, *If you want, I'll come to the beach with you this weekend. I'll help you carry in your mattress, and then we can sleep together on your little bed all weekend. You can sleep on top of me.*

I wrote back, *No, but thank you for letting me borrow your truck to get it down there. It's very kind.*

"Fuck kind," I heard Ricky grumble as he read the note. He crumbled it and threw it back over our cubicle wall. It hit me in the face right as I was telling an insured we wouldn't be paying his claim and that the four feet of water his nine-year-old Volkswagen Jetta was immersed in wasn't a covered loss on his policy.

I settled into my chair and prepared myself for the screams of damnation that were sure to come from the caller. I'd heard the response so many times I had a way of meditating through it. The harsh words and threats of battery couldn't penetrate the wall I'd erected years ago. I was the perfect claims adjuster.

Three

The Proper Way to Begin a Relationship

RICKY CAME TO my apartment before work and traded his truck for my car. He helped me tie down the twin mattress I'd bought, commenting several times how boring work was going to be without my being there. I dropped my backpack onto the passenger seat without responding. SafeOne Insurance would have to adjust Friday's auto claims without me. I needed to submit a claim for some floor space at a house by the sea.

The air conditioning was broken in Ricky's truck. I rode the hour and a half to Dewey Beach with the windows down and my hair blowing in my face. It wasn't until the final few miles where I hit bumper-to-bumper traffic that the heat lay in the truck cab like the foul smell of rotting fruit—the furry kind. There was nothing I wouldn't endure to avoid spending the summer with my mother.

We'd settled into a tolerable routine. I saw her on holidays and for dinner every other month. I thought we'd spend the rest of my life that way until my mother's desperate attempts to rebuild our family included a shore house rented for the summer. I was expected to spend every weekend from Memorial Day to Labor Day reconnecting and reliving my childhood along the coast in Cape May, New Jersey, but I'd left my childhood on the purple ruffles of my bedspread my French teacher had ridden her on.

"The house is enormous. We'll all have our own space," my mother said, but there wasn't a property large enough.

I passed the endless strips of outlets and restaurants and drove into Dewey, far away from the house my mother had rented for the summer. There wasn't an ounce of fear or nervousness in me. The beach house was less exciting than it was necessary. The driveway overflowed with cars. I parked behind the motorcycle on the lawn. I wasn't the only one seeking real estate. I eyed the twin mattress bungeed in the truck bed and pulled my backpack out of the cab.

This is it. This is my summer. At least, every weekend of it. I inhaled the ocean air in one deep breath and walked to the house.

"Nora, hey!" Heather said, surprised by my early arrival. She was smoking a cigarette in the front yard. Her cover-up was a plush white terry you'd only find in an expensive store. I'd have run my hand across the thick pile while it was on the hanger, but never have spent that much money on something to cover up. Heather's had a brown stain on the ruffle touching her upper thigh.

"Hi, Heather."

Her eyes darted around. She was jumpier than usual. Or maybe just high. It was hard to tell with Heather. We lived together for all four years of college, and the little I knew of her wasn't endearing, but it worked for us. Heather wasn't interested in a best friend, either. "Here. Let me help you with your bag." She smashed the remnants of her cigarette with her flip-flop and grabbed my backpack off my shoulder. She was barely taller than me, which was saying something, since by all standards I was short. She had the new cropped haircut that reminded me of the way she always used to tell me I should cut mine. We stepped through the front door and into the packed living room of the house. Admiring eyes stared at us from every corner of the room.

There were few variations in the muscular, shirtless torsos. All had shorts or bathing suits on, beer in their hands, and grins on their faces. Beyond the pack, my sight froze on Rob Holloway. The most gorgeous guy friend a girl could torture herself loving from afar.

"Nora!" He was hugging me before I had my fill of staring at him. He pulled me to his chest, and the hints of marijuana and coconut sunscreen lifted my nose to his neck. I didn't have to see him. I'd memorized his wandering hazel eyes and longish hair years ago. The feel of his arms surrounding me was forever engrained in my memory. Everything about Rob, from the guitar solos he played late at night to the way he said my name, was a magnetic force I fought against when I was near him.

"Would you let her go?" Heather teased as she hit Rob on the arm. She and Rob graduated from high school together and then met me at the University of Delaware. Every person in the shore house was from their hometown. I was the only outsider, which was perfect. I could hide out here for the summer.

"Sorry," Rob said, still beaming at me. "How have you been? Where have you been?"

"I've been good." I couldn't stop staring at him. He looked so happy to see me, almost like he loved me, too. Sort of. "Living the dream in Wilmington, Delaware."

"I'll show you your room," Heather interrupted and squirmed at the mention of *your room*. I dragged myself from Rob and followed her through the small living room and kitchen to an enclosed back porch with a twin mattress pushed against the wall.

The space on the other side of the porch was bare, presumably for my matching mattress in the back of Ricky's truck. "Sorry we're not together. Mila—you'll meet her later—begged me to share with her. She's not thrilled about the two half shares in her room and needs backup."

"Will this . . . room . . . be all mine?" The wood paneling covering the lower half of the walls unearthed memories of my grandmother's basement. The top halves of the walls were covered in slatted windows with cranks at the bottom. The air was thick with heat as the limited breeze from the kitchen window air conditioning unit fought to reach us.

"You're funny," Heather said as she placed my backpack on the floor. "Did you bring a bed?" I nodded, leaving the smile cemented to my face. "I'll get the guys to carry it in. You'll share this porch with two half shares. They can only come down one at a time." I peered through the window slats into the backyard. This wasn't even a room. It probably was only a patio at its inception, but it was still better than a summer with my mother. "Is that okay?"

"It's fine."

Heather looked at me, gauging my response.

"Really. I don't mind." The stifling hot porch was my safe haven until September.

"I told Rob you wouldn't. He said it wasn't fair. He doesn't know you at all."

It sounded like he had a better grasp on common human decency and me, but I wasn't about to linger on it. I needed this hot, old, exposed porch more than anyone else in the house.

Since my bedroom was basically a fish tank from the waist up, I changed in the bathroom. Rob introduced me to four guys and three other girls, and I forgot all of their names two seconds after hearing them. Two of the guys carried my mattress from the truck to the floor of my porch without ever putting their beers down in the process.

This will be fine. I lied, even to myself.

"HOW MANY PEOPLE are in the house?" I asked Rob on the way to the beach.

"Sixteen. Eight full shares and eight half shares." He said it as if it were a completely reasonable amount of people to crash in one house.

"Sixteen?"

"The half shares can't be here at the same time except holiday weekends. So next weekend there will only be twelve of us."

"Right. Twelve. Is there another bathroom I didn't see?"

"One upstairs and one downstairs, so don't wait until the last minute. We have an outside shower, too. God! There's nothing better than a beach house." Rob screamed into the air, ignoring everyone around us. "I love it!"

My oblivious father loved the idea of a beach house, too. He loved most of my mother's ideas. Poor guy. I'd considered telling him about her French lessons to avoid her all summer, but what would be *fine* about that? Instead, I'd called Heather and asked for a spot in her Dewey house. She gave me two options. A full share for twenty-two hundred dollars, or a half share for a thousand with no guaranteed bed and I'd only be allowed down every other weekend. I sent Heather the twenty-two hundred and told my mother I'd see her in the fall.

"This weekend's going to be crazy. I think our entire town's coming down." Rob was practically skipping as he spoke. He was having the perfect summer already.

"Great!" flew out of my mouth without the sarcastic ring in my head.

Rob slowed for a half step and studied me. "I'm glad you're

here, Nora. I never get to see you anymore. I miss you."

I stopped breathing for a few seconds. If Rob only knew how much I missed him. Four years he'd spent stopping by, dropping in, and passing out in my apartment. I could sit back and see everything I avoided in my own life in Rob. He was alive every second. He surrounded himself with laughter and excitement. He wouldn't be secluded by the mistakes of his mother or anyone else. It was Rob's life, and he was going to live it. There were nights I'd sip my beer and bask in the glow of his stardom.

Our feet sunk into the soft, hot sand as Rob and I climbed the dune. He pulled the sheet out of my arms as we descended toward the ocean, and I looked into the eyes of his girlfriend. The joy drained from her face as she recognized me. I knew exactly how she felt. Her presence deprived me of excitement, too. Blaire recovered almost instantly and waved to me.

It wasn't hard to understand what Rob saw in Blaire. Even from twenty feet away I could see her flawless body in her almost non-existent string bikini. She was long and lean and appeared to float weightlessly across the world. She had the body of a dancer, but as the universe could be cruel, she was rhythmless. Many a party at Delaware I spent in awe, watching Blaire fling herself in different directions, fighting the beat of the music. It was impossible to believe she wasn't perfect in every way, until the deejay arrived.

My arm rose and waved back as Rob spread out my beach sheet. He stepped to the side and motioned toward the magic carpet he'd laid out for me, right before he walked over to Blaire and kissed her neck until she forgot all about me. The sun went behind a cloud, and I forced myself to look away. I tried to forget that I'd been forgotten.

The largest person I'd ever been near, in any situation, paused next to my blanket. I'd met an ex-offensive tackle for the Philadelphia Eagles once, and this guy was bigger. My head tilted back to take in the whole of him. *Definitely over six-five.* He plopped down on my sheet, set down the white bakery box he'd been carrying, and waved his hand at the spot beside him, signaling for me to sit. Since I had no idea what was going on, I kneeled onto the sheet.

"I'm Thomas Kragler," he said and opened the lid to the box. "And these are filled with Boston crème."

I raised my eyebrows at the box. The smell of the donuts forced the sea breeze from my mind. "They're lovely?" I kind of asked, not knowing what else to say.

"What's your name?" He spoke slowly, as if training me in societal politeness.

"I'm Nora."

"Nora, I want you to eat a donut." I shook my head before he got the last syllable out. "I made them myself, and it's the proper way to begin this relationship." He was enormous, spread out across my sheet, and more comfortable than a family member before me. Just as though he'd known me my whole life and loved me every minute of it.

"Relationship?" I asked as I looked around to see if anyone else was listening. We were now surrounded by ten other housemates, not one of whom cared about us or Thomas' box of donuts.

"Yes. We're embarking on a summer adventure. Starting right now, we're going to be spending a lot of time together, and no matter what happens, we'll remember this the rest of our lives." Something about the way he laughed a little as he spoke made me smile. It broke through the absurdity of him perching himself here with me in the first place. "And I want you to call me Tank. Everyone else does."

I scanned the box of donuts and then my eyes found Tank again. He was waiting for me to bite. Waiting for me to begin our relationship. I reached in and picked the fattest donut in the box. "Thank you, Tank," I said right before taking a bite. He was pleased, and pleasing him had some appeal I couldn't place. If Thomas "Tank" Kragler wasn't happy in this world, why was there a world at all?

Tank took a donut and closed the box. He lay on his back and ate it, the chocolate sticking to his top lip. I took another bite of my own and stared out to the horizon. "You're pretty, you know?" he asked, and I stopped eating and shielded my eyes from the sun to see him better. "I'm not trying to pick you up. I just wondered if you knew. Most pretty girls know it. You seem a little lost in it."

"Lost in being pretty?" I laughed to make light of his question.

"Among other things," he said, and I stared out to sea. Tank dropped the subject and rolled over, turning his gaze toward the ocean as well. When I finished my donut, I laid down next to him. I closed my eyes and left him to the sunshine. I dreamed Rob and I were renting the house alone, and he was lying next to me instead of Tank. We walked back to the empty house, and he made love to me. It was perfect.

When I woke up, Heather was shaking out her towel, throwing sand in my face. Tank was nowhere to be found. The box of donuts was gone as well. In fact, almost everyone was gone. The sun dipped low over the dune; the air had cooled off. I thought how nice it would be to stay here alone with Rob.

But Rob couldn't stand to be alone. Most of his college visits had taken place when Blaire was otherwise occupied. Even when she was present, there had to be ten other people around to satisfy him. Intimacy was foreign to him. He was the party, in all its glory, and he owed it to his people to be present among them. His need for recognition was the cause of Blaire's unending misery. A hardship that was impossible to manage and a source of constant lingering doubt about her position in his life.

Rob's appetite for attention never bothered me. I wasn't supposed to be the center of his world. The very first night he'd slept in my dorm, while we ate cheese fries and drank from a bottle of

Jameson he'd stolen from his dad's house, he confessed he hated to be alone. When he fell asleep in my bed, I wondered which of us was worse off. The one who was terrified to be alone or the one who lived her entire life that way.

I couldn't dwell on that. Not then and not now. I pushed myself up and shook the sand off the sheet before climbing the dune back to the road. The house closest to the ocean was deserted. The windows were shut, the driveway was empty, and not a light shone from the rooms. It was beautiful and empty.

What a waste.

Ours was on the Bay side of Swedes Street, where there were no curbs or sidewalks. I cut across the grass and climbed the three brick stairs of the front stoop before opening the screeching screen door into the living room. There were bodies everywhere in different states of dress, or undress, depending on the individual's position in the shower line. Rob lounged on the love seat with Blaire draped across him, her eyes finding mine before the door slammed shut behind me.

"Blaire, you're up!" a guy called as he exited the bathroom wrapped in a towel, and Blaire's concern rested on me as if I'd steal Rob's affection while she conditioned her perfect hair. Rob didn't seem to notice either of us. Blaire's demotion to my equal struck a chord of sympathy in me.

"I should unpack," I said and smiled at her before exiting through the kitchen and onto the porch. The towel-draped guy from the bathroom was staring out the wall of windows when I walked in.

"Oh, hey," he said, turning to me with the easy smile of someone who generally liked people.

"Hey," I said dryly, demonstrating I was the opposite of him.

"I'm Jack Randall." He held out his hand, and I stared at it until he started laughing, and then I shook it.

"Are you one of the half shares?" I asked as he kept shaking my hand.

"No. I'm a full share, but twins were involved in my room, and you know how that goes."

"Sure." I had no idea what he was talking about.

"So, we're going to be together all summer." His eyes never left my hand as I took it back and returned it to my side. I felt as naked as he was standing before me still dripping. His chest and stomach were hard and already tan. He was at least eight inches taller than me, even without shoes. His comfortable nature made me uncomfortable immediately.

"Are you from Maryland, too?" I asked, running from the center of his attention.

"Of course. And you . . ." Jack dipped his head, waiting for something from me. I let my head follow his until I caught on that he wanted my name.

"Nora," I divulged.

"Nora." He nodded his head, pleased with the information. "Not a big sharer, are you, Nora?"

"I'm an open book." I laughed until I realized I was the only one who really got the joke. Jack watched me as if I'd been brought into the house solely for his enjoyment.

Without a word, he spun his finger in a circle asking me to turn around. I did as I was instructed and faced the windows. "So where are you from, Nora?" he asked. I could hear him moving about behind me.

"I live in Wilmington."

"And what do you do in Wilmington?"

I should have left the room when he'd first asked me to turn around. Now I was trapped by his nakedness. "I work at an insurance company. You?"

"I'm a teacher."

"Please tell me you're not a French teacher," I said before I could check myself.

His light laughter broke through my resentment of my mother that hadn't dissipated in five years. "Something against the French?"

"They're not our allies." I stared out the window at the beach towels strung across the clothes line.

"Well, you'll be happy to know I teach history. During the summer I work for a builder down here." A University of Vermont beach towel blew up and off the line.

"Can you build us some walls for our room?" I asked, and Jack came and stood in front of me, leaving mere inches between us. He was still shirtless and smelled clean. His easy smile promised a fresh start.

"I could, but I think it's going to get hot in here this summer." His smile disappeared. The look in his eyes stole my breath. I sunk deep into his stare and forgot to not care. "We might need the windows for air."

My eyes fell to his lips, and a chill danced across my hot skin.

Jack pushed the unruly strands of hair off my face and then reached behind me and gathered it all into a ponytail in his hand. He twisted it, his body even closer now with his arms up near my face, and pulled it around and rested it on my shoulder. "That's better."

I focused on breathing. He was right. It was so much better.

"Nora—" Rob started as he stepped onto the porch, surprised by Jack's and my proximity. He took a half second to scrutinize Jack and me before an annoyed expression replaced his usual carefree one. "You're up for the shower." His eyes darted from Jack to me again. "You should get in there while you can."

Jack was unaffected. He was enjoying the tension. Rob was never jealous. Certainly not of me, but not once had I let a guy close enough for anyone to be jealous. My mother predicted I'd act out sexually to rebel against her soiled authority, but I'd promised myself I'd never meet her expectations again. I was safe and careful and discerning. Three things that she was not. She'd taught me at an early age that sex had nothing to do with love.

"Thanks," I said to both of them and then grabbed my bath basket, towel, and a long dress for the night. I walked past Rob as satisfaction replaced displeasure in his eyes.

I showered faster than an inmate on her first day in prison. To free up the bathroom, I left my hair and makeup to do on my porch. I found my compact and propped it against the window. While kneeling on my mattress, I could see one square inch of my face at a time.

Jack was lying on his own mattress, shirtless. His eyes were closed, and I pretended he wasn't there. I assumed I'd spend most of my summer the same way.

The sounds of a beer pong game set up on the kitchen table burst onto our porch at different intervals, but Jack made no move to join the rest of our group. He just laid there looking fantastic. With one arm behind his head and his biceps in my face. Not really, but it felt that way. "Where did you grow up?"

"Huh?" I sighed. We were really going to do this conversation thing.

"You said you *live* in Wilmington. That's not where you're from?"

I silently cursed him for listening. "Pennsylvania."

"That wasn't so hard, was it?" Jack walked over and plopped himself on my mattress next to me. My makeup spilled from the insufficient bag that held it in the first place.

I placed the fallen eyeshadows in a stack on the window sill.

"What's your last name?"

I knew we'd come to this. My left eye stared back at me from the miniscule mirror in front of me. "Hargrove," fell from my lips.

"Nora Hargrove." He dragged out the last syllables of both my names. He was searching his mind for the reference. I thought there might be a chance, considering his age, that he wouldn't recognize the name. "Isn't that the woman who writes all the romance novels?"

"Yep." I dabbed the turquoise moon dust shadow over my eye the same way the woman who'd sold it to me had done.

"Is your mom a big fan?"

I laughed. I couldn't help myself. The idea of my mother reading a romance novel was absurd. Almost as absurd as me living months on a back porch to avoid her. "She'd never heard of her." I turned to Jack as the confusion set in.

"How could she not know?"

"My mother believes nonfiction is the only genre of books worth reading. She'd never heard of Nora Hargrove when she picked the name." I returned to the task of my eyeshadow. "I think on some buried level she still blames my father for the bitter irony."

Jack moved back so he was leaning against the half wall I had my compact set on. "And what about you? What do you think of romance novels?" He was really never going to stop. This conversation, or avoiding covering his chest with fabric.

"They're fine." I kept my voice light, hoping to end this exchange and all the future ones he might attempt.

Jack smiled and shook his head. He was annoyed with me, but not enough to leave me alone. Not yet. "What's your favorite part?" He raised his eyebrows, challenging me.

I searched for the answer that would end this conversation. "The beginning."

"You don't like the endings?"

"Don't they all end the same?" I asked, and Jack stared at me confused. "Happy?"

"Do you have something against happy endings?"

I rummaged through my memories for a happy ending. Some fairy tale connected to my existence.

Jack ran his fingers down the side of my face and pushed my wet hair off my neck. I inhaled deeply to bury the chill his touch left in its wake. "Feel that?"

I shook my head ever so slightly, and he smiled again.

"Maybe we should move the beds together." He was enjoying himself, and I was the wrong person to entertain himself with.

I found my mascara and applied it without peeking his way.

"It's going to be a long summer for you to have to deal with all this *tension* on our porch."

"And not for you?"

He stood and said, "I believe in happy endings," as he walked out of the room.

Four

It's Okay . . . We All Like Him

BY THE TIME we made it to the Starboard, there was a line. Besides having to pee, I knew the fresh air was preferable to being inside the packed bar on the first weekend of summer. Tank was bending down to step inside the doorway of the Starboard. He was at the front of our line and the first one in. The bouncers checked the IDs of the few half shares behind him, and they all disappeared inside. The rest of us waited for what seemed like an eternity.

Rob was only a few feet from me with Blaire practically stuck to his side. He waved his arms as he told a story to a few of the half shares next to them. The girls' skirts were short, but their attention spans were long, at least where Rob was concerned. They laughed when he directed them to and stayed quiet through the important parts.

Having witnessed Rob's effect on people for four straight years in college, it had finally lost its mystery to me. I'd accepted that he was a magnet, constantly connecting. He was the only person who made me believe I was okay. He could make a person believe anything. Even when he was wrong, I wanted him to be right. Rob was the sun the rest of us rotated around. Except for Blaire. She was adhered to the side of him.

Jack stood six people behind me. He was quiet and patient as he listened to two other guys talk about baseball. The way he crossed his arms over his chest brought him an air of maturity, but the tight fabric against his shoulders stole any compliments from my mind not related to his body. He glanced over and winked at me. Before I could act like I had no idea what he meant, he was engrossed back in his conversation.

A large group stumbled out of the bar, and finally, the rest of us were allowed in. While my housemates headed to the bartender, I found the bathroom and stood in line there, too. Heather walked up and tried to cut the line. The sweet girl behind us told her to "Fuck off" and to move her "Skinny ass to the back." I was then lucky enough to stand in front of her for the rest of my wait while Heather yelled obscenities like a child from the back of the line. She was belligerent and she was loud.

When I exited the bathroom, I walked in the opposite direction of her. Avoiding Heather was the only safe decision for the rest of the night. The first thing I learned after I met her was that there was always a time of the night when Heather switched from fun and outrageous to an all-out liability. She became impossible to talk to and even harder to reason with, which earned her the nickname Heather Hyde.

Tank waved at me over the mass of people between us. He held up a beer and beckoned me to him with a nod of his head.

I inched through the crowd. Bodies separated only by clothes surrounded me as I pushed one leg forward and then followed it with the rest of my body. A tall girl got in front of me, and I followed in her wake the last ten feet to Tank, who pulled me into a hug.

"Here." He took a step to the left, displaying an empty corner of the bar. "You stand by me."

"Thanks." I slipped into the open spot and was safely barricaded from the crowd by the enormous Thomas Kragler. I sipped my beer, happy to finally be settled amid the chaos of the bar. Our house was chaos; the bars were chaos. The only solace this summer would be the beach.

"It's too fucking crowded in here," one of my housemates said. I recognized him, but I didn't know his name, and based on the scowl covering his face, I was in no rush to introduce myself.

Tank kept smiling, bouncing to the music. He pretended the words had never been spoken, as if he could infect this miserable person with his own mood just by being near him.

"Stone, get me a beer," another housemate yelled over the people above me to the miserable oxen next to me. She stood out from everyone around her. Her olive skin heightened the drama of her ice-blue eyes. I'd never seen anyone in person with such striking features. If I'd seen her on the cover of a magazine, I would have sworn she was Photoshopped. I stared at her because I couldn't look away, and then she smiled so kindly I didn't even try to hide my gawking. Her chestnut hair hung down her chest and covered most of her halter top, making it appear she was walking around topless. She practically transformed the aged bar just with her presence.

Stone didn't hesitate before ordering another round at the girl's request. He didn't even roll his eyes. It wasn't like he smiled. I already knew that was out of the question. But his anger turned to a quiet absence when she moved closer to him. He was five-ten and almost as wide as he was tall. His chest was broader than two men standing shoulder to shoulder. Stone was a compact wall of muscle with an expression of disgust permanently attached to his face. I let my sight linger on him as he gingerly handed the beer over my head and took a sip of his own. The blue-eyed girl calmed him, and for that she calmed me, too.

Heather tripped between me and Tank. She was angry, or drunk. It was becoming difficult to discern between the two. Heather had little to be happy about, and yet, nothing to be concerned with all at the same time. I glanced past her to the door.

I searched for Rob in the crowd. I wanted him to rescue me from Hateful Heather the way he had a thousand times before. She rolled her eyes at me. My mere presence was pissing her off. It was definitely time to go. Heather huffed and shrugged, spilling her cranberry-doused drink down the front of the girl next to her. The yelling began. It was a series of demands of an apology and insults all slurred together, making both parties look ridiculous. Tank stepped between the girls and tried to end the discussion with his brilliant smile, but the victim's boyfriend became conscious of the situation and decided to get involved with some pushing.

Heather quietly stepped back from the turmoil she'd set in place. She was standing next to me and out of the way when Stone punched the girl's boyfriend in the face, starting an all-out brawl in the packed corner of the Starboard.

To say we were ushered out was putting it gently. Stone, who was still running his mouth, was thrown out onto his head. Heather and I were relocated to outside the door, but only because it was a toss between the police and an ambulance, and the bouncers didn't want to deal with the decision. Instead she was placed next to me with a stern word from the bouncer, suggesting she was now my problem to deal with.

I looked around for Tank. For help. Without hesitation, the blue-eyed brunette held one side of Heather up and waited for me to support the other. "I'm Mila, Mila Redd," she said, seeming completely sober.

"Nora." She didn't ask for my last name. I was in no mood. I probably would have lied. Nora Murvine, Nora Miles, Nora Monroe, whatever. Heather slumped over between us, and Mila picked up more of her weight as we practically carried her down the main street.

"Heather traded conversation for mixed drinks in eighth grade and never really returned," Mila said when we turned onto Swedes Street.

"You knew Heather in eighth grade?"

"Well, of course. We've all known each other that long. Stone, Rob, Heather and I have been together since kindergarten. We have the class pictures to prove it." Mila ignored Heather and happily basked in the memory of age five for a moment. "Tank, Jack, and Blaire joined our group in high school."

Heather fell to her knees. Mila and I caught her just before her face scraped the asphalt of the street.

"I'm worried about her," she continued. "I tried to tell her it was too much last month when she was hysterically crying after a bottle of tequila and a dozen pills, and that totally pissed her off. She hasn't been the same with me since."

"She's not into constructive feedback."

"No." Mila laughed, and I didn't say another word. Heather wasn't a good friend, but I never spoke of her or her excessive drinking to anyone. It hadn't been an issue in school. I didn't speak to anyone about anything of substance, because all roads of deep understanding always led me back to my mother, and *that* I wanted to forget. It should be the same way here. They all knew each other. *Talk among yourselves. Leave me alone.*

Mila and I dumped Heather on the chair before straightening and facing each other with looks of reciprocated gratefulness. Rob floated into the room, singing the latest insurance commercial at the top of his lungs. He turned it into a heavy metal rendition and then slowed it to a romantic chorus.

He jumped onto the couch for the finale and fell into a seated position with the air of a hawk settling onto a wire. Blaire came, handed him a beer, and nestled in beside him. Rob put his arm around her and pulled her close. It was as natural as breathing to him.

"You like him?" Mila's question startled me. I must have been staring.

I shook my head quickly. All denials should be swift. "No."

"It's okay. We all like him," she said and turned to watch Rob as he began singing a new song. This was the national anthem with electric guitar sounds in between the verses. "Just remember, you're too good for him. Poor Blaire forgot, and now look at her."

Blaire's eyes scanned the room as she sat perched next to her magnanimous boyfriend. He would always eclipse her. She'd spend her life trying to identify the next girl he'd love. It must've stolen her sleep every night she'd lain in bed next to him.

Rob loved her. Of that I was sure. He'd told me once. We'd drank too much and stumbled home to Heather's and my apartment because it was closer than his or Blaire's house. So much with Rob was locational, like a toddler whose playdates were scheduled based on convenience without regard for affinity. He'd said, "I love her. I really do. Life just feels unnecessarily long with her." I wasn't sure what he meant, but I'd wallowed in the disregard attached to it. I wanted him to choose me, but I'd never tell him that was an option.

"I'm glad to know you," Mila said and disappeared down the back hallway to the room she shared with at least three people this weekend.

When I glanced back into the living room, Blaire was staring at me.

"Good night," I said and made my way past the now raging beer pong game in the kitchen. I took off my shoes and makeup and dropped onto my mattress still wearing my dress. My pillow was only inches from the floor. The heat surrounded me. It was thicker than the hint of air blowing from the box fan perched on a wooden chair by the doorway.

Welcome to summer.

Five

Just Friends Forever

"I THINK WE should have sex in the shower." Ricky leaned into me at our lunch table. The cafeteria was packed today, and we were sitting with an entire shift that would leave in two minutes to return to their phones.

I kept eating as if Ricky hadn't spoken.

"Like, you can go in first, and I'll meet you in there after you're all wet." He bounced his eyebrows. It appeared he was imagining the entire scenario in great detail. "I could *wash* you." He was kind of a comedy skit. He forced me to acknowledge him with the threat that he'd never stop.

"I think we should be just friends forever."

"Please don't ever say that again."

Sharon walked into the cafeteria and sucked the joy from the room. Her gait was stilted by too-high heels that she could barely walk in. Her skirt was four inches shorter than appropriate, but her lipstick was perfectly intact. She smiled and laughed with the cafeteria staff as she paid for her lunch. The only thing more disturbing than *normal* Sharon was happy Sharon. Her laugh was too loud and felt darker than a theater the moment before a horror film began.

"She's a scary lady." Ricky shook his head and swirled his spoon in his chicken rice soup. We both watched as the broth circled the paper bowl. "I think she needs to have sex."

"You think everyone needs to have sex."

The guy sitting across from us glanced at the time on his phone and announced to the others that lunch was over. They stood, leaving Ricky and me sitting next to each other and staring out the windows. It was sunny out there in the place people could go who weren't given only thirty minutes to buy and eat their food and then use the bathroom before returning to their desks.

"You should have sex with me." He never stopped.

"I don't have sex."

"Yesterday, you told me you were a lesbian."

I'd forgotten. I smiled at myself. It was a good one. "I'm a sexless lesbian."

"Is that like a cell phone with a dead battery? What is the point?"

I pushed my tray a few inches away and leaned back in my chair. "You're like talking to a child."

"You don't mean that." Ricky leaned back, too. "How is your beach house? Are there a lot of beautiful lesbians in it?"

"Yes."

"You're lying again. You should invite me down. We can go for a swim, take a nap on the sand, and then make love in the moonlight. I'll bet everyone is having a lot of sex down there."

"I'm not sure."

"Of course they are. It's summer at the beach. It's a giant

party with sex. It's perfection."

"It wasn't really like that."

"In my country—"

"What country?" I sat up and looked at Ricky, who was smiling in the warm sunshine. "You're from West Chester, Pennsylvania. There is no 'my country.'"

"As I was saying, in my country we'd be making love at the shore."

I didn't want to check, but the time on my phone was calling me. I could feel my last seconds of freedom slipping away, and the thought of putting the headset back on my head dragged my spirits down. I reached for my phone, and Ricky grabbed my hand and stopped me.

"Not yet."

I closed my eyes again. "I don't want to be late."

"We won't. I promise," he said.

I DIDN'T HAVE to go back to the beach. I wanted to, and no one was more surprised by that fact than I was.

I ran out of my office building at four fifteen. My bag was already in the back of my car. My mind was already at the beach. Everyone would be cracking open a beer or riding the last waves of Saturday, making me one of the few stragglers racing there to catch Saturday night and Sunday day.

The steering wheel was warm to the touch, and the seatbelt buckle nearly burned me. It took my car ten minutes to cool off even with the air conditioner blasting, but by the time I pulled into the one stop I had to make, it was bearable. The animal shelter closed to visitors, even volunteers, at five on Saturday. Rufus wasn't going to like how the beach house affected our schedule.

"He's waiting for you," Janine said when I walked in the door.

"Sorry. I had to work today."

"Tell him that." Her smile put me at ease. Janine loved animals more than humans, and the longer I lived, the more I understood it.

I passed the other dogs as they barked at each other. A few stayed silent at the edges of their spaces, but most had something to say. Rufus, who was housed in the very last cage in the row, was huddled in the back corner. His chin lifted as soon as I sat down outside of it, but he didn't move an inch to greet me.

"Hey, buddy. How's it going? Have you made any friends?" His black fur was long. He was some unknown mix of a Collie, or Golden Retriever with a Black Labrador. He was beautiful and he was terrified. If he didn't find a way to engage with people, no one would ever adopt him. "I brought a new book for you."

The dog in the cage next to Rufus stuck his nose out and begged for attention. He'd be gone by the next week.

"It's *Scooby Doo and the Phantom Cowboy*." I looked back at Rufus, who'd returned his head to the ground but kept his eyes on me. "I mean, who doesn't love a cowboy?"

I read the book and stopped at each page to show Rufus the pictures. When I was almost to the end, Rufus stood and moved near me. He wasn't close enough to touch, but he was making an effort. I kept reading and when I said, "The end," he came and stood at the edge of the cage. I gave him a treat, and his tail wagged.

"I've got to go. I've got a beach house for the summer and I won't be able to come on Saturdays anymore, but I promise I'll be back." Rufus tilted his head as I spoke. "Be exactly like *this* when families come. You're the best dog here, and nobody knows it but me."

I stood up, and Rufus moved to the back of his cage and laid down again. I turned and walked out knowing if I didn't, I'd cry. If my landlord wouldn't evict me, I'd have brought Rufus home the first day I'd met him.

THE SUN WAS still high in the sky my entire trip down, and when I arrived at the house, half the people there were high in the sky as well. I opened the front door to a thick cloud. I waved my hand in front of my face, searching for some clean air.

"Nora." Rob's voice cut through the smoke. "You want a hit?"

"No. Thanks." I kept moving through the room. Four girls congregated around a pizza box in the kitchen. I thought they were half shares, but I was still far from knowing who everyone was in the house. "Hey. How's it going?" I asked as I slid past the only one I remembered. Her hair was cut into a pixie and her big brown eyes were unforgettable, unlike her name. I didn't wait for an answer before I stepped down into my porch.

The room, as well as the backyard, were empty. Everyone was inside getting ready to start the night. I leaned against the windows and stared at the empty picnic table in the center of the patch of grass we called our backyard.

Jack popped up in front of the screen door, and I jumped as he pulled it out toward him.

"Sorry." He laughed. "I didn't mean to scare you." He wore a gray suit and navy tie. My shock at the sight of him was replaced with admiration as I raked my eyes from his shoulders, down his arms, and then all the way to the dress shoes on his feet.

"You're so dressed up." The words stammered from my lips. I'd become accustomed to managing the effect his bare chest had on me. This was a new challenge.

"I had to go to a funeral."

"Oh. I'm sorry."

"Yeah. A teacher I worked with." Jack's expression turned serious. "He had a heart attack while tubing with his kids."

"Oh, man."

"I know. The funeral was really sad. He had eight-year-old twins." Jack's words were weighted down. "His wife's pregnant with twins again. Everyone at the service was a wreck."

"Oh my God."

Jack didn't move. I stood still, lost in the horror of his story. "I don't know why I'm telling you all this. Sorry."

Two eight-year-olds no longer had a dad, and I barely spoke to mine. I lowered my eyes and stared at the floor. I let in a hint of guilt regarding my denial of both my parents.

Jack took off his suit jacket and hung it on the hook on the side wall. "Where were you last night?" He was unbuttoning his dress shirt. I didn't look away. I welcomed the distraction from my mind.

"Um."

He pushed the shirt off his shoulders and then worked to unbutton the cuffs.

"I had to work."

"Last night?"

"No. Today. I have to work every other Saturday."

"Oh." Jack held out his arm to me, and I unbuttoned the cuff. "Thanks." When he held out the other arm, I did the same. Jack moved unbearably close, as if taunting me with his body. Which was ridiculous. What were we, fourteen? It was totally working, though. This summer was going to be impossible if he kept it up. "I was afraid you were going to tell me you have a boyfriend."

"Actually, I am seeing someone." I wasn't going to be the girl who had sex on the back porch of a summer rental. That sounded more like my mother's MO.

He leaned down until we were eye level. He brushed the hair away from my face and ran his fingertips down my cheek. When I realized I was holding my breath, I exhaled. "Who?" he asked, but I didn't know what he was talking about. "Who are you seeing?"

"Oh." I nodded my head in a trance. "Jackie." I wanted to

close my eyes and rest my face on his chest.

"Jackie?"

I sighed, frustrated that he was still asking questions. "Jackie . . . Robinson," I found inside my head.

Jack stopped caressing my neck. With a straight face, he asked, "As in Jackie Robinson, the first black baseball player to compete in the major league?"

I started to sweat. "Oh." I shook my head.

"Oh." He laughed and moved a few inches away from me, giving me room to think. "You know, you don't have to lie." His eyes were the color of the ocean just before the sun fully set. A deep mix of blue and gray. They almost made me believe him. "You're not easy to get to know, Nora."

"I know." I turned my back to Jack while he changed the rest of his clothes. My gaze fixed on the picnic table again.

"And now I find out you're not going to be here that much on the weekends."

"Well, on the off weeks, I get a three-day weekend."

"That's nice." He was so close behind me that I could feel his breath on my shoulders. "Does that mean you're going to be down here on Thursday nights? Or will you be stuck at home with Jackie?"

"I don't know. I haven't thought about it." I wasn't even sure I was allowed to be down here.

"Well, I'm going to think about it quite a bit. Do you want a beer?" He stepped back and walked toward the kitchen door.

I exhaled. "I'm good. I'm just going to change."

"I can't wait to see what you wear."

I thought of the taupe romper in my bag. It was cut low on the sides, but I was going to wear a tank under it. "It's pretty basic."

"I live for simplicity." Jack disappeared into the house, and I missed him immediately. He was beautiful to look at, but there was something even more appealing about him. It was an intangible quality that rested somewhere between making me feel safe and making me feel desired. I longed to be near him in spite of the fact that he always put me at the center of his attention. Jack didn't let me hide.

The screen door opened again, and Tank wandered in completely naked. He was enormous, yet walked into the room like an innocent child. He was a giant teddy bear with a large, flaccid penis dangling between his legs. The air caught in my throat.

"Hey, Nora!" He hugged me. His skin was still damp, and the scent of drugstore-brand soap permeated my nostrils.

My arms hung at my sides, leaving maximum energy for my brain to process the image of him naked.

"When did you get here?"

"I . . . I just got down."

Tank released me and stood with his hand on his waist in front of me as if one of us wasn't naked. "Perfect timing." He nodded. If he was waiting for me to say something, this was going to be even more awkward. I looked away. "We're going out to see Rob's friend's band. I think he might do a set with them."

"Awesome," I forced out and turned my gaze from the wall of windows to Tank.

"All right then. I've got to go find some clothes. Is that what you're wearing?" He pointed to the romper laying out on my bed.

"Yes."

"That's hot."

"You think?" It only felt hot if you were into the army surplus look.

"Oh, yeah. It's gonna be great with your green eyes."

I blushed at Tank's mention of my eye color.

"Do you have a necklace to wear with it?" The conversation was taking a strange turn, which was notable since Tank had no clothes on. *Maybe Tank's gay.*

I searched the pockets of my weekend bag and found a blue

arrowhead necklace that hung low on my chest. I laid it over the romper.

"Perfect." Tank moved the necklace around, and his naked arm touched mine in the process.

Tank left me alone, and I waited in line for the bathroom to change into my romper and officially begin my second weekend at the beach.

THE BARS WERE less crowded than the weekend before, which only made it easier to get the bartender's attention. The outfit had been a good choice because based on the amount we drank, someone in our house was being deployed the next day, or going to prison, or marrying an arranged suitor. Not one of us spoke a word of reason as shots were downed and intricate dance moves were performed. At least they seemed intricate in my head. The last thing I remembered was hating my bed for being so close to the sand-covered floor.

I didn't open my eyes when morning came. I wasn't sure I could. My mouth was dry, unbearably so. I reached up to the sill next to my bed and grabbed the bottle of water I'd left there. I unscrewed the cap and sat up to down it. The warm water sliding across my throat was like swallowing fire. Shots of Fireball and lemon drops cut through the pain.

This is the morning I deserve.

Jack stirred on his mattress across the porch. A slender leg slipped out from under his sheet. I visually traced it until the bedding hid the attached body and picked the image back up at a loose tank top twisted around Mila's breasts. She clung to the edge of the mattress. It appeared she'd slept with Jack, and they'd gotten into a fight, sending her to the farthest point away from him. Jack rolled again and encircled Mila with his arm. She moved closer to him and melted into an obviously familiar position.

My cheeks flushed. How did I not see they were together

before now, and why didn't they just share a room in the first place?

I stared at Jack's arm around Mila. The sight made me feel worse. My lip curled at the romantic picture across the floor from me, and I lowered my gaze to avoid it. It was ridiculous. I couldn't be jealous of Jack. He barely knew my name. He touched my hair. Once. *This* I had to stop.

I managed to stand. Once steady, I made my way to the bathroom with my toothbrush. The inside of my mouth needed some remediation. Because if the inside of your mouth hurt, you hurt. My mother had always said, "Take care of your eyes, your mouth, and your vagina. The rest will work itself out." She'd also said yes to my French teacher when he'd asked her to have sex with him, so whatever.

The house was asleep. The only sound was someone snoring from the second floor. A half share probably, because the noise was foreign. I knew so little of all these people, but I knew how they sounded when they slept and what type of beer they drank. I knew Stone was a breath away from a fight, and I thought there was one raging inside him at all times. Tank could light the world up like a fireworks display, and Mila made people stop and stare. Heather was the physical embodiment of anger. Jack was her opposite in every way. He was calm and strong, and Rob, my lovely Rob, could capture my attention by reading the Sunrise Restaurant's breakfast menu.

"Nora," Tank whispered as I stepped out of the bathroom.

"What are you doing up?"

"What are you doing up?" He mocked me and made me laugh.

"Shh." The pounding in my head increased.

"Let's go swimming."

I shook my head, still holding it. "No. I'm not well."

"You'll be fine. I promise."

I needed drugs, preferably some painkillers.

"I can't sleep," Tank pleaded.

He reminded me Mila was in Jack's bed. And I couldn't sleep either. "Okay. Give me a minute. I'll change, but I'm not swimming. My head is killing me."

"Meet you outside."

I nodded and slipped onto the back porch. I changed into my bathing suit, watching for movement from Jack the whole time. He was passed out. I was taking a chance he'd stay that way. I found my bottle of Advil in my bag, wincing as it played like a maraca as I tried to get just three pills out of it. One, four, fifteen. Finally, I managed to separate three from the rest and swallowed them with the dredges of water left in my bottle.

I stood up, and Jack opened his eyes. I felt like I should say something, but I didn't know what, or even why I felt that way. There was some strain in our non-existent relationship that I would have denied except for the way he was staring at me.

Whenever Heather had brought someone home in college, I just wanted the guy to leave. If they'd come home with her, I assumed they were bad news. But I liked Jack and I liked Mila. Still, their tangled bodies left me feeling alone.

Jack's expression stayed the same. He didn't smile. He didn't wink or make some funny face. He seemed disappointed in me for seeing them. I was disappointed in myself for not having a clue they were together. I left to meet Tank in the front yard.

Six

She was Just Lonely

ONE BY ONE, they dragged themselves to the beach. Stone carried a chair and a bottle of water. He forgot a towel. Rob was whistling, completely unaffected by his hangover, and Blaire was a mere inch from him at all times, as if she needed to share the air he breathed to exist. Mila came next. She carried a large bag and a chair. And finally, Jack arrived. His chair was rusted at the joint and creaked when he opened it and sat down. He pulled his hat low and opened the memoir on Truman he'd started reading the weekend before.

"Where's Heather?" Rob asked, and it was the first time I noticed she wasn't with us. I should have recognized the quiet calm her absence allowed.

"She was talking to a guy when I left her at Mama Celeste's. She said she was fine, and he bought her pizza." Mila shrugged, offering pizza as the great influencer of safety ratings.

She was always fine. Heather took care of Heather.

What a strange thought. I still viewed my former roommate—who was often too fucked up to know what was going on around her—as one of the most self-centered people on the earth. She held the spot right next to my mother.

In that moment, I realized why I never really fell in love with Heather. It wasn't that she was such a liability. She was too much like what I was running from. Maybe that was why I kept coming back. Heather was the perfect substitution. I lowered my head and closed my eyes. It was too sunny out to consider my mother.

"Text her," Tank said, stealing me from my internal therapy session.

Mila pulled her phone from her bag and texted Heather. "I'm sure she's fine," she said as she pressed the last few buttons and then rested her phone on her bathing suit bottoms.

Tank stood and surveyed the group of us. The wounded soldiers of our battalion. "You guys look like hell." Not a word was spoken from any of us. "Seriously, you're the walking dead. Let's go in the ocean. It'll heal you. It'll cure the injuries of last night."

"No way. I'll drown," Mila said, and lowered the back of her chair, ending her portion of the conversation.

"Come on!"

"I'll go in with you," I said but didn't move. My mind craved the ocean, but my body was revolting.

"All right! Let's go." Tank turned toward the ocean but noticed I was still settled comfortably in my chair. "Come on. Let's go," he repeated as he returned and held his hand out for me to take it.

I rested mine in his and let him pull me to my feet. He held it the entire walk to the water and then let it drop without a hint of significance. Tank and I were childhood friends who'd somehow just met.

"I saw you had a roommate last night," he said as we stopped and let the surf hit our feet.

"Ah, it's cold." I winced. "It's too cold to swim."

"It's the cold that'll make you feel better. You're hung over and foggy. Your body needs to be shocked. It needs to feel something." Tank shook his fists in the air.

"My body wants to go back to sleep. Now that my room's empty." I smiled at Tank, letting him know I didn't think of Mila as an intruder. "How did you know Mila stayed over?"

"I snuck into your room last night to ask you to smoke, but all three of you were passed out."

"Why weren't you passed out?"

"I couldn't sleep. My mind was racing."

"Do Mila and Jack hook up a lot?"

Tank took two more steps into the freezing water until it was to his knees. He waved me in with him, and I followed, certain that was as deep as I was going to go. "They have a history. They were the king and queen of the prom." Laughter shook my chest. "What's so funny?"

I stifled my reaction. "I don't know." I actually couldn't place the humor myself. "I just can't see Jack as the prom king." Part of his appeal to me was his seeming unawareness of how other people viewed him, or maybe he was aware and just didn't care. He never seemed to be fighting for attention. Prom king sounded like an honor Rob would campaign for, not Jack.

"It was a long time ago. I don't think he really cared. That's what happens when you're quarterback of the football team. The byproducts are unusual."

"Did they date?"

Tank walked deeper into the water, and I winced as I took another step into the frigid ocean. "One drunken night, Mila thought she was in love with him, but he cured her of it when he explained he didn't want a girlfriend."

"Oh." I dwelled on my own disappointment for a moment.

"We were all getting ready to leave for college. Mila was just scared to go. She needed an anchor to our hometown, which Jack was smart enough to see before the rest of us. He's always been the smart one." Fear of what Jack saw in me took my mind off the icy water for a moment. "He's an old soul. He sees things the way they're intended to be, not necessarily the way they've turned out."

I wanted to stop talking about what Jack saw. The beach house was my hideaway, not a place to be *seen* by the hot guy I was sharing a porch with. "Tank, I'm freezing."

"We've got to run in. This tiptoeing just makes it harder."

"No. I think I should get out."

"Don't give up, Nora. Let's go!" He ran into the next wave and dove before it crested above him, disappearing under the water. He finally came up for air, shaking his hair out of his eyes and smiling at me as though life had just been injected into every inch of his body.

He drew me to him. I was miserably cold but content as long as Tank was near me. I dove in, too, but came up wrapping my arms around my chest. My hard nipples rubbed against my arms, reminding me the water was too cold for swimming.

Tank dove into the water toward me and pulled me into a bear hug when he surfaced. My teeth chattered.

"Think warm thoughts," he said and rubbed my biceps.

"Maybe we could get out and think warm thoughts on the hot sand?"

He released me and dove under water again. He came up floating on his stomach with his head up, facing me. "Swimming is the human equivalent of flying." I just watched him as he turned over, rolling like a torpedo through the water. "Suspended above the earth, moving through space . . . it's amazing, don't you think?"

I'd taken swimming for granted.

Tank's smile infected me with enthusiasm. I dove into the

water and followed him deeper into the ocean.

"Do you realize there are some children who will never learn to swim? Never feel this?" Tank and I floated next to each other with our toes facing the sun. "They'll forever have their feet on the ground and never soar through time like you can do only in the water. It's tragic."

I lifted my head to see the face that had spoken such somber words. Tank's mood changed quicker than I could keep up. I was still marveling at the wonder of swimming, soaring through time, and now he was pulling me deep into the realization of our privilege and the divisions that displayed it.

"I need to get out," I said, and when Tank finally smiled again I caught the next wave to shore. I tightened my core and rode it until it died out in the shallow water. I straightened my bathing suit and stood. Tank was still floating on his back out past the breakers. It seemed the sun was only shining on him.

"YOU DRESSED?" JACK asked as he peeked onto our porch from the kitchen. I was buttoning my denim shorts. I'd just completed an eighties aerobics routine trying to exchange my tank top for my towel without all of Dewey seeing me through our walls of windows. "I'm collecting money for dinner." He stopped as a thought occurred to him. "Are you going to be here for dinner?"

I brushed my wet hair. It would be so much easier to shower and get ready to go out if I had my own room. Or a room. "Yes. How much do you need?"

"Everyone's putting in ten dollars. Tank and I are going to go shopping and grill."

I dropped the brush and searched through my bag for my wallet, which was painfully thin after last night. I took the remaining bills out and counted them. "How about nine dollars, and I won't eat that much?"

"Perfect." He took the money and put it with the stack already in his hand. "Any requests?"

"Nope. Whatever you make will be fine."

Jack just stared at me as though he hated the word "fine", which was ridiculous. "Of course." He still didn't leave. "I feel like I should say something about last night, or apologize maybe."

"Last night?" I tried to sound nonchalant.

"Yeah, the way you looked at me this morning. You seemed . . . uncomfortable with Mila in my bed."

I couldn't shake my head fast or hard enough. My hands flew up in front of me. My eyes partially closed. I was a poorly managed puppet. "Who you have sex with is none of my business."

"We didn't have sex."

Oh, God. More head shaking. *Please make this stop.* "Really. This conversation is the only uncomfortable part of Mila being in your bed." Jack half smiled and put me at ease. "Or should I say on your mattress, because we porch people aren't good enough for actual beds." Jack scanned the pathetic sleeping arrangements we shared. "Do you want me to switch rooms with Mila? Maybe give you guys some privacy?"

"No!" he practically yelled at me. "There's nothing going on between Mila and me. She was just lonely." I cringed at his words and then regretted sharing that with him. "Look, Mila has always been about the moment. She likes to *feel* things and experience sensations. She's going to go through life talking like she's high all the time." I took in his expression. He was being both critical and sweet at the same time. He could say the same things in front of Mila without a hint of criticism. "She was lonely and wanted a warm body to sleep next to. That's all last night was."

"What if she's lonely again?"

Jack stayed silent, and I tried to figure out what I was saying. More specifically, what I could say next to end this conversation. "Where's your phone?" he asked. I stared at him as if he were crazy. "I think we should exchange numbers." I raised my eyebrows at him. "And if either of us is going to have company, we can text and let the other know." I sighed, finally realizing this plan would make things less awkward. "Although, if it's Mila, there's no reason for you to avoid us. We're just friends."

I shook my head again and said, "None. Of. My. Business."

"Phone."

I unlocked it and handed Jack my phone. He dialed his own. We stayed looking at each other as it rang behind us. There was something about him that rose above the rest of this. Tank was right. He was an old soul. When the ringing stopped, Jack placed my phone in my hand, grabbed his, and left me standing alone in our screened-in porch.

"WHAT THE FUCK? Can these assholes play their music any louder?" was Stone's way of drawing our attention to the hip-hop anthems that had been our dinner music for the last two hours. The house behind us was nothing if not dedicated to the genre. "Seriously. If I go over there and kick their asses, maybe they'll turn it down."

"Would you calm down?" Jack said, and Stone stopped talking. "Seriously, it's the beach. It's happy hour. Be happy, man."

Stone took a swig of his beer and rubbed his temples. There was a storm brewing inside him. He left me tense in the same way Heather left me disappointed. They never did anything directly to me; just being in their presence had the overwhelming sense that what you thought might occur, would.

Mila stepped out of the back porch wearing a long navy sarong wrapped and tied above her chest in a way that made it appear like a well-constructed dress rather than one large square she'd whipped into shape. That was what she was wearing to drive back to the real world in. Some homegrown runway-worthy frock. Her hair was still damp from the shower and hung down her back perfectly.

I, on the other hand, had on a pair of cutoff jeans and a gray tank top with "Slightly Dark and Twisted" written on it. I was a black cloud next to the Saudi princess who'd recently flown in from Paris for a reading of some kind.

Mila stopped and rested her hand on Stone's shoulder. His face softened and he reached up and held her hand there. Just her touch soothed him, and her presence soothed me. She was pure light in a house sometimes filled with darkness.

Heather stepped into the backyard, still wearing the clothes she had on last night. Her hair was a mess, lying flat against her face, which was almost unrecognizable without her signature makeup.

"Well, well, well, look what the cat dragged in," Stone said, pleased with the topic.

"Fuck you, Stone," Heather said and picked up a kabob from the table. She bit into the chicken on the end and winced because it was too hot.

"Those just came off the grill," I said too softly for anyone to hear.

"How was last night?" Mila asked with a collusive voice. She knew before she'd left Heather at the pizza place exactly how last night was.

"Uneventful." Her words were drowning in sadness. She walked into the house through the porch that was my bedroom.

Rob sat on top of the picnic table right next to the food, assuming no one would mind. He played his guitar and sang, sometimes joining in with the hip-hop songs in the background and other times switching to some of his original compositions.

I recognized all of them. I stared as he shut his eyes when he sang the high notes and leaned back during the instrumentals. He was a born performer. His father had given him one year to explore "this band thing" and then he was required to report to his uncle's brokerage firm for an entry-level position. Since Rob took five years to graduate college with his communications degree, his year of exploration had just begun last month.

Blaire coughed. The noise stole my attention from Rob, and when I looked up, she was staring at me. She hated me. Couldn't say I blamed her.

Tank was grilling, wearing an apron that said "Kathy's Kitchen" over his boxer shorts, and when Heather walked past us to her car he yelled, "Hey! It's the fantastic eight." Everyone turned to him. I wasn't even sure what question was most prevalent in my mind. There was a lot going on in my vision. "The eight full shares in the house." Heather paused and examined us. Based on her glare, she hated every single one of us. "We're all here. You never know when that's going to be the case again. We should take a picture."

It should be every weekend, but I let Tank go on. He seemed to have a better grasp on the universe than I did. Tank stuck his head in the house and yelled for a half share to come out and take our picture.

Blaire rushed to sit next to Rob on the picnic table. Stone turned his chair around to face the camera. Mila and I leaned into Jack, and Tank put his arm around Heather, who stood with her arms crossed at her chest and hatred occupying her face. Tank looked like he'd never been happier with the tiny bit of horror wrapped in his arms. As soon as the picture was taken, Heather walked into the house without a word to any of us, and I followed her.

"Hey," I said when my three-step-behind-her stroll became weird.

Heather kept walking but turned around in her stride. "Yes."

"My work schedule has me working six days one week and four the next. It alternates."

"So?" Heather didn't waste either of our time acting like she cared.

I followed her into her room and watched as she took off her shirt and threw it on the floor next to her bed. She had on no bra, and a deep purple bruise—a hickey—covered the area above her left nipple. It was violent rather than sexual on Heather.

I made eye contact again. "So I was wondering if there's any problem with me being here some Thursday nights."

Heather took off her skirt and scraped a dried spot of sauce stuck to the hem. She wasn't wearing any underwear, and I was tired of being with my roommates without their clothes on. "No one will care, Nora." My name added on the end of her statement was said with the same tone as "you complete fucking dumbass."

"Great. Thanks." I turned to escape her presence.

"Oh," she said as she wrapped herself in a towel. "Do you remember Lionel Hall?"

"Lonnie?" He'd lived down the hall from us freshman year and was the kindest person I'd ever met. Lonnie existed only to make other people happy. He never once was in a bad mood. He'd hold the door open for you and say good morning before your eyes adjusted to the sunlight outside.

"Yeah." She stopped moving and looked me in the eye. "He's dead. Died in a car accident last week."

My breath lodged in my throat and choked me. I couldn't swallow. Heather picked up her shampoo and conditioner and passed me in the doorway of her room.

Heather wasn't just deteriorating. She was barely human.

Seven

The Beginning was Great

I TOOK MY bag and my half-gallon water bottle out of my car and tilted my head as I closed my car door. There wasn't a sound except the squeaking of the front screen door. The beach house was completely unlocked and, from what I could tell, abandoned. I left my water in the refrigerator and stepped past the box fan that was on a chair blocking the doorway from the kitchen into my porch and stopped short.

The bed—beds—took my breath away. On each side of the porch, there were beds Jack had made out of stacked pallets and painted the most perfect sky blue. He'd brought the sunshine into our dark-paneled porch. My mattress was not only off the floor, but it sat higher than a regular bed. I almost had to climb into it. I ran my hand across the quilt lying on top of it that never touched my skin because of the ever-present, stifling heat in our room.

"Do you like it?"

I inhaled sharply and turned to Jack, who was standing behind me. His feet were covered in sand, which no longer mattered since my bed was off the floor, and his sunglasses were still on.

"Let me guess. It's fine."

I turned back to the bed. It was so much more than fine. "I love it." Jack was stunned. Almost as much as I was. "Thank you." I rested my bag on my bed.

"I, ah . . . just got home from work a little while ago. I was going to go down to the beach if you want to come."

"Yeah," I replied.

Jack was just standing there, smiling at me and making me feel more comfortable than I did even alone in my own apartment.

"That sounds good. I just have to change," I added.

"Of course."

I left Jack standing by my bed and changed in the bathroom. The house was a different place without the rest of the people crammed into it. No yelling or loud music. There was no tension, no darkness. Only Jack, and he was peaceful.

I stood on my tiptoes to see my chest in the mirror and arranged my bathing suit, making sure everything that was supposed to be covered by the red bandeau top was. I left the bathroom and practically tripped over Rob's guitar and wished it was Rob here with me instead of Jack. I was ridiculous. Rob had a girlfriend. He was always going to have a girlfriend, and it was never going to be me. I gathered my clothes in my arms and returned to my bedroom where Jack was waiting for me.

"You ready?" he asked.

"Yes." Jack was holding a sheet and a bottle of wine. "Wine?"

"I think a half share brought it down last weekend." He read the bottle in his hand.

"Cabernet. Do you like wine?"

"Wine's fine. You're going to need to uncork it, though."

Jack pointed at me. "Smart."

We both searched the drawers for a bottle opener. I finally found one behind the butter door in the refrigerator. Because of course. I shook my head and handed it to Jack.

"Glasses?" he asked.

"I don't think we should take glass to the beach." The bottle was enough of a hazard. I searched for disposable cups.

"Good thinking. We'll share the bottle." Jack started toward the front door.

I grabbed my tank top and followed him.

"How was work today?" he asked as we waited for the traffic on Route 1.

"It's like we're married. Hi, honey. How was the office?" I mocked him.

"It should be like we're married. Maybe have sex after we put the kids to bed." It made perfect sense to him. I opened my mouth to tell him I'd taken a vow of abstinence when he said, "Don't bother lying." He stopped walking and stared at me. He'd never seemed so serious. Possibilities flew through my head. They all ended with me in Jack's bed instead of Mila. I was a high school girl in my mind. "It's Manifest Destiny." Jack took my hand, and we started walking toward the beach.

I gathered my thoughts and circled around the concept of Manifest Destiny. "As in I'm territory to be occupied in the name of God?"

"As in, it's inevitable. I haven't heard from Jesus himself. Yet."

We climbed the dune. The beach was nearly empty. The sky was a red hue that reflected off the ocean. The gray-turquoise water sent pink waves crashing to the sand. "Wow. It's beautiful out here."

"It's my favorite time of day. I come a lot during the week."

"Why don't we ever come at this time on the weekends?"

"Because there'd be no water left in the entire town if we didn't go back and shower early." I helped Jack spread out the sheet and sat down in the center. "I'm going for a swim. You want to come in?"

"No. I'm going to stay right here."

"Keep an eye on me. The guards left." The stand had been abandoned in the soft sand. It was after five.

"Afraid you'll drown?"

"The Coast Guard helicopter dropped divers in to save a guy last week, but he didn't make it."

"Here?"

"Right down the block. Undercurrents. They'll kill you. That's why it's best to keep things obvious." Jack turned around and ran into the ocean. He lifted his legs high above his knees when he reached the breakers and dove into the coming waves.

I didn't take my eyes off him. Fear gripped me. If the Coast Guard couldn't save someone, I doubted I could. I didn't even have my phone with me to call 911. I walked to the edge of the water and wanted him to come out.

He's fine. He's not going to die. I picked up three perfect shells and a broken one from the surf.

Jack dodged a couple of waves and then rode one to shore. Relief filled me when he finally stood next to me at the water's edge. "You coming in?"

"No. I want you to come out."

"Do you miss me?" He was grinning as if I'd told him I loved him.

"You scared me with all that talk of drowning. I can't save you."

Jack held me at the waist and rested his forehead on mine. "You could save me."

I was the one drowning. This was perfectly normal for Jack. A girl in his arms on the beach. His closeness was a shock to my entire system. Nothing about it was normal. "No, I can't." I stepped away from him and walked back to our sheet. I took a huge sip of the wine and sunk the bottle into the sand behind us.

Jack plopped down beside me, soaking wet and oblivious to how his closeness made me anxious. Or maybe completely aware and enjoying it. Either way, I was unnerved. "Look. We're going to be together."

I nodded. "Manifest Destiny. I heard."

"So now you know." He took a sip of the wine and handed me the bottle.

It was thick and I craved a glass of ice water. I drank more, hoping to douse the need, but it only made me thirstier.

"What you probably assumed, but can't be certain about, is it's going to be incredible." I laughed a little at him. "I'm serious." His voice steadied and was completely void of any humor. He wasn't the cocky cartoon character Ricky was. Jack was a man with the secret that I'd want him for the rest of my life if he had me just once.

I had a secret, too. I wasn't going to hook up with some guy I'd met at the beach, or in a bar, or my daughter's school.

"I'm going to make you forget your name."

"That would be great."

"You won't be able to remember what anyone else was like." I could feel my cheeks blushing. "Have you had a lot of lovers?" He was so incredibly likable.

"I stopped counting at eighty-nine."

Jack paused. He appeared disturbed until he took another sip of wine. Then he seemed like he didn't believe me. "I feel like we're wasting precious time." He smiled, placing the entire conversation within the gentle space of Jack Randall.

"Wasting time and missed opportunities are my hobbies."

"I'm not surprised." Jack stared out at the horizon. He was quiet, and I hoped this conversation was over. He rested back on the sheet and stared at the sky. I laid back, too. "Did your parents take you to the beach for vacation when you were young?"

The shore houses my parents had rented were some of my happiest memories. We'd go the same week every year, and some of the families in the surrounding houses came down the same week, too. It was a giant block-wide vacation. Those days seemed a lifetime ago. "Sometimes."

"Where else did you go?"

"We went to Disney World when I was little. My mother was aghast at the commercialism, so the next year we went to the Rainforest in Jamaica, but the political and economic depression appalled her there." I sighed. "Then we went to Paris. See how this is going?"

"Quite well, it sounds like to me. I had a few day trips to Ocean City, Maryland and once a summer we got to ride the rides. Was she satisfied in Paris?"

My mother was never satisfied. I stared at the sky and hated her. "She's a big fan of the French."

"But not you?"

"Can we talk about something else?"

Jack turned on his side and rested his head on his bent arm. "What do you want to talk about, Nora?"

I wanted to stop talking. Why did everyone in the world want to talk so much? Get to know one another . . . Couldn't we all just be near each other? Share an experience without delving into each other's fucked-up stories? I took a deep breath and asked, "Why did you make us beds?"

Jack froze, and I took some pleasure in finally finding a topic that made him uncomfortable. "I made the beds because I thought it would make you happy."

I rolled on my side and faced him. "Did I not seem happy?"

"Since the first minute you set foot in the house, you've looked like you might drive away and never come back."

I was surprised. The thought had never crossed my mind. And I was a runner.

"I thought maybe if you had a bed, you'd stay," he continued.

"I wasn't planning on going anywhere."

"Not yet."

The sun was low behind us. The moon rose over the ocean. Thursday was coming to an end. Jack and I stayed next to each other until darkness surrounded us.

"Are you hungry?" he asked.

I was content. There was nothing I needed in the world. I could lay there next to him until the end of time as long as he didn't ask me to have sex with him. I let myself off the hook of how fucked up that thought was. "I'm good."

Jack turned his head toward me. "That almost sounded sincere."

"It was." I let the wine warm me until my eyelids were a thousand pounds and I couldn't hold them open any longer. When consciousness became painful, I closed them and fell asleep next to my roommate.

MY EYES DIDN'T open again until the moon was high in the sky. The breeze blew the sheet I'd wrapped over my shoulders off me. I stayed still for a few seconds, trying to recollect where I was and how I'd gotten there. I was too groggy to be scared. I just was. But I wasn't sure who I was, or where I was. The first memory that came back was of him. My head rested atop his chest, and his arm was around my back.

"Jack?"

"I'm right here. I was just about to wake you up." He pulled me closer to him and I closed my eyes again, feeling safe in his arms. "We fell asleep."

That little moan escaped my lips. The sound you made when you were asleep just inside the gates of heaven and nothing would drag you out. Jack squeezed my shoulders and ran his lips across my temple. The touch of his lips pulled me from sleep and delivered me right to him.

"What time is it?" I asked.

"I don't know, but I think it's late. We should go back."

"But it's perfect here."

Jack ran his hand through my hair. He pushed it back off my shoulders with a light touch. "It is." He pulled me on top of him, and suddenly, I was awake.

I lifted my head and faced him. I let my legs fall to his sides and sat up, straddling him. I could do this tonight. I could do Jack. I stared into his eyes and thought he was thinking the same thing, but the possibility of Mila sleeping in his bed tomorrow stopped me. I leaned over to climb off him, and he grabbed me and pulled me back.

"What's wrong?"

"Nothing." I smiled to hide everything I was thinking and moved next to him. "I think we should go back, too."

"What happened?" Jack sat up next to me. His glare dove into me, opening me up and searching for the answers I'd never give him. "What changed in the last ten seconds?"

"Nothing. I swear. I just woke up." I stood and found my flip-flops. "Let's go back to the house." My heart pounded against my bathing suit top. The throbbing crept up my neck and lodged in my throat. He was confusing me, and I hated him for it. "I need to go back." Suddenly, the situation seemed urgent. He asked too many questions. He actually listened to the answers. He refused to let me hide and he was right here with me. I swallowed hard.

"Nora?" The moonlight shone on him. His beautiful chest was a stark contrast to the bewildered expression on his face.

"What? What do you want from me?"

"I want you."

"Why? Because you can't have me?"

"Is that what you think?" Jack stood and violently rolled the sheet into a ball. "You think you're some acquisition?"

"Aren't I? We're at the beach. Isn't everyone?"

"I don't know." He stood waiting for me to say something, but I had nothing to share. "Yeah. I guess. But that's not why I want you."

"You don't even know me."

"Whose fault is that?"

"Can we just go?" I pleaded with my eyes and the tone of my voice and the look of pure torture I knew was covering my face.

Jack stretched out his hand toward the dune, beckoning me to lead the way. He let out a frustrated sigh. "After you."

I walked forward through the soft sand, taking deep breaths with every stride. By the time we reached our porch, I regretted every word that had come out of my mouth, including the initial acceptance of his offer to go to the beach. He was my roommate. I wasn't going to have sex with him or anyone else in this house. I dropped my shells in the pile at the end of my bed with all the broken ones I'd found before.

I locked myself in the bathroom and tried to sort through my feelings. It wasn't as easy as usual. They were layered on top of each other, and their uneven edges couldn't be piled together perfectly. The people here were driving me crazy.

When I returned to our room, he was gone. I was alone again. I laid down on my bed and let my feet hang over the edge. I heard the outside shower and knew he was in it. He didn't sing at the top of his lungs the way Rob would have. He was just there, and I knew it because he was Jack.

The water turned off. I waited for him to return. I wanted him near me. I shut my eyes and tried to fall asleep, but the thought of him wouldn't allow any peace in my mind. Maybe he wasn't coming back. Maybe he slept in another room during the week. Maybe he hated me.

The back door creaked, and my eyes shot open. Jack walked in wearing only a towel, and I stared at him like some lovesick puppy. I couldn't look away.

Jack smiled and put me at ease. "What time is it?"

"A little after four," I told him.

"I have to get up for work tomorrow."

"I'm sorry I fell asleep on the beach. I was exhausted from adjusting insurance claims all day." I exaggerated it, knowing my desk job was nothing compared to the physical exertion Jack had every day at work.

"How is that? Claims?"

"It's okay." He stopped smiling. He was sick of my vague answers. "You've got a nice life down here all summer."

"It gets a little lonely." Jack pulled on a pair of underwear and dropped his towel on the floor. He ran his hands through his hair and hung the towel on the hook at the end of his bed. The slats of pallet caught my eye. I was thankful not to be at sea level.

"Jack, thanks for the bed. I love it."

Jack lifted my sheet and slid in my bed next to me. He rolled on his side, and I did the same. My back was to him. Every inch of me was touched by Jack. He was warm from the shower, but I didn't mind. "Someday, you'll tell me all the things you're running from," he said and rested his chin on my head. "But until then we can just be friends if that's what you need."

I wasn't sure what I needed, but his words made me feel nothing but love for him. "Thanks."

"To start," he said and pulled me tighter against his body.

"Of course."

That night, I fell asleep with Jack in my bed and I knew I'd want him there every night after it. I also knew he'd sleep in other girls' beds, and that the touch of him meant something completely different to me than to him. I was his conquest. Unsettled land of the west. He was my warmth.

I COULD BARELY open my eyes to say good bye when Jack's

alarm sounded at six in the morning, and I fell back to sleep before he even left my bed. I dreamed we were driving cross country, and he kept introducing me to strangers as Mrs. Randall, or the missus.

A slight breeze flowed through the windows and skipped over my skin. Air had been forsaken us while we'd huddled on the floor. My phone rang. It was lying next to me on the windowsill with my car keys. The caller ID read *Therapy*, my code name for my mother. As in, I'd need therapy from having her as my mother. "Hello."

"Hello, darling." It was roaring '20s actress accent time. "What are you doing? Where *are* you? *When* are you coming to see us at the shore?"

I waited for her to take a breath. Surely, she wore on herself as much as she did the rest of the world. "I don't know, Mom. I'm at my shore house."

"But your father and I miss you. He hasn't been feeling well, you know. He could use a visit to cheer him up."

"What's wrong with him?"

"Colitis. We think. He hates to go to the doctor, so I'm left with WebMD and the years I spent at grad school to diagnose him."

"Maybe he's just exhausted."

My mother's chatter stopped. She knew what I meant, that maybe he was sick of her shit. Even if I couldn't stand her, she knew me better than anyone.

"I'll call him."

"When?" She'd lost her theatrical tone.

"Maybe tomorrow on my way home."

"You can't call while you're driving. Seriously, Nora. Has working auto claims taught you nothing?"

"Okay." Hearing from her was worse than missing her. My mother should stay in a constant state of absence. It was our only hope. "I've got to go."

"Pick a weekend to come down. You can bring someone with you. Maybe a boyfriend."

"Good bye, Mom." I hung up the phone and stared at the stains on the ceiling above me.

Two deep breaths . . .

She couldn't bother me from another state. She didn't have that much control over my emotions. I controlled them.

I wandered through the quiet house. The living room seemed twice as big without the dozen bodies that usually inhabited it. Shoes littered every corner of the room, and beach towels hung from the back of every chair. A bookcase with only two shelves sat below the living room window, filled with old books. It was like the free books bin at the library. I ran my finger over the spines, absorbing the titles and the colors of each until *The Commander's Capture* stole my attention. Its author was Nora Hargrove.

"Unbelievable."

I carried my selection back to my porch. By the third page I was asleep with the book lying next to me on the most wonderful bed a girl had ever slept in.

The beginning was great.

Eight

When it Rains, Things Slow Down

"YOU NEED TO get your shit together," Stone said, and thank God he wasn't talking to me, because just the tone of his voice scared me a little.

"Whatever, Stone." Heather slurred through his name. I could see her propping herself against the kitchen counter. Stone grunted and huffed away. Or maybe that was how he walked. He settled into the last open seat on the couch.

It was raining out, trapping us all together in our over-occupied cottage and robbing some of their civility. Stone and Heather weren't made for small spaces. She tripped on her way through the living room.

"Keep drinking," Stone said without moving an inch to help her.

I leaned down and extended a hand to her, which Heather sneered at and walked away.

"Man, she's drunk early," Mila said. Her voice was full of worry.

"Is that drunk?" It was a valid question. Could she have consumed enough alcohol by six thirty to make her incapable of speech or walking? I'd only seen her with one beer in her hand. She was on something; I just wasn't sure what.

A few minutes with Heather made me crave solitude. I followed the sound of the rain hitting the porch windows to my bedroom where Tank was lying in my bed. He was so comfortable it appeared it was actually his and I just stored my things near it.

I climbed on next to him and laid down too, feet-to-head, head-to-feet. "What are you doing in here?"

"I'm bored. I was going to smoke and wanted to see if you did, too."

"Why didn't you just ask me?"

"I was in no rush. Time doesn't seem to move when it's raining. The world flies by in the bright sunshine, but when it rains, things slow down." Tank rolled on his side and lit the bowl in his hand.

I reached over him and cranked the windows open a half inch. Without a word, he handed me the bowl. I loved this version of him. He was peaceful. The gentle kindness flowed from him and covered me on top of my quilt.

We passed the bowl back and forth until Tank rested it on the window sill by my pillow. I stared at the ceiling. It amazed me it wasn't leaking. Not one drop entered the porch.

"Tell me something," he said.

"What?"

"Anything."

I believed he meant anything. The first thing that popped in my mind was Jack, so I skipped to the second thing. "I hate my job." Until that moment, I hadn't let myself grasp the depth of my disdain for it. It was as if Ricky and I'd been arrested for underage drinking and our claim rep jobs were the community service we were sentenced to complete. Not once had I considered it, or Sharon, a real part of my life. It just was. Like me.

"You should quit." His words were definitive. It was obvious to him.

The rain drove harder, and I looked to Jack's empty bed. I hadn't seen him since he'd left for work. Wherever he was, I hoped he wasn't on his bike.

"Where's Jack?" I asked. My throat was dry and my voice sounded rough.

"Don't know. What do you want to do?"

"Right now?" I couldn't imagine doing a single thing besides lying in my bed.

"No. Instead of your job."

"Oh." I was too busy enduring my job to consider a new one. I was void of passion. I'd spent the years in college hiding from myself rather than finding myself.

"There must be something. Kids, animals, books, the outdoors . . . what do you love?"

His certainty made me nervous. My complete failure as a human being was bubbling to the surface. Rufus understood. Being alone was less terrifying than being with some of the people who you were supposed to love.

Lightning blinked through the room, and I braced myself for the thunder. I jumped from the initial clap and slowly exhaled as the rumble continued. The storm must have been directly above us. "Can we talk about something else?"

"Close your eyes. I'll tell you something." Tank turned in the bed, making it easier to hear him over the storm raging around us. He lifted his arm over my head, and I rested on his shoulder. Us lying together was the most natural thing in the world. "There are, like, seven billion people on Earth. Three hundred million of them just in the United States. And out of all them, in an old cottage in a beach town just one mile long, you and I met two weeks ago."

I opened my eyes as Tank's free arm waved across the air in front of our faces.

"Just two tiny humans, spinning on a sphere, circling the sun, aligned with eight other planets, and holding down our own as a galaxy in the universe. You weren't living in Brazil. I wasn't backpacking in Colorado. You hadn't been sold into the child sex trade." I shook that from my head. "I hadn't been born to a crack head who never let me go outside." The rain drummed, not caring if Tank was speaking. "We're mere specks, and yet it all means so much."

The idea that our interactions, regardless of how small, were a purposeful part of our existence, lodged in my mind. If Tank and I meeting meant something, the depth of my other connections was inexplicable. It left me with one thought—my mother was my mother for a reason. I was overwhelmed by it.

"That's deep," I said.

He leaned his head down to mine. "That's life."

Nine

You Can't Fly Unless You Believe You Can

"SIR, I UNDERSTAND your frustration."

"Bullshit. You don't understand anything."

Hang up, Ricky mouthed from over my cubicle wall. *Just hang up.*

I can't hang up, I mouthed back and rolled my eyes.

"For the tenth time. And I mean tenth, maybe even the eleventh time, I'm going to tell you how stupid you guys are," Mr. Watkins said.

I paused for a second. "Thank you."

"My agent just informed me that you're going to pay the claim of the imbecile who hit me, and now my rates are going to go up."

I maneuvered through the computer screens, trying to catch up on the investigation. The claim had been paid and closed. "Mr. Watkins, it appears from the notes in your file that the decision was made to pay the claim based on the police report and witness statements."

"What police report?" he screamed into the phone. "That fucking car hit me in my driver's side door. He nearly killed me."

"According to this police report, he had the right of way."

"That's bullshit! I could have been killed." I kept reading. "That accident was not my fault, and that damn cop wouldn't believe me."

"Sir, it says here that you were ticketed for driving under the influence at the accident scene." For the first time in our conversation, Mr. Watkins was silent. "Sir?" I could hear him breathing. "Sir, are you still there?"

"No," he said, and when the following silence became too awkward, I hung up.

"You okay?" Ricky asked.

"Why do I get these people?" I kept typing. "And how does someone not *know* they've gotten a DUI? Like, is he drunk now?"

"You get them because you're the best at handling them. He's having a bad day. I would have hung up on him, but you . . . you were nice to him. That's why the universe sent him to you." Ricky was unusually enlightened today.

"Did you smoke at lunch?"

"No." He stood up straight. "I fucked a yoga instructor last night, and she made me meditate with her before work this morning."

"Oh, how nice."

He nodded. "She's very flexible." He stared at the ceiling with satisfaction covering his face.

"Ricky, have you ever just slept with a close friend?"

Ricky perked up. "You want to sleep with me?"

I shook my head. "No."

"This is how it starts. First we sleep together and then we"—he bounced his eyebrows—"Sleep together."

"You're not understanding me. Like, if we were friends for, say . . ." I calculated Mila and Jack's acquaintance in my head, "nine years. Do you think we'd ever sleep in the same bed together but not have sex?"

I could tell by the look on his face I was confusing him.

Sharon cleared her throat and glared at us.

Ricky smiled at her and said, "We should discuss this in bed."

Ricky was my sanity. He kept the job from becoming real. "Do you ever think about the fact that in all the offices of all the world, you and I sit next to each other in this one?"

He lowered his brow and let his mouth hang open. His head tilted as if he needed to hear me better. "Are you guys eating shrooms at that beach house? What the hell has gotten into you?"

"Like, it's all a huge master plan that we were meant to be together here, in this specific situation."

He nodded his head as if he were catching on. "Okay. If I actually let myself think this horrible job was part of a master plan for Ricky, I'd drown myself in liquor until this life ended."

"So, no?" I shook my head.

"No." Ricky turned and sat down at his desk.

I still believed in Tank's theory. Ricky was ridiculous, but he wasn't random.

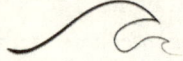

RUFUS WOULDN'T COME to the edge of the cage. Not even after I read Scooby Doo to him twice. His big, sad eyes just stared at me from the back wall.

"I know what you're thinking. That you're better off alone. But you've got to trust me on this."

His head tilted to the side, and then he rolled over until I couldn't see his face anymore.

We were moving in the wrong direction.

On my way out, I stopped to talk to Janine. "I'm worried about Rufus. He's worse than ever."

She shook her head. "He didn't eat this morning. I'll have the vet check him out when he's in this afternoon."

I glanced back toward the dog room. "Okay. I'll see you Monday." I wasn't sure I should leave.

"See you." Janine patted my shoulder as if she'd read my mind.

"Call me if he gets worse?"

"You got it." She smiled at me. She knew how much I loved him. Now, if I could just get him to believe it.

Rufus stayed on my mind the entire drive to Dewey. When I stopped at the last traffic light before our street, I thought of my housemates. They were either at the beach or in bed. Some of them would be in bed together. Last night was the second Friday night I'd missed since the summer began. My seven to three fifteen shift on the phone today had kept me home. Making this also the second Saturday I hadn't woken up with cotton mouth and dry eyes.

My car just fit into the last parking spot on our lawn. Technically, it was on our neighbor's lawn, too, but I hoped they'd let me slide since I was just arriving, and they'd already had an entire day of fun.

"Why did you invite her?" Blaire's shrill voice carried onto the front lawn from inside the house. It sounded like she might cry. It sounded familiar.

"What's the big deal? She's meeting us at a bar. It's not like I invited her to a wedding. She's my sister's best friend."

"That you fucked!" A door slammed inside the house and followed the noise of their latest fight into the driveway. "You left that part out. 'She's my sister's best friend *that I fucked*'. That's the big deal."

"You're ridiculous. We were fifteen and on a ski trip."

"No, you're ridiculous. You never consider me." Blaire would wait the rest of her life for that. Yes, he loved her. He just didn't want her to come before himself.

I stopped next to my car, unwilling to move my feet forward toward the house. What if no one else was in there? What if I was trapped inside with them?

Stone came around the side of the house, shaking his head and carrying a beer. "Here." He handed the bottle to me. "They are a *fucking* nightmare." I took a sip of the beer. A long one. "Like, literally. They're fucking each other, and they give me nightmares." He leaned back against the quarter panel of my car. "Why are you just getting down?"

"I had to work."

"Ew. Gross. Sorry." He stood straight and turned toward the house. "You coming in?"

"Fuck you, Rob!" Blaire's shriek could shut down happy hour within a two-block radius.

Stone turned around and came back to me. He took the beer from my hand and finished it. "On second thought, let's just go out."

My choices were limited. Try my luck with Rob and Blaire, who were hitting a new level of screaming, or Stone, who was always one beer away from being a complete prick.

"I promise I'll be good." He stood very still. He was calm and serene and appeared sincere.

"No fighting."

He held both hands up. "Promise."

I looked at Stone and back at my car. I took a deep breath. This was a mistake.

"You're smothering me!" Rob yelled at Blaire before another door slammed.

"Okay." I unlocked my car and threw my bag back into it, letting it fall to the floor of the back seat before relocking the car. I put my small cross body bag over my head.

Stone smiled. Not kindly. More like he was satisfied that I'd finally figured out he was smarter than me and had let him make the decision. He was smug. I preferred it to him being angry. "Why is there a Scooby Doo book in the back of your car?"

I wasn't used to sharing Rufus with anyone, but now that Stone had asked, I wasn't sure why. "Why do you care what's in the back of my car?"

"Okay." He walked toward the curb, and I followed him.

Tank and Jack were walking back to the house barefoot with boogie boards under their arms and towels around their necks. They were joy and happiness. I was out with the heat miser. This weekend already made no sense. The only thing I knew for sure was that I didn't want to be anywhere near Blaire. I hoped the fight escalated to the point of her going home, and then Rob could come out and party solo. That never happened though. Blaire's tolerance for annoying arguments and wasted time was higher than any other human being I'd ever met. She'd rather ruin her own night and be present than salvage it and be away from him.

"Hey! Where you guys going?" Tank asked with a huge grin on his face. He was pleased Stone and I were together. Jack appeared confused, which was the more appropriate response.

"I can't listen to those idiots argue about who Rob's fucking anymore."

"Oh," Jack said, knowing exactly what Stone was referring to.

"It hasn't occurred to either of them they should break up?" Stone asked, and my mind lit up with the thought of it. I was about to suggest that Stone should sit them both down and calmly and rationally explain why they'd both be happier apart, but then he finished his thought. "Fucking morons, they are." And I bit my tongue. Maybe someone other than Stone should do it.

"So where are you going?" Jack asked. He was looking at me.

"Jam Session?" Stone asked me, and I shrugged. I was still in shock we were going anywhere.

"You are so fucking selfish!" Blaire screamed from the house. We were half a block away and could still hear her.

Stone rolled his eyes.

"We'll catch up with you guys," Jack said.

"I'd hurry if I were you. It's like watching your parents fight when you're twelve and you lie in bed and pray they'll get divorced." Stone's laugh was sinister and filled with his usual anger. It was a rare glimpse into the darkness inside his head.

I let Stone lead the way down the sidewalk. A mixed crowd surrounded us along the walk. Some people were sandy and wet having just returned from the beach. Others were half ready—as in they appeared clean—and were roaming the streets searching for food. Some had already begun their night. They wore wedges and short skirts. Their faces were painted; their hair was gelled.

After a block and a half, Stone stopped and turned to me. "Why are you walking behind me?"

I shrugged, because admitting I felt more comfortable three feet behind him seemed like the wrong choice.

"Come here." He was annoyed. He had no more patience for me than he had for anyone else. I checked the time on my phone and wondered how long it would be before Tank and Jack showed up.

I took a deep breath and caught up. "Sorry."

There was no line at the Bottle & Cork. Stone and I paid our ten dollar covers and walked through the door and onto the patio. He ordered us each a beer with a rock face, not even smiling at the attractive girl leaning over to hear him. He was immune to arousal.

The air horn sounded, and we all stood in silence as the band played "The Star Spangled Banner," commencing this afternoon's session. Even our country's national anthem and the cheers it evoked didn't change Stone's unenthused expression.

I willed the others to come. Jack and Tank could handle Stone. Mila was great at it. I was terrible. I could barely handle myself, let alone this fire head. I tried to maneuver us into a spot that was less crowded. Less chance of someone bumping into us and setting him off. The band played, and everyone around us was happy. Stone was, too. I just wasn't sure how long it would last.

He smiled the same way he had in our driveway. He was try-ing. "Are you seeing anyone?" Stone asked in the exact way you would expect him to. He demanded the information. It wasn't sly or suave. It was an interrogation.

"Ah. Yeah. On and off." Stone didn't move any part of his face. "Sometimes."

"You sound like as big of an idiot as Blaire."

"Thank you?"

"You talking about Jackie?" Jack's voice asked in my ear.

I closed my eyes. I was equal parts annoyed with his assess-ment and thrilled he was there with us. I sighed. "Yes."

He reached up and squeezed Stone's shoulder, and then Mila and a gaggle of half shares surrounded us.

"Where's Tank?"

Jack shook his head. "He's working on something back at the house."

"Like what?"

Jack took a sip of his beer. "Some masterpiece. He's going to meet us out in a little bit."

"Oh."

Mila danced around. She moved to the front of the crowd and made love to the lead singer as he belted out the lyrics. He sang them directly to her and pointed as he did. She enchanted him in less than three minutes. She was wearing a cropped top tied under her breasts and a pair of black short shorts. She was cap-tivating even to me. Stone watched her dance, waiting to erupt.

After an hour, the band took a break, and the singer escorted

Mila to the bar for a drink. Stone and Jack were discussing the Redskins, and the rest of the house was pulling me into their circle and singing at the top of their lungs to the deejay. I stepped away when the song ended and snuck out of the bar so I could breathe. I stopped three feet from the door and did just that. I faced the line of people waiting to get in and inhaled deeply. I needed space. I sought the distance that I was always able to control, and that living with this group of strangers threatened every weekend.

Instead of going back inside, I turned and walked home alone without a fear in my body. The street was bright and full of people. Groups, singles, couples, all of them laughing too loud, enjoying their weekends as I hid from mine. If I got home early enough, before the rest of the house, I could be asleep prior to their arrival and absent from the after-party. My pace quickened with the thought of it. They had to leave me alone if I was unconscious.

I opened the door, and Tank turned to me with surprised joy covering his face. There would be no escape from him. "You're home!" he said and walked over to me. He had a long joint hanging from his lips. He pulled me by the elbow to a chair he'd positioned in the center of the kitchen facing the doorway to my porch.

"Tank, what are you doing?"

"Shush. I need you to see something." He sat me down in the chair and leaned over so he didn't tower above me. "But first you have to smoke some of this."

He handed me the joint. I held it in my hand as the end burned from the barely present night air touching the paper's edge. Weed seemed simple compared to my roommates, and I suddenly realized what plagued every thought of them. They were advanced. They were into things I wasn't. Like white powders, and pills, and bar fights . . . and engaging each other with the sole purpose of getting to know each other. "This is just weed?"

Tank stopped moving and looked from the joint to me. He wasn't offended. He was almost curious. I'd shared a secret with him, but the secret was about himself. Tank did other things besides smoking marijuana.

"Just weed." He watched as I inhaled deeply. "I'd tell you if there were something else in there."

I took two more hits and coughed until I thought I might never stop.

Tank reached over to the sink and poured me a glass of water. "Here."

"Thanks," I said through the coughs. I handed the joint back to Tank and took another deep breath. The clean air filling my lungs soothed my throat and my mind. Tank sat on top of the kitchen counter and smoked. He studied the end of the joint, the ceiling, and finally me. He smiled like he'd just discovered I was there with him. I inhaled and felt the breath travel down to my lungs and the oxygen reach every inch of my body. The world was moving in slow motion, or so I thought.

"Here." He hopped off the counter and handed me the joint.

"I'm good. Very good. You finish it."

Tank licked his fingertips and put it out. He placed it on the counter and poured himself a glass of water. When he saw my glass was empty, he refilled it, too. We drank our water pleasantly until I forgot about the bar I'd been in earlier.

"Now sit still and don't take your eyes off the doorway," he said.

"What are you going to do?" I giggled. I felt eight years old every time I was with him, but now especially as I couldn't stop myself from laughing.

"I'm going to fly." Tank turned up the speakers in the kitchen, and the bass of the music centered in the bottom of my stomach as it thumped louder than the rest of the song. My eyes focused on the damaged molding around the door. The wood was frayed on the bottom; the paint was missing. The work of a puppy with sore gums.

His fingertips appeared first, stealing my concentration from the molding and centering it on the left side of the doorway. Ever so slowly, he moved forward until his hands, forearms, and elbows were visible in the middle of the doorway. Tank was flying, and I was laughing. It wasn't until the first of his hair was visible that I could see he'd turned Jack's fan toward him, which blew his hair back wildly as he careened through the sky. When his face finally came into view, he was as serious as a super hero.

The sight of him mesmerized me, as if he were truly flying and the chair I was sitting in was somehow in the sky, too, allowing me to watch him from above the earth. Tank's flight was one of the most amazing things I'd ever seen.

"Nora, I'll be back," he yelled over the music and closed his eyes. He swayed slightly to each side, countering the wind in his imaginary flight and staying his course.

Tank inched out a little farther until his entire torso was flying through the doorway and then, when the angle was too far to hold, he fell forward and landed on his stomach, ruining the illusion and making me return to uncontrollable laughter. I threw my head back and laughed at the stained ceiling. I doubled over, letting the hysterics infect me until I held my stomach to control myself.

Jack appeared in front of my chair. I didn't know how long he'd been watching us, but he was clearly intrigued by what he was witnessing now. He was the perfect addition to our theater.

"Hi," I said to Jack, and Tank came back into the kitchen. He nodded at me, giving me permission to share his new skill. Tank handed Jack the roach and the lighter.

Jack stared at both of them and then looked back at me quizzically. "Well, well, well, what have you two been up to?" His words sunk into me and made me warm.

"You'll see." I laughed again at the memory of Tank flying through my bedroom. Jack held the joint in his hand and stared at me until I stopped laughing and lowered my eyes. I couldn't stop smiling though. Tank had permanently affixed it to my face.

Jack smoked the roach. The bright red of the paper as he inhaled held my mind hostage until he moved the joint from his mouth and the red dimmed. He smoked until there was only paper left to hold it between his fingers without burning himself. He placed the remnants on the counter with the lighter and turned to us, awaiting his directions. I took his hand and led him to the chair in the middle of the room.

"Here. Sit down for a minute." Jack paused with his eyes fixed on me, and his gaze took my breath away. The weed was good. I felt everything deeper. I couldn't hide from him or myself. With a hand on each of his shoulders I pushed him into the chair. "Down, boy."

He broke into laughter and released me from his scrutiny. Tank was selecting a new song on the CD player. He turned back to us as the music filled the room and walked out the doorway onto my porch.

I stood behind Jack as Tank's fingertips appeared. I thought I'd only witness it this time. After all, I knew what was coming. But the sight of him as the rest of his arms came into view had me laughing again. I forced myself to watch. I didn't want to miss the moment when his windblown head flew by. Tank was a born performer, not breaking his role for a second as he soared in front of us. He kept his face toward the wind blowing at him and slowly moved farther into the doorway.

Jack watched Tank the entire time. He was used to Tank's art. He'd grown up with him. To me, Tank was special. When Jack started clapping and whistled, I realized Tank was special to him, too.

Tank fell forward on his stomach, and I leaned over the kitchen counter, laughing until I began to cough. I reached over and grabbed my glass and then filled it with water. When I turned around, Jack was standing next to his chair staring at me.

What did I do?

He didn't look away. Nothing was funny anymore.

The screen door opened, and voices filled the room in the front of the house. Tank disappeared out the back door of my bedroom. His shadow moved toward the lounge chairs near the clothes line.

"Why did he leave?" I asked and turned back to Jack.

"Sometimes he doesn't like crowds."

The rest of the house was loud. They were drunk and oblivious to anyone outside of their vision. I returned to my original plan of avoiding all of them. I moved toward our bedroom, but Jack stepped in front of me. He was only inches away. My face was close enough to rest on his chest. Exhaustion took over, and I imagined lying down with him. I let the sensation of wanting him spread through me.

"Ask me why I was looking at you that way," he said and reminded me he was dangerous.

"No thanks." I moved to the left to go around him, but he blocked me and held me close with his hands on both my arms.

"Ask me, Nora."

I let my head rise. I couldn't turn away. He stole me from myself. "Why were you looking at me that way?" The openness of the question turned in my stomach.

"Because when you laugh like that . . . when you let yourself go, you're the most beautiful thing I've ever seen."

He took my breath away. The honesty in his eyes was breaking me. I believed in him. I believed in me. "Thank you." I stood still in his stare. I couldn't find another word inside me to say aloud.

Outside, a bottle crashed against the side of a car and set an alarm off.

"What the fuck?" Stone yelled from the front yard.

"Shit," Jack said but didn't move from in front of me. "I've got to go check on him."

"You do?" I was having trouble breathing. I was shallow. I searched my mind for the logic behind not hooking up with him. Every shred of evidence that it wasn't a great idea was lost to me.

There was more yelling out front, followed by a police siren. Jack half smiled at me and walked out the back door.

I laid in my bed and listened as Jack pulled Stone together. He had him sit on the front step and told him, "If you move, I'm going to kick your ass." I didn't hear a response from Stone but assumed he was sitting down. The thought of Jack kicking Stone's ass made me smile.

The police radio clicked in and out with short phrases I couldn't make out, and Jack's voice randomly came through the screens, calm and in control. It was almost forty-five minutes before Jack had convinced the police and Blaire that no charges were going to be filed regarding her broken passenger car window. "Stone would happily pay for it," Jack had assured them both.

Jack came to our room and collapsed in his own bed. I wanted him in mine.

Ten

Animal Instincts

"WHEN I CLOSE my eyes, I see us having sex."

I stopped chewing my slice of pizza and stared at Ricky, utterly disturbed.

"What? We would be beautiful together. I don't understand why you keep saying no."

"Is there anyone you wouldn't be beautiful with?" I went back to my lunch. The only thing Ricky longed for more than to fuck me was to shock me.

"You know, just because I have sex with a lot of people doesn't mean I have low standards." I regretted responding in the first place. "You're . . ." He searched for the words. "Petite, and yet your breasts are the best I've ever seen. They're real, aren't they?"

I looked down at my chest and back up at Ricky without changing my detached expression.

"I knew it. Oh my God, what I would do with them." Ricky

fisted his hands and closed his eyes. The inside of his head must be a terrifying place.

"Are you ready to go back?"

"Why do you always do that?"

"What?"

"You ruin my fantasies with work."

"We are *at* work." I stated the obvious. I scanned the cafeteria and assumed no one else was talking about having sex with each other.

"Besides your boobs, it's your hair."

"Are you done?"

"No. And your eyes. It's the brown hair, green eye combination." He leaned toward me across the table and took my hands in his. "Nora Hargrove, I think we should make babies. They'll be gorgeous."

I confirmed no one was watching us. "You've lost your mind." I took back my hands.

"I haven't. Something about you makes me want you more than anyone else."

"Did you ever think it's because you can't have me?"

"I have considered it. The only way to know for sure is for you to have sex with me." I rolled my eyes at his words. "And then we'll know."

"You never stop." I stood and grabbed my tray, but Ricky stayed in his seat. "Are you coming back?"

"I'm going to go jerk off in the bathroom first. All this talk about you has left me . . . unclear."

I rolled my eyes and walked away.

"PLEASE," TANK BEGGED, and I couldn't resist. "I haven't slept in three days."

I laughed while he was busy packing his bowl.

When I'd left the Starboard, Mila was in love with a half share whose name I couldn't remember. I only recognized him as a housemate because of his red hair. He and Mila were mismatched together, but in an interesting way. She could make anything look right.

Jack was leaning on the bar, barely drinking his beer. We'd all been drinking for hours, and he seemed like it was catching up to him. I moved in his direction to see if he wanted to get pizza, but a half share swooped in on him before I made my way through the crowd. I caught his eye right before I walked out the door and left my housemates to follow the rest of Dewey home. I didn't realize until I was halfway down the block that I wanted Jack to follow.

I smoked with Tank until my eyelids slid shut, threatening to take my consciousness with them. He was still singing to the latest song he'd selected on the old boom box on the kitchen counter. His energy was endless. I didn't even say good night. I couldn't. I slithered into my bed and passed out. When I woke Saturday morning, Tank was sleeping in Jack's bed. He was sprawled across the top of it with the covers bunched beneath him like he'd actually crashed into it.

No one was where they were supposed to be. Except for Blaire and Rob. They were constantly in motion and always at the exact same place—fighting. I was standing in the kitchen, watching the coffee drip into the pot when Jack walked by me. He didn't even raise an eyebrow at the angry yelling coming from Rob's bedroom next to the kitchen. No one reacted to Rob and Blaire, whether they were fighting or happy. I suspected the lack of relevance bothered Rob more than the fighting. What was the point of a spectacle if it had no audience? Rob had to be in the center of the ring, and he was willing to torture Blaire to get there. He wasn't used to being inconsequential and he wasn't comfortable with it.

My stomach felt like an empty tin cup, and Blaire's shrill voice made it feel like acid was being poured into it. I swallowed and held my hand to my head to steady my shaky existence. It was going to be a long day.

The half share who was hanging on Jack when I'd left the bar the night before stopped by our room twice throughout the morning. Both times to giggle and shake something. Her hair once, her ass another time. She seemed nice, although I hated her laugh, and the way she talked, and her hair color, and pretty much everything about her. Other than that, she was perfect.

She hung on Jack as we walked to the beach as a defeated bri gade. In fact, she was the only one talking. Her energy and the sound of her voice pounded against my aching head like a drum. Jack was silent, and I knew she was grating on his nerves the same way she grated on mine, but he deserved this morning for having her the night before.

"Ow! Fu—" I hopped on one foot as a pain stabbed through the bone of the other. "What the—" Tank stopped and looked at me. "I hurt my foot."

"I can see that," he said, as I continued to hop around. Tank dropped his boogie board and towel and came to help me. I steadied myself with a hand on his shoulder as he lifted my foot and turned it toward him. It was covered in dirt and blood.

"Ugh. That's disgusting," I said and turned my head away from the damage.

"Shells . . . or a piece of glass." He searched for the weapon that had attacked me.

"I have flip-flops on."

"Just makes it more impressive. Here." He handed me the string attached to his boogie board and leaned down with his back to me.

"What are you doing?"

"I'm giving you a piggy-back ride. You need to stick your foot in the water so we can see the wound better."

I turned to the house. The ocean was closer. I climbed on Tank's back, and he shifted my weight higher up on him. We bounced to the bottom of the dune with me dragging his boogie board behind us.

"What are you doing?" Mila asked us when I dropped my bag from the safety of Tank's back.

"She stepped on something."

Mila's face twisted in disgust as she noticed the blood covering the bottom of my foot. Tank ignored her and walked toward the surf.

"This is going to hurt," I said near his ear.

"Nah. The salt water is good for it."

"It's going to hurt. The air hurts it."

"You're going to be surprised."

"By how much it hurts?"

He leaned down, and I slid off his back, still holding my right foot in the air. He laughed a little and gently pressed my knee down until the water reached my wound.

"Ah!"

"Just a little bit more. Move it around. Clean it out."

I did as I was told, and the pain dissipated with the blood. When I pulled my foot from the water the second time, the gash was visible and clean. It was an inch-and-a-half slice across the bottom of my foot. Tank examined it. It wasn't bleeding until he pressed on both sides of the cut.

"It's up to you if you want to go to the hospital. It might need a stitch, but what do I know? We can bandage and elevate it." Bandage and elevate made him sound like he knew something.

"What's your degree in?"

"Biochemistry."

"I don't even know what that is." I laughed. "You're really smart."

Tank straightened and looked me in the eyes. "Why do you sound so surprised?"

I stopped laughing. "I'm not." I wasn't. "I'm really not. How come you work at the bakery, though?"

"I'm kind of between jobs. The first one didn't work out." Tank bent down, ending our conversation and offering me a ride back to the rest of our group.

"I think you're very smart," I said before we reached them. I needed him to know. I didn't want there to be any question of how impressive I found Tank to be.

Mila had Band-Aids in her bag. I covered the cut with a tissue and then secured it with the Band-Aids. It would suffice until I drove offshore to the drug store on Route 1. I'd wait until later in the day when all the weeklies were safely parked at their rentals.

"What are you reading?" the half share asked Jack. I couldn't stop laughing at the torment on his face. She wouldn't even be quiet long enough for him to read.

"I found this novel in the house. It's a mystery, I think." He held up the book for her to see.

"Read it aloud," Tank demanded.

"I'm on vacation," Jack said and returned to his book.

"Yeah. We can all listen and try to guess who did it," Mila said.

"Who did what?" Jack's brilliant half share asked.

"According to the back cover." Jack was patient as he answered. "'Who dared to murder the last living member of the Cromwell Clan?'"

"Oh, that sounds like a good one," I said. I couldn't help myself.

"Read it." His new friend interrupted our moment.

Jack sighed but read aloud beginning with, "Chapter one, The Rise of the Unknown."

We all laid around him on our towels or perched on our chairs and listened as he read through the first few chapters of the novel. As I listened to the words, I surveyed our group. The only person missing was Heather, but unlike the last time she hadn't made it home on Friday night, no one seemed to notice.

Jack's voice and the story of the Cromwell Clan soothed my thoughts and carried me away to Europe in the eighteen hundreds. The last time I remembered being read aloud to, I was in elementary school. Maybe that was why it had such a calming effect on all of us. No one said a word until he stopped near the end of chapter three.

"Why did you stop?" Mila asked.

"A page is torn out." Jack held up the book, displaying the missing page.

"Interesting." Mila nodded, noting the missing page as part of the plot.

"The girlfriend did it," Tank said and broke all of our concentration. "Someone write that down. It was the girlfriend."

I mulled the idea over in my head. I liked the theory, but I thought it was Cromwell's partner who killed him.

Jack dropped the book on the towel next to his chair. A dog ran up to our group and excitedly greeted each of us as if he'd been waiting for a break in the story to introduce himself. He cocked his leg and peed on the corner of Stone's chair.

"What the fuck?" Stone roared, and the dog ran over to me. He cuddled next to me as I rubbed him behind his ears.

The dog's owner was apologizing as she ran to us. He wasn't even allowed on the beach until after five thirty, and Stone's chair was the reason why.

"I'm so sorry," she said over and over again. Stone never accepted her apology.

"He's so cute," I said more to the dog than to his owner. He was a beagle, and his sweet little face was impossible to be mad at. "Aren't you?" I asked him. He moved even closer to me.

"He's cute, but he's bad," his owner said and hooked a leash to his collar. When I stopped petting him, he ran alongside his owner to the dune.

"I fucking hate dogs," Stone said. I rolled my eyes. *How can someone hate a dog?*

"I think that one has excellent taste," Jack said and stared at me.

"Animals can sense the good in people," Tank added. Every word from his mouth sounded like the absolute truth on a subject. I wondered if Rufus would ever be able to run up to a group of people like that dog had.

The tide poured onto our towels and into our bags. It surprised all of us before it pulled stray flip-flops and boogie boards out with it as it rescinded.

My towel was soaked. My foot hurt. My beach day was done. I wrung the excess water from the towel and grabbed my bottom-soaked bag before limping over the dune and back to the house.

The shower set my foot on fire for the second time. I washed my hair furiously and dragged conditioner through the strands. I needed to get to the pharmacy for proper bandages as soon as possible. I wrapped myself in my towel and stepped out onto the concrete surrounding the side of our house. I kept my weight off my foot as I walked to my porch.

Jack stood next to my bed with a bag in his hand. "I got you some bandages."

I glanced at the bag and back at Jack. "You didn't have to do that."

"I wanted to. I figured you'd need them as soon as you got out of the shower."

I was a little overwhelmed. "Thanks," was all I managed to get out.

"I brought you some shells, too. I put them in your pile." He motioned toward the mound of shells on the floor. I could barely take my eyes off him to look their way. He'd brought me shells. "A lot of those are broken."

"I know. I love them anyway."

"Sit down, and I'll help you."

I tightened the towel around myself. Jack appeared as if he were holding back his laughter as I did it. I sat about three feet from him, and he picked up my foot and placed it gingerly on his lap.

He grimaced as he used his thumb to move the cut around.

"Gross. I know."

"I've seen worse." He opened a few large sterile pads and placed them on the bed next to us. He grabbed the corner of my towel and dried my foot completely. I winced and pulled my foot back.

"That didn't hurt," I said. "My feet are really ticklish."

"Interesting. What about the rest of you?"

"I can do this myself."

Jack silenced me with a wave of his hand. He squeezed anti-biotic cream onto the cut and then covered it with several pads. Relief flowed through me just from not seeing it. He wound tape around the pads and the top of my foot until everything was secure.

"Thanks. I owe you."

"You know how you can pay me back?" I only raised my eyebrows at him. "Marry me." I was dumbfounded, and so was my expression. "Or at least lie and tell people you married me. Like, today."

I finally caught up. "Your new friend driving you crazy?"

"It's not funny."

"It's a little funny. She seems great," I said with overt sarcasm.

"She's insane. I shouldn't have hooked up with her."

"Why did you then?" I heard the words but couldn't believe I'd spoken them. They'd chipped away at my insides until I'd finally set them free.

Jack held my foot in his hands and looked at me, surprised. "I don't know." He slowly spoke. It sounded like a response that would come from me rather than Jack. I held my breath until he continued with, "It was late . . . and she was persistent. She smelled nice." He sighed. "It sounds very animalistic, I admit. It was far from intelligent."

I don't know what I was hoping for, but his honesty left me cold. I needed to change the subject. Anything to make him stop regarding me as if he'd disappointed me and was apologizing. Jack didn't owe me a thing. This was the summer, and we were at the beach.

"It's not even the Fourth of July. You guys still have months together," I joked, and Jack pushed against the bottom of my foot. "Ow!"

"Sorry. You okay?"

"I'm fine." My voice was terse. I pulled my foot back from his hands.

"I'm really sorry." He ran his fingertips up my ankle. "You probably want me to have sex with you now," he said and immediately repaired my hurt feelings. "Please don't beg me."

"I'll try to control myself." I reached into my bag for my brush and began brushing my hair. Jack observed me. It was like being at work. I wasn't sure he was ever going away. He might hide in my bed for the rest of the summer. "You're going to have to deal with it. She's here every other weekend. Give it a chance. Maybe she's just excited. Maybe she really likes you."

Jack fell back flat on my bed and covered his face. I used the time to stand and slide my strapless dress on before letting the towel drop to the floor. I slipped my foot in my flip-flop and placed my full weight on it. It hurt like hell.

"This weekend sucks," he said without uncovering his eyes.

"Yes." I hated the girl he'd hooked up with. "It does."

Eleven

And Then there Were Seven

EVEN BEFORE THE large drunk man stepped on me, I couldn't take it any longer. I was sure my foot was bleeding. I couldn't stop the tears from streaming down my cheeks. I knew without looking that it had to be re-bandaged.

Mila stood next to me at the scene of the crime, the three-deep line for a beer at the Starboard. "You okay?"

"I'm maimed." She laughed at my statement that wasn't meant to be funny. "They might have to amputate." She passed back shots Jack had bought and a beer. I waited for the house to regroup, and I slammed the shot down my throat to dull the pain. It didn't touch it. "Here." I handed my beer to Jack.

"Where do you think you're going?"

"To redress my wound." I lifted my foot out of my shoe and turned it so both of us could see it. Blood covered the bandage.

"Do you want me to come with you?"

I shook my head. "No."

"Text me when you get home."

"I'm sure I'll be fine."

"Of course. You're always fine." He took a sip of the beer I'd just handed him. "Text me anyway."

I walked through the crowds. The one in the bar, the groups waiting to get in, and the throngs of people filling the sidewalks of Dewey Beach. No one noticed I was limping. Every step was a knife stabbing into the bottom of my foot. I sat on the front stoop of the house and crossed my ankle over my knee. I had to take the weight off of it. I removed the dressing and washed my foot under the hose. Based on the pain that caused, the cut hadn't closed at all in the last few hours.

I walked on one foot and a tiptoe through the front door. The house was deserted; the quiet engulfed me. Jack must love it down here during the week. He probably dreaded our arrival every Friday.

The bag full of medical supplies still sat on my bed. I bandaged my foot the exact way Jack had, except I doubled up on the gauze pads. Apparently, one layer wasn't enough.

A low, almost knocking sound came from the silent kitchen. I leaned over to see what was making it, but the noise stopped as soon as my awareness arrived. I'd imagined it. I rested on my pillow and wallowed in the silence of our shore house.

The knocking came again. This time it was two distinct bangs without much humph. It wasn't coming from the kitchen. It was farther inside the house. My heart raced in my chest as I mentally recounted each roommate's attendance at the Starboard. No one else should be in here.

Two more knocks.

I followed the sound, hating myself for being afraid.

"Hello," I said and felt ridiculous. This was Dewey, after all. I should be running toward the sound.

A pale hand shook against the doorway of Heather's room. The nails were painted a bright blue, which was the same color the sky had been earlier in the day. The hand jerked again, and I ran to it, ignoring the pain that shot through my foot.

Heather laid on the floor, her dress from the night before half off and her makeup smeared across her face. Vomit pooled next to her. The smell repulsed me more than her appearance.

"Heather?" I stepped over her so I could see her face better. Her lips were dry and cracked. I wanted to run out of the room and somehow take Heather with me. "Heather, can you hear me?"

"Fuck you, Nora." There was no strength in her horrid words, and my name hung on a dry heave. Even with her hate-filled sentiment, I felt for her, and I wasn't sure what to do.

"Maybe I can help you into the shower." Her eyes closed and her arm jerked again. Something was very different about this hangover and Heather. She'd been sick for three days after her twenty-first birthday. Hadn't eaten a thing. It was all I could do to force her to drink so she wouldn't become dehydrated. But even after her twenty-one shots, she didn't look like this.

I found my phone and called Jack.

"I didn't expect a call. Is this you begging?" His smug voice, a vital distinction from the lifeless body in front of me, made me realize Heather was further gone than I'd thought. The sounds of the bar a few blocks away invaded the silence of our house.

"I need your help. Can you come home?"

"You are begging."

Heather's head shot to the side and vomit flew out of her mouth. It was a white liquid mixed with bright red that I thought was blood. I flinched and forced my eyes shut.

"Nora?"

I opened my mouth, not sure if I was going to scream or cry, and pleaded, "Jack, come home right now!"

I hung up and stared at Heather's lifeless body. I knew what to do. I called 911.

They were unsettlingly calm and professional on the phone. This was their shift. I was their customer calling, and they showed as much urgency on the phone as I did when an insured called me. I gave them my name, our address, Heather's condition, as much as I could tell them, and pleaded with them to hurry.

Heather dry heaved twice more before I hung up.

"Heather, can you hear me?" I ran my hand roughly up and down her arm.

Heather jerked forward; she was shaking and then engrossed in a seizure, kicking her legs wildly to the side as her eyes rolled back in her head. She was a terrifying movie hurling toward me, and I was paralyzed at the sight of it.

Oh my God . . . she's going to die.

"Heather!" I screamed.

Jack ran into the room and stopped short at the sight of us. Heather's seizure was subsiding. I moved her legs out straight.

"I called 911," I said to Jack without taking my eyes off Heather.

"Jesus." He scanned the room, and my eyes followed his inspection. Her purse was on the bed. Her stomach contents were everywhere. "Is she breathing?"

I watched as Heather's chest barely rose and fell. Peace had descended upon her. I thought she was dying. This was what it looked like. It was violent and wretched and then it was quiet before you were gone. "Barely."

"Stay with her." Jack ran through the house. Noises came from the kitchen, the living room, and all of the bedrooms. He stopped at the door midstep. "Still the same?" Car keys jiggled from his finger and his arms were full of bongs, bowls, prescription bottles, and bags of drugs.

"I think so."

"I'll be right back." The screen door on the front of the house screeched when he opened it, and then I heard a car trunk close. The car chirped with locked doors seconds before Jack was on the floor next to me. "I don't know if the police are going to come." He took his phone out of his pocket and texted a message. "I'm telling Mila. If you're okay in here, I'm going to go out front and wait for the ambulance."

I was kneeling in a pool of vomit mixed with blood. I was holding the hand of a friend who I wasn't even sure if she liked me, and I was terrified she was going to die. "I'm fine."

It was as if he'd heard every thought. Jack rubbed my shoulders and took one last look at Heather before walking out of the room.

I thought they'd never come. As soon as they walked in with all their equipment, I knew I'd made the right decision. Heather was well beyond my level of responsibility.

"Do you know what she ingested?" the female paramedic asked us.

"No. We haven't seen her since yesterday afternoon." I stared at Jack, wanting someone to share the shame of not even knowing where'd she'd been. "I came home early and found her on the floor like this. I have no idea what's she's taken. If anything."

She inspected the room and Heather's purse while the male paramedic worked on Heather.

I moved out of the room. I didn't want to be near Heather or the people who would save her. Eventually Jack met me in the living room. I was sitting on a wooden kitchen chair in the corner of the room.

"I almost didn't see you there. You're so quiet."

"I'm here," I said and wished more than anything that I wasn't.

"They're prepping her for transport. I'm going to follow the ambulance to the hospital."

"On your motorcycle?" Jack nodded at my question. "I'll drive.

My car is the last one anyway."

We rode in silence behind the ambulance. When it ran the red lights, we stopped. Jack's presence was the only thing keeping the tears from pouring from my eyes. What had happened to Heather to turn her into this? Halfway to the Beebe Medical Center in Lewes, I turned to Jack and he was staring at me.

"What?" I asked, but he didn't move. "What? You're scaring me." Everything scared me. I'd never known anyone who'd died.

"Nothing." When he still didn't look away, I braced myself for what he'd say next. "Don't ever be afraid of me."

I was too exhausted to engage in any real conversation. "What time is it?"

He turned his phone on. "It's nine thirty."

"It feels like three thirty." I inhaled deeply and exhaled as I pulled into the entrance of the hospital. "What did you do with the drugs?"

"I put them in the trunk of Rob's car."

I nodded and parked in the first empty spot in the visitor parking lot.

Jack and I sat in the hospital waiting room next to each other. There was one other man in the room with us, but he was called to the desk and then disappeared behind double doors that automatically opened toward him. Neither of us was related to Heather. Neither of us was old enough to be responsible for her.

"I've never been in a hospital." The time didn't move here. I never wanted to come back.

"I broke my collarbone playing football sophomore year. That was enough for me."

"High school or college?"

"High school. I didn't play in college."

"How come?"

"Because I went to Alabama. I tried to walk on the first two years, but every player there is phenomenal." Jack abruptly leaned over and pulled his phone from his pocket. He read the screen and typed something. "Mila's calling Heather's parents. This should be good."

"She hates them." Heather and I spoke about our parents less than we spoke about any other subject, but I knew she hated them. Her dread at their arrival on the day of graduation told me everything I needed to know.

"You know that's not her dad, right?"

"What? No."

"Her mom left her dad for that guy. Heather hates both of them. That was in . . ." Jack thought for a moment. "Ninth grade."

"You guys all know so much about each other." There was no follow-up. I had that one observation. I wasn't longing for close friends who'd known me my whole life. In fact, I'd run from every single person I had known before I'd caught my mother with my French teacher. Their faces reminded me of that day. Their references brought back the lost year of high school, and I'd chosen to be as far from it as possible.

I yawned. The memories were exhausting me.

"Come here." Jack raised his arm, beckoning me to the perfect resting spot on his shoulder.

I could lean over the thin arm of my chair and fade away on his chest, but I glanced down and saw the vomit crusted on my skin. It was particularly bad around my knees. "I smell."

"It's okay. I can smell you from here."

I'd gotten so used to the odor. Our house must've reeked of it. I leaned against Jack and tucked my feet under me in the chair. He pulled me closer with his hand on my shoulder. The last thing I remembered was his fingertips gliding back and forth across my vomit-covered forearm.

It was two in the morning before I moved again. Jack shook me awake upon the arrival of Heather's parents, or her mother and stepfather. They thanked us for bringing her in and promised to call when they knew more. I followed Jack to my car, and when he held out his hand, I handed him my keys without argument. I was only half awake. I couldn't shake the fog surrounding me. The entire night had been a bad dream, and I couldn't quite remember the details to tell anyone about it.

Jack drove us home and parked my car in the exact spot it had moved from earlier. The windows were all open in the house. It was hot and smelled of bleach. Mila had cleaned the floor I'd found Heather on earlier.

"Do you want to take a shower?" Jack asked as I stumbled onto our porch.

"Yes."

He rummaged through the pile of clothes on the floor next to his bed. "You take the bathroom. I'll use the outside shower." He pulled his towel off the hook he'd hung in the corner of the room and vanished into the darkness of the back door.

I found my shampoo and conditioner, a towel, a pair of underwear, and my nightgown. It wasn't my usual just-drop-in-the-dress-I'm-wearing sleepwear, but I packed it every weekend and just never wore it. I was definitely *not* sleeping in the clothes I'd worn through our ordeal.

Chunks of throw-up slid from my skin as the hot water assaulted me. I couldn't get it hot enough. I feared I'd forever smell the odor of what I'd thought was Heather's death. I scrubbed myself and drenched my hair with shampoo. It would have to be enough. The sun would be up soon.

I brushed my hair and put the nightgown on while still in the bathroom. Through the wall, I could hear Blaire and Rob fighting. *Does it ever stop?* Was this what it was like to be in love with him? Because to the outsider, it sounded like pure hell.

I stepped out of the bathroom at the same time Rob slammed his bedroom door behind him.

"Hey," he said when he noticed me.

"Hi." I walked away. I could feel him following me, but I was too exhausted to be with him.

"I need to talk to you," he whispered as he followed me onto the porch. Jack was lying in his bed with the sheet covering the bottom of him. It was hot, and without the air conditioners the rest of the house was stifled under the heat we dealt with every weekend.

"It's late," I pleaded with Rob.

"I know." He ran his hand through his hair in frustration, and I thought he was going to make the decent choice and say good night. "Why didn't you call me?"

I was wrong. I threw my towel over the door to the porch and walked past Rob to my bed.

"When you found Heather, why didn't you call me instead of Jack?"

Jack didn't move.

"I don't know." I shook my head and found a plastic bag to put my clothes in from the night before.

"Because you, Heather, and I spent a lot of time together at Delaware, and you've known him less than a month."

I pulled the covers back on my bed.

This annoyed him. "Nora?"

"What? I don't know why I called him." I was whisper-yelling. "I needed help, and he came, and he helped. That's all I know." I calmed down, and the sadness of the night hit me again. "It wasn't a popularity contest. I thought she was going to die."

He should have hugged me or apologized. I'd been through a lot. He'd had his latest fight with Blaire, and I wasn't going to let him take it out on me. I climbed under my sheet, and Rob huffed his way off my porch. He was selfish. I wasn't impressed. I'd never been more grateful to be alone. I closed my eyes and thought of the sky. The stars, the moon, anything but Rob and Heather.

"I love your nightgown."

I opened my eyes and turned to Jack. He was smiling, completely awake and beaming like he'd won a prize. The fact that he could still make a joke, combined with the kindness in his eyes, made me believe the world wasn't all bad.

Without a word, I drifted off to sleep.

I WOKE TO the sound of Blaire yelling. Their voices drilled through the house and out the door. I could hear them through the side windows near my pillow.

"Why are you so pissed off? She's fucked up."

"It's not about Heather!" he screamed. I was sure the whole block heard him.

"What the hell is it about then?"

The car doors opened and slammed shut, and the house was returned to the calm Blaire and Rob always ruined.

Jack was asleep in his bed. His head was turned away from me and his tanned biceps held my attention for much longer than I'd ever admit to him. His feet hung off the end of his bed. It was as if last night had never happened.

I sat up in bed and straightened my nightgown that had ridden up on my waist. It had happened, all right.

I walked through the trashed kitchen and past the unconscious housemates strewn across the living room furniture and floor. I opened Heather's door a few inches and poked my head in the crack. The room was empty. The windows were open, and a fan was blowing, trying to dry the floor and remove the odor of bleach from the scene.

I found Heather's bag on the floor by her bed. I turned it over in my hands and, inconceivably, there was no vomit on it anywhere. I packed the clothes I knew were hers inside of it.

"What are you doing up?" Tank walked into the room and shut the door quietly behind him.

"I couldn't sleep anymore."

"I know the feeling."

I opened the top drawer of the dresser and found six prescription bottles. Four with Heather's name on them and two with the name *Cirillo* that I didn't recognize. "I figured I'd go see Heather and take her stuff. She'll probably want it with her."

"Last night was crazy."

"Yes. What should I do with this?" I held up a bag of weed and a bowl and a few small packs of white powder that Jack hadn't found in his rushed cleaning of the house.

Tank stared at them in my hands. "Here." He waved a hand at himself. "Give them to me. I'll hold on to them until she comes back. You shouldn't transport that."

I handed him the drugs. "I don't even know why I'm going. It's just going to piss her off."

"Why are you then?"

"Because she's alone. She had a horrible night. I think she'll want her stuff."

"Someone else should take her stuff."

"Heather and I go way back. This is our day-after routine."

"Have you guys had a lot of those?"

"No." The memory of her lying on the floor struck me. "She scared me."

Tank pulled Heather's bathing suit off the doorknob and folded her towel that was lying across the back of the chair in the corner. "Her shampoo and stuff are in the bathroom."

"I'll grab them on my way out."

"You okay?"

"I'm not the one you should be worried about."

"Yes, you are," he said, and I turned to him. He was half smiling and all-knowing.

"I'm fine." I walked out of the room with Heather's bag in my arms.

Twelve

Signs of Abuse

"DID YOU EVER see someone die?" I asked as Ricky and I walked the hall to our cells. It'd been a week since I'd found Heather on the floor. My foot was healing, but I wasn't sure I could say the same for Heather. She didn't even acknowledge my presence in her hospital room when I dropped off her things, and she hadn't answered the two texts I'd sent her since.

"On television?"

"No. In real life. Like, someone you knew."

"One time, my mother and I were sitting on Navy Pier in Chicago and we saw the police pull a body out of the water."

I stopped walking, stunned.

"What?" he asked with both hands in the air. "You brought it up. I don't know. No. I haven't seen anyone die." I shook my head a little and followed Ricky again. "It was totally gross. Some of his skin was coming off his face."

I had three more hours before I could leave and drive to the beach. I sat on the bench and searched for apartments on my phone. If Rufus didn't start opening up, he was going to need me to adopt him. I needed an apartment that would accept dogs. Really, I needed a dog. I thought I'd lived alone long enough.

"Why are you asking me this?"

"Because my friend Heather was hospitalized for drugs and alcohol last weekend."

"Sounds like a fun friend."

"We're not really friends. I don't know if she has any." I stopped reading and considered it. Heather spent most of her time away from anyone who knew her that well, and she wasn't easy to get to know. Another reason we were so compatible.

"There's something terrifying about a girl with no friends. People don't want to take a chance on the person who's alone, because deep down they know there's a reason."

Ricky's words hit eerily close to home. "But what if it's not their fault?"

"Not their fault, or not their doing?" I stared at Ricky, confused by his question. "You can't control everything that happens to you, but you can control how you move forward."

I turned my attention back to the safety of my phone.

"What are you reading?"

"I'm looking for a new apartment. One that will let me have a dog."

"You can move in with me." He tilted his head and grinned in his playful way.

"I only want one dog."

I finished my shift and practically ran to my car. One stop to see Rufus and this girl was headed to the beach for the Fourth of July weekend. Janine met me at the front desk of the shelter. "Wait a minute before you go in," she said.

Fear gripped me. I should have come back on Monday. "Is he

still sick?"

"No. He's better. There's a family in there."

Janine and I watched from the window in the door. The little girl and her parents walked slowly in front of the cages and stopped to talk to several dogs. When they reached Rufus, all three of them tried to coax him to the front. I knew he was huddled far away.

Janine's head shook in frustration. "That doctor we recused him from should be executed." He'd kept Rufus chained outside and barely fed him. The shelter had found out about him when the neighbors called because the doctor was shooting BBs at him.

"Poor guy." I wanted to kill the doctor, too. The little girl walked back to the Chihuahua three cages down from Rufus. "I'm trying to find a new apartment so he can come live with me."

"You might be his only hope."

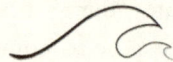

THERE WERE BODIES everywhere. It was an exact replication of Memorial Day weekend. I sipped my beer in the corner of the kitchen because there was no place else to stand. These weekends I was grateful for our porch. No half shares would dare sleep out there. Even atrocious was good, if it was only yours.

The leaves of the old wooden table had been extended once again for a beer pong tournament that would have no end. The results would be forgotten as soon as the music was turned down and the house emptied into the bars down the street.

I'd heard the name of Heather's rehab facility once and forgotten it immediately. I didn't care where she was. If I searched hard enough for an emotion that pertained to her, it was exhaustion, and now that she was gone, there was only relief.

It was a four-day weekend for everyone but Tank and me. I'd requested it off and had shockingly been granted the time, but then Sharon had decided we'd open the claims unit on Sunday and put me back on the schedule to be on the phone by ten. Tank had to make the donuts Sunday morning, so he'd leave Saturday night.

"And then there were seven," Tank said, surveying the room. It felt more like seventy now that every half share was down for the weekend, but without Heather there were only seven full shares left.

The refrigerator door had the recycling schedule, a magnet for Grottos Pizza, and three pictures from my housemates' youth. They were the kindergarten class picture of Mila, Stone, Rob, and Heather, a high school graduation picture of all of them in their caps and gowns, and a picture of the king and queen of the prom—Jack and Mila. It was impossible to look at them and not smile.

"Girls' night. Girls' night. Girls' night," a few of the half shares chanted. One stood right in front of me, smiling and pumping her fist.

"Tonight, we're going out just girls," Mila leaned around the half share and said.

I want to stay with the boys. Tank lounged on the couch, taking up the room of four people, and I should be sitting next to him when Girls' Night walked out the door.

"I've almost talked Blaire off the ledge. It took forty minutes to convince her she could exist without Rob's presence."

It'd been years since I'd had the freedom to just be with him without the ever-present ominous cloud of Blaire around. I wanted him to be the way he used to be instead of the ass he was down here. I missed the way he made me feel in college. He was the only safe place for me to hide and still feel the sunlight on my face.

They wouldn't let me bow out of girls' night, and eventually I was herded out the door. We arrived at Taco Toss when the line was just forming. I texted Jack and let him know the male contingency of our separate parties should move soon. The entire town would be a giant line by the end of the night.

I followed the girls to a sliver of space by the railing of the outside deck of the Lighthouse. Mila came and stood by me. Together we downed a round of shots and were engulfed by the group of guys standing next to us. There were only five of us and at least eight of them. I stayed close to the edge of our group. I was almost invisible. The world was an amusement park, and I was trapped, watching the merry-go-round. The guy to my right spilled his beer down the side of my shirt. I still preferred it to small talk, or any talk.

"Oh man. Sorry," he said and swiped his hand across the beads of liquid that hadn't soaked in yet.

"It's okay." I stepped back from him into the few inches not occupied behind me.

"'Trust no one,'" he read from the front of my shirt and smiled at me as if the directive was some inside joke. "I'm so sorry." He was stricken and genuine.

"Really. It's fine. You barely got me."

"Let me get you a beer." He walked away and ordered two beers. He wasn't my type. He wore a button-down shirt and khaki shorts. He wasn't too buttoned up, but he definitely wasn't the slightly dirty, band T-shirt, long-haired Rob I'd adhered my obsession to for the past few years. This guy was corporate or maybe an attorney. He was different.

"Here. I owe you at least one more, too." He handed me my beer. "I'm Derrick." I smiled to put him at ease. "The guy who spills liquor on you."

"Nora. The target." Knowing the questions would begin—the getting-to-know-you series of torture—I went on the offensive. "Where do you live, Derrick?"

"DC."

I nodded in appreciation, and Derrick smiled slightly. He was quiet, which I liked. "And what do you do in DC?"

"I work for Senator Aldrich."

"Now, that's interesting." I meant it. I couldn't stand the constant discussions with my mother about gun laws, global warming, health care, and terrorism, but with anyone else I was fascinated. Especially someone close to my age. My Uncle Dick had always spouted off about the Democrats as he drank too much Scotch during the holidays. The only value to his visits was watching my mother boil from his claims. As Derrick chatted on, I realized quickly he had a passion for politics and had been raised in a family of activists. I'd been raised in a lie. My mother was an activist when being one made for provocative dinner conversation.

"Are you down here for the summer?" he asked.

"Just on the weekends. Unfortunately."

I think.

"What do you do? Where do you live? Tell me something about you—"

"Nora!" Rob yelled from the other side of the deck. "Nora." He sang my name like the chorus of a heavy metal love song. He was alone, and I'm sure uncomfortable because of it.

"Friend of yours?" Derrick asked. He was suddenly less excited about me.

"Yes," I said. "I'm going to go see what's up, or else he's never going to stop. It was nice to meet you."

"Yeah." Derrick paused. He was going to ask for my number. I inched further away. He didn't need my number. He'd find someone else before the night ended. This was the beach. There was always a Plan B. "Hopefully I'll run into you again. Without spilling my beer on you next time."

"Sounds good."

The crowd was now immense. Stories of the line to get in and the sobering wait monopolized the conversations as I pulled myself through the inner circles of friends and housemates. I emerged from the last one as Rob put his arm around my shoulders and pulled me close for a hug.

"Man, you are a sight for sore eyes."

"Where is everyone? Why are you alone?"

"I don't know. After waiting forty-five minutes to get in here, I had to go the bathroom. I thought I was going to piss myself and die of dehydration all at once." He sucked me into Rob's world. "So I left everyone at the bar and by the time I waited in line at the bathroom, they were all gone."

"It's this weekend. Fourth of July isn't easy."

Rob's attention abandoned me and fixed on his hair as he ran his hands through it to perfect his unkempt look. I stared past him at the water and tried to remember what it was I loved about him.

Blaire walked up beside us. She was angry. At least that was what her glare and quiet hello depicted. I was never sure what Blaire was. It never seemed to be her own emotion, always an extension of Rob in some way. She was a moron and pathetic, but I was worse than her. At least she allowed her emotions to hinge on *her* boyfriend. Mine had been attached to someone else's for far too long.

The night continued, and we moved on to Que Pasa and Northbeach and finally the Starboard. I was drunk and tired by the time Andrew from Baltimore hit on me. He managed to only spill his beer on himself, but the constant threat of being doused twice in one night left me on edge as the words slurred from his lips. He'd been abandoned by his friends who were probably equally as solid in their form at this, the eleventh hour of their partying.

"We've been drinking since noon," he kept saying. Not repeating it one sentence after another, but with every lull to our painful chat, he'd interject it.

"Andrew, I'm going to go. Maybe you should, too."

"We've been drinking since noon."

"I heard. It's impressive," I said earnestly. I didn't want to wound him any more than he had himself. "I'll see you later maybe." I turned to walk away, and Andrew grabbed my arm. I knew this wasn't going to be easy.

"Where are you going? Do you want to get some food?"

I took a deep breath. If I didn't lose him now, he'd be with me forever. "No. My head is pounding. I need to go home and get some Advil," I lied.

"I've got some right here." Andrew reached in his pocket and pulled out six pills. Four were small blue ones and two were Advil gel caps. He ran his finger over the group of them, trying to decipher through drunken eyes which ones I should take.

"Everything okay over here?" Jack asked and stood next to Andrew. He towered over him. His height plus his obvious ability to better manage his liquor were a strong contrast to Andrew, who barely acknowledged Jack when he'd spoke.

"Hey," I said, so thankful he was there.

Jack's eyebrows lifted as he noticed the pills in Andrew's hand. He looked back at me, questioning my participation.

"I was just telling Andrew I had a headache, and he was nice enough to root through the apothecary in his pocket for some pain relievers for me."

"Oh." Jack nodded as if the idea of me taking one of those pills wasn't ridiculous. "I need to talk to you." He grabbed my hand and pulled me through the unbearable crowd. I glanced back to make sure Andrew wasn't following us, and he tilted his head back as he swallowed some pills and downed them with his beer.

Jack pulled me all the way to the front patio, where there were six inches for us to share. I stood in front of him. The crowd behind me surged, forcing me to lean against his chest, and I lost myself there. Somewhere between his shoulder and the rough fabric of his T-shirt that dragged against my face. I could have stayed until the bar emptied. Until we were the only people left in the night.

"Drugs are bad."

His words pulled me back. "I've heard that."

"I'm serious. Don't take anything from that guy."

I laughed right in Jack's face. Well, more like his chest, because he was a normal size and I was an elf. "I wouldn't take directions from him."

He pulled my hair off my shoulders and gathered it in his hand behind my head the same way he had the first day we'd met. He kept pushing it away as if he didn't like the sight of it, but the way he fisted his hand made my head drop back and my eyes close. I wanted Jack to control me.

I inhaled deeply and forced myself to face him. "Do you prefer girls with short hair?"

He rested his forearm on my shoulder and leaned down until I could feel his breath on my cheek. I closed my eyes and let it dance across my skin. "Your hair is perfect." He wrapped the ponytail around his hand and tightened his grip. "It makes me think of all the things I want to do to you." Jack pulled me back by the hair, and I opened my eyes again. I lost myself in the deep blue staring back at me.

I longed for him to take me home. I stepped back from him as the idea washed over me, leaving me with a fresh feeling of want. Jack didn't smile, he didn't make a joke, and he didn't look away. I was sure he knew it, too. No matter what I said to hide it, I felt his understanding of what I needed from him.

It scared me through three more beers, until the crowd thinned out and most of the people we lived with found us. They were a wave of exhaustion. Falling, yelling, singing, slurring. All of them were out well past their bedtime, but happily among their equals. I walked home with Tank and a half share.

"Tank, remember the time you kissed me on the back of the bus on the way to our senior trip?" the half share asked.

He smiled at her like he was tasting her. I should have turned away, but they were enticing in their flirtation. "Yes. You dared me to."

"I might dare you again," she said, and I felt the heat rise to my cheeks. I fell back two steps and let them walk alone the rest of the way to our house. By the time I arrived, they were carrying a beach blanket and walking back toward the bay.

I sunk back into my invisible place and fell into my bed.

I AWOKE TO the sound of Mila's voice and a banging on the side of the porch. She was outside. I rolled over and found Jack's bed empty. I wished he were in mine, but I wouldn't think about that. He'd either met someone or found somewhere else to sleep.

"Not here," a guy said not far from my head.

"What's wrong with here?" Mila was seductive. There were pauses between her words, and I imagined her kissing him. Whoever he was. I leaned up to hear better.

"Um, we're outside. Standing up."

Relief flowed through me at the realization that it wasn't Jack.

"Haven't you ever had sex standing up?" she asked.

There was a thump on the side of the house just past the wall of windows I slept under.

"This is what you want?" he asked, and there was a longer pause. I fought against the muscles in my arms and legs not to stand up and watch them. "You want me to *fuck* you right here against the side of this house?" Oh . . .

There was silence and then the sound of a zipper. It was followed up by some short, stifled grunts.

"Ah, yes," Mila said breathless. "Just like that."

I was mortified, and disturbed, and aroused. I could have crawled under my covers and died. I hid my head beneath the quilt, and the heat almost suffocated me. In the darkness of my porch, and during the performance outside my window, I slipped my fingers inside my underwear and touched myself. I was gentle. Mila and her friend were not. They thumped against the wall again, and my pace quickened. I thought of Jack between my thighs on the beach, and lying next to me in the bed he'd made for me. My breaths were deep as I listened to the sounds from outside. The heat rose up inside me as I closed my eyes. I arched my back chasing the heat as the muscles in my thighs tightened. I played until I was on the verge of coming and then slowly caressed myself until I heard Mila say, "I'm about to come," from outside my window. I finished, shaking beneath my covers and squeezing my thighs together in silence.

When my breathing steadied, I pushed the home button on my phone, and it doused my bed tent with light. I quickly turned it off. I tilted it down toward the mattress and hit it again. It was four thirty in the morning, and Mila was having sex against the side of our house.

I was alone.

Again.

Thirteen

I Think it's a Bad Idea

"YOU ARE SUCH a selfish bastard!" Blaire said in a hushed fury just inside the kitchen. This was why a porch was not a bedroom. It should have four walls and one door. We could never shut our door because we were always trying to steal air conditioning from the kitchen. Blaire should close it now.

"Shh. My head is killing me."

"Your head." This apparently infuriated her more. I opened my eyes and found Jack in the bed next to me. He was back. He didn't stir from the fight. "Where were you last night?"

"What are you talking about?"

"You didn't come home until five. That's what I'm fucking talking about. You weren't with Nora, because I checked her room. She was asleep. Alone." *That hurt.* "You weren't in any of the other rooms, either. Not in your car, not passed out on the lawn, not asleep in the hammock. Where the fuck were you?"

"You're crazy. I ran into some people I knew, and we partied. That's it."

"What people? We've been together for four years. Any people you know, I know."

"That's the problem with you. You think you share my life."

"I'm supposed to share your life. That's what being in a relationship means."

Their voices trailed off as they mercifully left the kitchen. I closed our door and moved the chair holding the box fan in front of the windows near my bed. It pointed mostly on Jack, but at least one of us should get some air. I didn't want to hear another word from the house.

I closed my eyes and fell back asleep. I didn't wake up until three thirty in the afternoon. I'd slept the day away, and so had Jack. It felt like he was avoiding me, even in his sleep. He hadn't come home and climbed in my bed. There were no funny comments from him in the morning about how he knew I wanted him. When he finally woke, he was quiet and evasive as he stood from his bed and went directly into the shower.

I found a leftover pizza and put the whole pie on a sheet in the oven, knowing someone would finish the rest. Food and liquor didn't go to waste here. Even day-old food. I took a slice and left the rest of the pizza on the stovetop next to the beer bottles with cigarette ashes dotting the rims.

When Jack got out of the shower, I got in. I let the water wash away the day before that had felt like a week. I let it drown out the questions of why I was alone and every other person around me had found someone, at least for the night. In Rob's case, at least one person.

Because it seemed as if everyone else in the house was still passed out, I took my time. I dried my hair in the bathroom and put on my makeup.

The dresses I owned were mostly plain. I was a shorts and tee kind of girl. Soft fabrics, clean lines. I'd brought my one red dress because it was the Fourth of July, and some juvenile parade-wear still pervaded my packing. Heather had made me buy it. It was more her than me. It was more everyone than me, but I was tired of being me, and I was sick of being alone. I slipped the dress over my head and let my towel fall to the floor at my feet.

"What is that?" Jack said as he opened the back door to our porch and stopped just inside, staring at me. I straightened the dress. It was short, but not tight. The neckline was plunging, and it laced up the back. "Happy birthday, America."

I pulled my hair to one side and ran my hands up and down the back of the dress, searching for the strings that cinched the corset effect. I found one and leaned to the side, hoping the other would fall like a pendulum into my hand.

I could feel him still watching me, but I couldn't let what Jack did move me. I'd learned a lot of things last night, and that was the harshest. He was, as he'd said a hundred times, on vacation, and that included many nights that I wasn't going to be a part of.

He walked behind me to see what I was doing. "Oh my," was his reaction to the back of the dress. "Are you taking a Taser out with you tonight?" I ignored his statement, and he took the string from my hand. He pulled both sides tight. "Good?"

The bodice floated on top of my skin. It was wearing me instead of the other way around. "A little tighter."

Jack groaned and tightened the corset. His cold fingers grazed the minute areas of skin still exposed by the ties. My thoughts were grounded exactly where his fingers touched. The sensation terrified me. I couldn't let my body respond to him this way. He'd be touching someone else's body in a few hours.

"Thank you," I said when he finished.

Jack ran his fingertips from the tops of my shoulders down my arms, sending heat through me as they traveled. A sudden resentment filled me. He could have anyone. He came and went as he pleased, leaving me trapped here alone. I blamed him for something he'd never done, and I'd punish him with the things I'd never do. I stepped away at the exact moment Tank popped his head into our porch.

"We're taking the Jolly Trolley into Rehoboth to get an early dinner." Jack and I only stared at him. "You're both coming."

"I just ate," I said and increased the distance between Jack and me. I caught the rejected look in his eyes. Something had changed between us the night before.

"Doesn't matter. You're coming."

"I'm not hungry."

"You can watch us eat."

Tank left Jack and me alone. I glanced at my car out the window. It was pulled in so far that four other people would have to move their cars for me to escape this place.

"Come." Just one word from Jack sent a tingle down my spine.

"Who else is going?"

"Me."

He was all that mattered.

I rummaged through my bag for my ID and bank card. I had two dollars left from the night before. At this rate, I'd spend my rent if I were here the entire weekend. Just one more night, I told myself. I left all my jewelry in my bag. The dress didn't need a thing to draw attention to it.

"Let's go," Mila yelled into the porch. She came out and shooed me into the front of the house.

There we were joined by Tank and Stone. We waited in the front yard until Jack came out of the house, and then we walked to Dickinson Street to catch the trolley to Rehoboth.

The trolley was open air, and to Jack's and my delight, there was some wind. I held my skirt down and let the breeze blow through my hair, not caring if it looked crazy by the time we got to the restaurant.

I knew we were going to Dogfish Brewery before the trolley even entered Rehoboth. I'd heard it mentioned enough to know it was only a matter of time before they went. The only surprise was that I was with them.

We filed into our seats at the restaurant. Mine was between Tank and Mila, directly across from Stone.

"Nice dress," Stone said.

I tried to decipher if it was sarcasm or serious. I couldn't tell. "Thanks."

"Why do you seem like you hate me?"

I was shocked. I tried so hard not to seem like anything. "I don't hate you."

"You sure?" Stone took a sip of his water, and Tank began to laugh.

"Yeah. I mean, you seem wound a little tight." I saw Jack out of the corner of my eye. He was reading his menu and listening to every word. "Like, maybe you should smoke some pot, or not drink . . . or try some yoga."

"Yeah, try some yoga," Mila added and winked at Stone.

"See? You sound like you don't enjoy my company."

"It's fine. Just maybe not as relaxing as it could be."

Stone sneered and focused his attention on his own menu. I inhaled deeply and avoided the sight of Jack.

"It sounded like *you* were doing some yoga outside last night," Tank said, and we all turned to him, but he was looking directly at Mila.

"You're one to talk," she quipped back.

"I'm just saying, taking advantage of these poor beach boys with your downward facing dog moves. Doesn't seem fair."

"What the fuck?" Stone put down his menu. "Is everyone getting laid around here but me?"

"Maybe that would help," I said, and he turned his anger on me. "Or yoga . . ."

I ordered the seventy-five minute IPA and the crab-and-corn chowder before escaping to the bathroom. I stared at myself in the mirror. Stone didn't bother me. As long as he wasn't starting a fight next to me in a bar, he didn't bother me at all. Jack looking at me from the other side of a packed table was what bothered me. I straightened my dress. Stone wasn't the only person who needed to get laid.

"Hey," Mila said as she opened the door to the ladies' room. "You okay?"

"Yeah. I'm fine," I said and meant it.

"The guys were just having a huge argument about whether you're a lesbian or not."

"What?" flew out of mouth before I could contain it.

"It's okay." She stood next to me looking in the mirror. Her deeply tanned skin was visible from her sleeveless dress. Lean muscles, fitting her career as a yoga instructor, defined her body. "Either way, it's okay. Stone thinks you are. Jack swears you're not."

Change the subject. Change the subject. Change the subject. I laughed a little. It was still awkward. "Hey, Mila, what was your major at Penn?"

"Mathematical Economics."

I nodded, seeming completely unsurprised.

"I know. I know. Yoga helps me think, and I need to take some time and really consider what I want to do with my life, you know?"

I stared at her in the mirror. "Why is Stone so angry all the time?"

"He's the youngest of four brothers and the only one to not graduate from West Point. Stone went to the University of Vermont."

I stood in shock. Assigning any reason to Stone's anger seemed impossible, but now the deep-rooted nature of it began to make sense.

"He felt some relief for the first thirty seconds after he decided he wasn't joining the army, but he's been trying to make it up to his father ever since." Mila reapplied her perfect pale-pink lip gloss. "He should be brewing his own beer somewhere but instead he's atoning for the one decision he made on his own five years ago."

"Like, stop being sorry for something that wasn't wrong."

"Exactly, but back to you, I just want to make sure you know that if you are a lesbian, or anything else, that's totally cool with me. In fact, in that dress it's more than cool." She kissed me on the cheek and walked out of the bathroom.

I wanted to leave. I needed to leave.

I forced myself to walk back to my table and ate in pleasant silence. I wouldn't let them bother me, and I wouldn't engage with Stone again. Nothing good would come from it, and now that I understood a little more of how deep his anger was buried, there was no point to it. I wasn't looking to fix anyone.

"How's your soup?" Jack asked.

"Good," I said instead of fine, just to mix things up a bit. In the pause where a normal person would return the question, I checked my phone, which said absolutely nothing but five fifteen.

Two rounds of shots were ordered as dessert. I did mine and placed the glass on the wooden table next to the other empty ones. There was no turning back. My last night of the holiday weekend had begun.

The shots diminished my discomfort with my roommates, but left me feeling less than sober. I was still bopping my head and singing along to the vocalist from the Dogfish when I was standing on the curb out front.

He touched my arm first. Before he said a word, he wrapped his hand around my elbow to steady me. His grasp pulled me from my tipsy song and landed me square in front of him.

"I was hoping I'd see you tonight."

It was the politician from the night before. Derrick was his name. "Hey." His recognition threw me. I was so used to seeking anonymity, and yet, I kind of liked Derrick knowing me. He was less corporate-looking today in a T-shirt and camo shorts. I liked them better on him since I could easily see his fit body defined under his slightly tight tee.

Having realized I wasn't with them when they reached the corner, Jack yelled, "Nora." My entire group stared at Derrick and me. All of them except Mila appeared concerned. She was grinning wildly and winking at me, hoping Derrick and I were going to have sex right there on the street.

"Want a ride?" he asked me. "We're headed back to Dewey."

I peered past Derrick at the shining Chevy Tahoe behind him. Four guys were opening the doors and getting in.

I turned back to my housemates. Their questions, their sharing, their debates about my sexuality were exhausting me. "I'll catch up with you guys later."

Derrick helped me climb into the Tahoe and closed the door. We pulled out and passed my housemates as Mila waved excitedly to the tinted windows of the car and Jack stared, disturbed by my departure. I inhaled and enjoyed the space.

DERRICK'S HOUSEMATES WERE eerily similar to my own. There was the angry girl, who seemed like she might have fucked him the night before, and the happiest guy alive, who was passing a bowl. Derrick declined, and I followed his lead.

Derrick kept a beer in my hand at all times in his house and at the Rudder. He was attentive and trying to get me drunk, neither of which I was opposed to. He was also intelligent and funny. Two things rarer than a twenty-three-year-old virgin at a beach bar on the Fourth of July.

We danced along with the music, and even that he did well. In the seven hours we'd spent together, I became certain I could spend the rest of my life with him. I hadn't fallen head over heels. My feelings were nowhere close to love at first sight. Our connection was a glorious compatibility that could endure the next five decades.

The drunker Derrick got, the more he liked me . . . and my dress. It was a crowd pleaser. As I walked through the hoards to the bathroom, several people commented on it. Some were even girls. I searched each face for one of my housemates, knowing there were only a few choices in bars. Where were they? More importantly, why did I care so much? Derrick's house was a much safer group for me to be with. I was still new, and besides Derrick, none of them cared who I was.

We lingered too long and I was exhausted. Derrick was unsteady on his feet. The Rudder was throwing us out. The lines for pizza had already formed, and half the town had properly passed out on their couches, floors, and back lawns. The time had come to go home.

We turned on New Orleans Street and left the stragglers of the main road behind. Next to a restored Volkswagen bus parked outside his house, Derrick stopped walking. My mind raced. Was I spending the night? Was I walking home tomorrow morning in this dress?

Were Derrick and I about to have sex?

He kissed me. He held my head in his hands. He was gentle and kind. Even as he forced my head back and leaned down on me, he made me believe I was the most cared-for girl in the world.

My arms hung at my sides. I liked the taste of him. His hands on me left me wanting more, and I told him with my tongue matching the force of his own. I reached up and pulled him down to me. I pressed myself against the front of him, my heart pounded against his chest.

Derrick released me. "Come inside with me."

I forced myself to stop thinking, to stop wondering if it was a good idea. I was just going to enjoy the moment. My phone dinged with a text as I followed Derrick. I pulled it from my purse and saw it was from Jack. He must have been bringing someone home, or found one of the half shares in our house who appealed to him.

The text read, *I know it's none of my business, but I just wanted to make sure you're okay. You've been gone a long time.*

To me, it felt as if I'd been gone forever. The time was a peaceful break from the never-ending drama the house created. Or was it the people in the house?

I texted back, *I'm fine. Don't wait up.*

I didn't linger on the message. Jack had his life, and I had mine. The phone went back in my purse as I followed Derrick to an empty bedroom on the third floor of the house. I scanned through my memories of the night for messages or signals he might have given his roommates requesting privacy.

Derrick kissed me again, reminding me of why we were here. In his bedroom. He was far less gentle than he'd been in the street. His hands slipped under the straps of my dress and pushed them off my shoulders. The front fell to the portion held up by the corset. He paused and gazed at my breasts as my nipples hardened from the exposure.

"You're so hot." He reached for one, taking it in his hand and caressing my hard nipple as he kissed my neck, and something shut down inside me. There was a moment, and I was no longer a part of it. I inhaled deeply trying to go back, but it was lost to me. Somewhere between the driveway and his bed, I'd run away.

"I need to go to the bathroom," I said.

Derrick stood straight and faced me. He was pleased, probably thinking I was going to insert some type of birth control or complete some other pre-coital preparation.

I grabbed my purse on the way out, which only added to Derrick's anticipation. I didn't need it. I didn't know why I'd brought it, except when I was safely locked in the bathroom I took out my phone and read Jack's text again. He was worried about me. His tongue might have been down some idiot's throat at the time, but he was worried about me, and that mattered.

I used the bathroom and washed my hands with the urgency of a person driving to the dentist to have a root canal. I took one last look in the mirror and solidified that I was going home.

"I'm going to need you to listen to me and not say anything," I said to Derrick, who was now lying on the bed, facing me. "I was just going to leave, but I thought I owed you this conversation—these words." I pointed to Derrick. "I'm just not sure if this . . ." He was still comfortable, not yet realizing my ramblings were our eulogy. "Is a good idea. It might be. It probably is." I shook my head in self-doubt. "You're a great kisser, so the potential is surely there, but I'd rather be sure." I was rambling. "Like, certain." The smile drained from his face. He was catching up. "So I'm going to go." I exhaled, thankful those statements were over and certain I'd meant every word now that they'd been said.

Derrick sat up in bed and pulled me to him with both hands on my waist. He kissed my stomach and peeked up at me. "I've got a ball gag in my duffel if that's what you're into."

I stopped moving and breathing. "Um."

"It has a harness, which I don't exactly know how to use, but I'm up for it if you want to try it out."

"No. Thanks." I shut my eyes and shook my head.

Derrick shrugged. He was completely fine with me wanting to be gagged, or not. "You can just sleep here."

"I think that's a bad idea."

I walked out the same way I'd come in twice that night, or was it the day before? According to my now-dying phone, it was three thirty in the morning. The streets were almost empty. The few people left wandering them made me question whether Dewey was ever fully asleep. It was like a giant birthday party everyone was invited to.

My house was dark. The only sounds were Blaire's voice yelling at Rob. Had she kept that up for the last twelve hours? I poured myself a glass of water and carried it past the chair with the fan blocking the doorway to my porch. Jack was asleep in my bed.

I could have climbed in with him and finished what I'd started with Derrick, but that was what my mother would have done. She wouldn't have cared that Jack would be in bed with someone else next weekend. It wouldn't have mattered to my mother that he wasn't in love with her.

This was a beach house, and he'd rented it for the whole summer. There were other full shares in plenty of other houses. Jack didn't stir as I placed the glass of water on the sill next to his bed and plugged in my phone. I set the alarm for seven and fell asleep alone. The same way I always did.

Fourteen

First Words

I LEFT WORK and drove to the shelter. I'd barely made any progress with Rufus in the past few weeks. He was one of the worst cases I'd ever seen. It made me thankful he couldn't tell me everything that had happened to make him distrust people so much.

"Hey, big guy," I said and kneeled down next to the wall of Rufus's cage. "How's it going in here?" His chin rested on the floor; his eyes peered up at me. "I brought the cowboy book and a new one." I pulled the books out of my bag. *Scooby Doo and the Weird Water Park.*" I smiled as I showed him. The little dog from the cage next door was gone. He'd been adopted and replaced by a small hound breed that howled whenever the dog on the other side did.

"If you think about it, all water parks are weird." I shrugged. "I mean, large slides, water, a bunch of strangers frolicking around together in their bathing suits. It's kind of an odd gathering."

Since meeting Tank, I was beginning to see things differently than I had before, or rather, I was beginning to *see* things.

I read Rufus the books, and he finally moved toward me. I gave him a treat, and he let me reach in and pet his head right between the eyes. He was such a sweet guy under his miserable exterior.

"I get it. You need to be friends with me first before you can love me." Rufus tilted his head from side to side, listening as I spoke. "You've got to talk to them," I whispered, even though the dogs around me were barking like crazy. "You've got to let them see how sweet you are, because I haven't been able to find an apartment yet that will let you stay with me."

I stood to leave, and Rufus returned to the corner of his cage.

"THE GUY WHO'S always lurking in the background did it," Stone stated his assessment not as part of a conversation. Jack had just finished reading us the last words of chapter eight and was folding down the corner of the page when Stone made his proclamation.

"Who? The butler?" Mila asked.

"Yes. He's always just there."

"I think that's what butlers do. They lurk. For a salary, of course."

I rolled onto my back and let the bright sunshine warm my face. The story was coming together. The Cromwells were a sordid bunch. Each more depraved than the next. There were glimpses of light in some of the characters, but mostly the dark was written in the pages Jack read to us.

I followed the story, but it was the sound of Jack's voice that held my attention. I rested my head on my arm and slid my fingers around in the sand next to my blanket as the words fell from his lips. The ocean waves crashed behind us. The sun shone above us, and my housemates surrounded Jack as he read about people we'd never known.

"Fucking keep reading," Stone demanded.

Jack put the book on his towel beside his chair and walked into the ocean without acknowledging Stone had ever spoken.

Mila stood, too. The fringe on her bathing suit moving in the warm breeze. She turned her head from the blowing wind and appeared as though the intrusion of the air was expected and welcomed. She walked over and laid on the blanket without an invitation. Mila was welcome wherever she landed. My sheet was no exception. She was warm and gentle, lying next to me and smiling at the sight of Blaire cuddled up against Rob on the beach blanket facing us.

Rob was lying on his stomach. Blaire was on her back, unbelievably close to him. He was looking at us and when Blaire noticed his sight line, she leaned in and whispered something in his ear. Rob grinned and kissed the side of her neck, confirming whatever she'd said was sexual. It was the only language she alone shared with him. She was smart to speak it rather than yelling at him in the words we could all utilize.

I turned to Mila. "Why don't you have a boyfriend?"

She smiled. I wasn't sure if she was pleased in my interest in her or if I'd just stumbled upon her favorite topic. "You know that feeling you get when you meet someone intriguing? That little rumble in the back of your mind?" She widened her eyes, pulling me into her thoughts. "It's always followed with: does he like to hold hands? Is he a good tipper? Can he speak about something I don't know about?" She moved closer to me. "You lean in and inhale him, and all those questions are replaced with, *Is he good in bed?*"

I stayed silent, and Mila stared at me. I searched my mind for evidence of a prior rumble. There'd been several, but I'd never explored the answers to the rest of the questions.

"That moment of uncertainty," she continued, now lost in her own memories of conquest. "That will either blow you away or leave you disappointed."

She paused, and I felt obligated to contribute. "I guess," I weakly added.

"Well, I'm addicted to it. I love to meet new people. I love their reactions the first time I touch them. I love the feel of their arms around me before I really know who they are. It's intoxicating. My drug of choice." Mila rolled over onto her side and faced me. "But I haven't found anyone who made me *need* seconds. So, I keep moving on."

"Does your family pressure you to settle down?" I had the strange urge to pressure her myself. Mila was my favorite.

Jack walked out of the ocean and picked up the football. He tossed it in the air until Stone rose out of his seat, too. They went behind us to the soft sand and threw the ball back and forth. The sun glistened on Jack's wet skin as the muscles in his arms flexed with every throw. Maybe Mila was *one* of my favorites.

"No." Her laughter pulled me back to the blanket and the topic of commitment. "My mother abandoned me and my father when I was seven." I reluctantly left the image of Jack and turned to Mila. She wasn't crying or sad. She was watching for my reaction. The one I was sure would be inadequate. I stayed very still.

She continued, "She left him a note that said she couldn't discover herself while being buried with us."

"Oh my God." The words repulsed me as soon as they reached my ears but had no effect on Mila. She'd known them for fifteen years. I was scarred after fifteen seconds. "Incredibly selfish."

"Debilitatingly so. It almost killed my father." Mila's face hardened at the mention of her father's pain. "Since then, he's let me explore every interest, answer every question."

"That's good." Words were coming out of my mouth, but I

really had no idea what I was saying, or what I should be saying.

"He does it out of fear that one day I'll walk away, too. He'd never survive it."

"That's horrible."

"I know."

My own mother's choices flashed through my head and my utter disdain for everything she'd ever touched, including myself. "Do you hate her?"

Mila laughed a little. "I had a therapist once who told me I could either choose to hate my mother or love my father. I chose to love him and let her go."

"Wow." The air I inhaled sank down deep into my body. "That's amazing."

"I went to several. He was the best." She rolled over onto her back again and added, "Then he killed himself. Isn't that an odd thing for a therapist to do?"

I focused on the sound of the ocean. I lifted my head for the breeze to run across it, and I wondered why it was called *living your life* when we were basically just surviving it.

"You guys, it's the Running of the Bull," Tank yelled as he ran from the ocean. "Get up. Let's go."

No one moved. Not even me. I turned north where Tank was pointing at two people in a bull costume, followed by hundreds of people in costumes of all sorts, including many who looked like matadors. They ran between cones near the water and had obviously been drinking for a while. Several spectators stopped the bull and participants for pictures. It was a drunken, pageantry-filled family event that could only exist in Dewey, Delaware.

"Seriously, guys. I'm going." Tank ran down to the crowd by the water and immediately integrated into the masses. My sight followed him as far down as I could see him.

"Where's he going?" Jack asked as he and Stone stopped playing ball and witnessed the running next to us.

"He's running with the bull," Mila said. "Obviously." Jack laughed as Tank disappeared a few blocks away.

I left all of them on the beach, trying to figure out whether to stay in the sun or go meet Tank at the Starboard. The show continued as stragglers tried to keep up with the crowd, and the early starters demonstrated why drinking in the sun could be challenging. No one noticed I slipped away.

Even though our house was empty, I sat in my car with the AC on, the windows up, and the doors locked. These people shared everything. I wanted to be left alone.

I found my phone in my beach bag and dialed my father's number. The guilt of leaving him because of my mother's indiscretion tore through me. I needed to hear his voice.

"Nora?" he answered the phone, and the uncertainty in his voice hurt me.

"Hey, Dad." I kept things light. He was my dad. We'd never had anything but a good time together. "How are you feeling?"

"I'm okay. Except for this pain in the ass."

"Mom?"

He laughed at me. "I tossed that one to you," he said, and I missed him. I missed her, too, but I wouldn't let myself think about that. "Did your mother call you? She's bored and torturing me because of it."

"She called, but I was planning on calling you anyway." I missed lying around watching C-SPAN with him, and building the model of the water cycle, and making my mother a wine opener—or simple lever, as my father always called it. "I miss you."

"Aw, sweetie. I miss you, too. What have you been doing? Why haven't you come to the shore? Your mom rented a great place."

"I know. I'd like to see you."

"Well, come down."

"Just you."

The silence from the phone was a deep tunnel into the center of the earth. It had no end until he gently said, "She loves you." My father, who never really knew why I hated my mother, had just witnessed us growing apart and avoiding each other. It started one day before he'd gotten home from work and hadn't ended five years later. He was lost to the why of our misery, but never unaware.

I wanted to say, *I know,* but how does one know their mother loves them? It should've been a given, but it apparently wasn't. Because when she was fucking my teacher, it had everything to do with me. Why else do it on my bed? And if it weren't about me, then it was the absolute denial of me, as if the center of where I lived meant so little it was the perfect place to break the only vow she'd ever taken. My anger was boiling over. I feared I might take it out on my dad. "Dad, I'm gonna go. I love you."

"Love you, too, Nora. Come see us." I pulled the phone away from my ear and heard, "And call again."

I put it back near my mouth. "I will."

I went for a drive and hid from my life in a parking lot in Ocean City, Maryland. I didn't go back to the house until I was sure everyone was out. Jack texted to make sure I was okay. I told him I'd run into an old friend and I'd be back later. For the first time it wasn't a lie. I'd run into my father.

I FELT HIM near me before he said anything, and yet he still startled me.

"Nora," he whispered. His presence again registered. How long had he been here? Tank was sitting on the edge of my bed. "Nora, wake up." He rubbed my arm, and I opened my eyes.

"Tank, what are you doing?"

"I want you to go in the ocean with me."

"What time is it?"

"It's four fifteen." Tank didn't check his phone. He didn't lean back to see the clock in the kitchen. He'd been waiting for four fifteen to wake me. As if that was our departure time.

"Are you okay?" I asked, because something didn't seem right about him. His words were urgent. I sat up and rested on my forearms. He stood up and gave me some room.

Jack half opened his eyes and rolled over to avoid waking up.

"I'm good. Please come with me," he whispered. I couldn't think of a way to say no to him.

"Okay. Let me change. I'll meet you outside."

Tank's smile lit up his eyes. "Meet me at the kayaks."

I stood on wobbly legs and searched around the porch for my bathing suit. The green one hung from the door knob to the backyard. My red one was at the bottom of my backpack.

With Jack's back to me, I slipped off the T-shirt I'd worn to bed a few hours before and stepped into the bottoms. The top was twisted and knotted together.

"It's dangerous to swim without a guard." Jack rolled over and faced me, and I didn't move to cover my chest. Him seeing me excited me more than it embarrassed me. I took a second to wallow in that realization.

"I know," I said and finally untangled the top. I pulled it over my head and hooked it behind my back. "Call the Coast Guard if I'm not back when you wake up."

"Your boobs are beautiful."

I stopped and looked down at my breasts and then back at him. There was no urge to roll my eyes the way I would have at Ricky. Jack's admiration was different. I welcomed it instead of the shunning any similar comments would receive.

Since Jack was already awake enough to appraise my breasts, I went out the door between our beds. Tank was pulling the kayak off the shelf in the shed. I rushed to get behind him and take the weight off one end, but he didn't need my help. To Tank, the kayak was like tossing a banana in the air. He picked it up and rested it on his shoulder.

"You know, I could help. Those little handles on both ends are for two people to carry it."

"You are helping." Tank passed by me without any other explanation, and I let him.

We walked in tandem over the dune in the darkness. I could hear the water and feel the wind, and suddenly it seemed very dangerous.

Tank turned to me when our feet touched the surf. "Here." He handed me his bowl and a lighter.

"Oh, I don't know. It's really dark out." I could see the whites of the waves as they crashed against the sand.

"Since you've already decided not to fully participate in life, you should at least enjoy the parts that you do."

I stood still in his analysis. "What does that mean?"

Tank put the bowl to his lips and took a hit. I waited for him to inhale a few times. The red glow from the bowl was the only light on the moonless night. When Tank finally exhaled, he said, "Life is deep, Nora. Dive in."

I let his words in. They sank all the way to my heart. I swallowed and held out my hand for the bowl. When Tank handed it to me, I took a hit, too.

I returned it, and Tank smoked again. He was relaxing in front of me, leaving his urgent demeanor with the red glow of the bowl.

"More?" he asked and held it up. I shook my head. Tank stashed the bowl under the towels he pulled from the body of the kayak. "Let's hope the tide's going out."

"And that we don't drown."

With a sly smile, Tank pulled the kayak into the water, and I pushed it from behind. We took it out past the breakers, and Tank climbed in. When he was steady, I climbed in the front and we paddled away from the shore.

I tried to memorize the pattern of lights. I searched for

something out of the ordinary to lead us back, but I stopped after they all started to appear the same. What was the worst that could happen? We'd go ashore a few miles from the house and have a long walk back?

The worst thing that could happen was that we'd never make it back.

I stopped paddling. Jack would find us. He'd send the Coast Guard or take the other kayak out if he had to. Jack took care of things. He took care of people. He probably got that from his mother.

"Tank?" I laid my paddle across the kayak and rested my legs over it. I leaned back toward him. "What's Jack's family like?" I turned a little so I could just see him out of the corner of my eye. "What's your family like?"

"Poor."

I turned fully toward him. "Really?"

"Yeah. We're the lower middle class of this group." Tank paddled farther away from the shore. "They hang out with us because we're cooler than them." I hung my hand over the side of the kayak and let the water flow through my open fingers. "And because Jack and I took our high school football team to the state championship."

"Did you win?"

"The game? Yes."

"I had no idea you guys weren't from affluent families, too."

"The first clue should have been we're the only two of this group working our asses off. Did you notice the rest of them seem to be taking time to figure things out? That's the type of behavior money indulges. Rich people should be the most self-aware in the world."

I sat up and slid my legs back under my paddle. "Why don't you rest for a while and I'll paddle us around?"

"Let's both rest and see where we drift."

"I don't want to do that."

Tank turned his head. I couldn't see him in the dim moon-light. I couldn't tell if he was disappointed. I turned my gaze to the moonless sky as a star shot across it.

"Tank! Did you see that?"

"Shh. I'm making a wish." He sat silent for a moment. "You should, too."

"I don't know what to wish for."

"That's tragic."

I knew I was tragic, and in the kayak with Tank, it bothered me.

I wished for Rufus to open up, and for him to be adopted by a nice family with a child who would adore him, and for a new apartment in case that didn't happen.

"You're different, Nora."

"Does that mean fucked up?"

"We're all fucked up. That wouldn't make you different." Tank laughed a little as he spoke.

"You seem to be better off than the rest of us," I said.

Tank's laugh bellowed through the empty sea air. It had an edge of horror to it as though I'd uncovered the secret to his sad existence. He stopped abruptly and said, "You're okay. You're like a string of Christmas lights." I stayed still. "If just one bulb was re-placed, you'd shine bright." I blushed at his words. "We just have to figure out which bulb it is."

"So, I'm salvageable?"

Tank paddled instead of answering. "Tell me something. Anything you want," he said. I stared down at the black ocean beneath us. "Share this moment with me. Like old times."

"We have no old times."

"I think we do. Maybe in another life, but we've been together for a while."

I inhaled deeply. I believed him. I believed in him.

When I couldn't fit any more of the atmosphere inside me, I closed my eyes and said, "I'm still a virgin." I shut them tight. The only sound was the water lapping against the side of the kayak. When the isolation wore on me, I forced myself to look back at him. No one else in the world knew, and I wanted to see his reaction as well as hear it.

"Wow. Now, that's something."

"I know."

"Such a heavy weight," he said, and it felt like he'd always resided right inside my mind. I relaxed in his understanding. "Most people drop it early because it's too difficult to carry."

"Yes. It's a horrible burden."

"Are you waiting to fall in love? Because that would seem like a mistake."

"Why?"

"Because when the love goes away, you'll have that tied to it, too."

"Who says the love will go away?"

"It comes more than it stays." With his words, my mother and my French teacher flashed through my mind, followed by my father. "The first person you have sex with touches your soul."

"Tank—"

"I'm serious. You're the virgin here. Remember? You need to listen to me." I rolled my eyes, but he couldn't see me. "You'll never forget your first. *He* should be amazing even if the sex is not."

"Who did you lose your virginity to?"

"The first girl who said yes."

"Was she amazing?"

"Not really, but neither was I, I'm sure. I don't want you to make a mistake."

I nodded. "Why do you think it's taken me this long? I don't want to make a mistake, either." I began to paddle again, and

Tank joined me. Together we raced through the water until I stopped and let the current take us.

Tank paused and said, "Okay. I'll do it." I turned back to him, already knowing what he was offering. I didn't have to say a word. Not one rejection. He was watching me and smiling like I was his favorite toy. Tank was innocence and love. "I'll have sex with you."

"You're very kind."

"I know it's not supposed to be me." There was no sadness to his words, only understanding. "There are so many decisions. Logistics, you know? Should it be daytime or nighttime? Raining or sunny? Are you into the verbal thing or quiet?"

"It's not that big of a deal."

"Of course it is. It's the deepest part of your being. The last physical home of your soul. You've carried it this long. It's a big deal." Tank beheld the sky. "Each of us has our mind and our body to share. Most people are willing to give away their body before their mind, but you've held on to both."

For too long, I thought.

TANK AND I stored the kayak in the garage, and he left me alone in our yard. I rinsed off in the outside shower, letting the water pour over my bathing suit before I slung it over the wall of the shower. It slapped against the rotting wood louder than I'd expected. It was just before dawn, and I hoped everyone would continue sleeping. I rung out my hair and wrapped myself in the first towel I'd found on the clothes line.

Rather than opening the back screen door that I knew would screech and wake Jack, I walked around to the front of the house and went in that way. Rob was passed out on the floor half sitting up with his lower back leaning against the front of the couch. There was an ashtray overflowing with cigarette butts next to him and a beer between his knees. I fought the urge to help him to bed. We were no longer at the University of Delaware, and he was not my responsibility.

"I think I'm pregnant." Blaire's voice startled me.

My head shot up in her direction. Her eyes were fixed on Rob. "What?"

She left the corner of the hall she'd been leaning against and walked into the living room lit only by the television on in the corner with the sound turned down. It flashed light across the paneled walls and her ethereal skin. "I told him tonight that I think I'm pregnant, and this is where he slept."

We both turned our attention to Rob. Even in his sleep, he had the delighted boyish grin that always made me feel there was still joy in the world waiting for me. All I had to do was join him and I'd have that grin, too. He was too young to have a baby. I was pretty sure men with babies slept in beds. Fathers of children quit smoking and got jobs. She must have the wrong guy. But Rob was the only guy Blaire had.

"Are you sure?" I asked.

Without a word, she turned and disappeared into the hallway. The light from the television echoed its silence across the walls of the room, and I heard Blaire's door shut.

I abandoned Rob to find my bed. My feet stuck to the beer-stained floor of the kitchen. The newest photo on the fridge was of Blaire and Rob at a University of Delaware formal. She was gazing at him as if he'd just risen, and he was smiling at the camera or whoever was holding it. I slid past the box fan that attempted to draw the cool air from the kitchen and deposit it into my porch. Jack's bed was empty.

He was in my bed. I tiptoed around him and silently rummaged through my bag at the end of my bed. I found shorts and a Blue Hens T-shirt and exchanged my towel for both. The towel I hung over the door to the kitchen to dry. When I turned, Jack was staring at me, completely awake.

"What are you doing up?" I asked.

"Waiting for you," he said, and need poured over my exhausted body.

"What are you doing in my bed?"

"I missed you." He held up the covers, beckoning me in beside him.

I climbed in, and he turned on his side and pulled me close to him. My arms were folded at my chest. In the silence of the morning, it was the safest I'd ever felt.

"Don't worry. I'm still not going to have sex with you until you beg me."

"I wasn't worried," I said, and Jack kissed the top of my head.

I closed my eyes.

Fifteen

The Hole You Left Behind

"SAFEONE AUTO. THIS is Nora." There was a pause on the other end of the line, and I hoped more than anything to hear a dial tone. *Please hang up.*

"Hello." The voice was frail. The man on the other end of the line was weak.

"Hi. Can I help you?"

"Yes. My son—" He took a deep breath and exhaled. "There was an accident. I believe I'm supposed to call this number to find out what's being done about the car. And the other driver. And his truck."

"Sure. Do you have the claim number?" I typed in the number as he read it off wherever he'd written it down. His claim must have been recent. I hadn't heard of the queues being backed up. "Is this Mr. Howe?"

"Yes. Steven Howe, my son . . ." He choked up a little and

cleared his throat. "Was driving the car."

My eyes scanned over my screen. Vehicle One: Honda Civic. Vehicle Two: Eighteen Wheeler. Total Loss. Fatality. "Mr. Howe, have you been contacted before regarding this claim?" It was miscoded. The fatality was only identified in the comments. The claim should have been in a complex unit thirty-six hours ago.

"No, and I'm sorry to bother you with this. My wife is beside herself, and she's taken to worrying about the car and the other driver to keep from going insane."

"Please don't apologize." I read more as I spoke. *Named insured's seventeen-year-old son head-on collided with eighteen-wheeler.* "We were just about to contact you regarding the same." *No skid marks. No signs of averting the loss.* My head pounded. "From the information in front of me, we've spoken with the driver of the truck. He sought medical attention the night of the accident and was treated and released from the hospital. He was only sore as of yesterday." *Driver of Vehicle Two stated he was unable to stop his truck in time. He could see into the insured driver's eyes as they collided. Insured made no effort to avoid the collision.*

"Oh, thank God."

"Mr. Howe, we have a specialized unit at SafeOne to handle serious accidents such as this. They're experienced with injuries and total losses." *And deaths.* "I'm going to transfer your claim to that unit, and someone will be in touch with you today."

"That's fine."

Fine. I knew what fine meant. "Are there any questions I can try to answer for you before we hang up?"

"The answers I need only God has. So, no."

"I'm so sorry, Mr. Howe."

There was a click on the other end of the line, and I feared I'd worsened his pain. If that was even possible. I logged our conversation into the file comments and wrote the claim number on a Post-it note. I put my phone on send and removed the headset that was chained to my head day after day.

Sharon was eating her lunch at her desk the same way she did every day. It was egg salad on wheat from the cafeteria. She sucked Diet Coke through a straw and raised her eyebrows as I approached her desk. "Yes? What are you doing off the phones?"

"A claim was misrouted. It's a fatality and needs a call back immediately."

"Did you note it in the file?"

"Of course."

I waited for her to request the claim number from me. I expected her to pick up her phone and call her counterpart in the complex unit and make something happen for Mr. Howe. Sharon took another bite of her sandwich. Her bright blue sand pail and shovel earrings laid flat against her lobes.

"Do you want the claim number?" I was appalled.

"The claim will be moved to complex based on your notations. Now get back on the phones. Our numbers are up."

I fought against the rage brewing inside of me. Sharon took another bite and chewed her food with her mouth open. I turned and walked out of our unit. I followed the hall to the other end of the building, where Complex Claims was housed, and found the only manager I knew in the group.

He was perched at a cubicle in the center of the room with all the claim reps' desks surrounding him. He was the command center. "Nora, what brings you over here?"

"I have a claim."

"Your own?"

I shook my head. "It was misrouted and it's a fatality."

"Have a seat." He waved his hand to the chair in front of his desk.

"I spoke to the insured on the phone. His son was driving and was killed in the loss."

"Oh. That's terrible." He held out his hand, and I placed the

Post-it into it. He entered the numbers into the keyboard and read the file information on the screen. "Oh," he said as he read. He'd gotten to the heart of the claim. He called over a middle-aged claim rep and handed him the Post-it note. "Whatever you're doing, I want you to stop and work on this. Read the file first and let me know if you have any questions."

The claim rep took the file number and returned to his desk.

I stood up to leave.

"You seem upset," he said, stopping me. "Nothing seemed to upset you when you were in my training class."

I didn't know what to say. It didn't feel like he was done dissecting me.

"It's okay to feel something."

"It's tragic."

"Thanks for bringing the claim over. We'll take care of him."

I walked back to my desk, wishing I could walk home.

ACCORDING TO TANK, I'd bared my soul to him. He now knew more than anyone. My mother assumed I'd had sex years ago. In between her awkward offers to help me obtain birth control, she'd ask if I was gay. Once she even tried to find out what I was "into." I was into *not* talking about my sex life with my mother, who'd probably forever ruined me for intimacy. There was no one else to tell.

With our alcohol-filled stomachs calmed by slices of pizza, Tank and I began the rest of our stumble home. I nearly fell off the curb waiting for the light to change, and Tank took my hand and wrapped it around his elbow for the rest of our journey.

"Did you have fun tonight?" he asked, sounding completely sober. He made me think he was.

I tilted my head to see him better, but I couldn't tell. "It was good. You?"

"Great friends, great weather. Great time," he rambled.

"Amen."

"Nora." I knew from his tone that this was important. Tank said so many words in a day, but I was getting accustomed to the highs and lows, the important and the entertaining. "What do you think happens to us when we die?"

"I have no idea."

"You've never thought about it? Not even for a minute?"

"I can't fathom it. I can't even grasp the idea of not living, so the afterlife is beyond me. Literally." Tank smiled at my words and kept us walking. "Why? What do you think happens to us?"

"I think when we die, it blasts a hole in the people who love us. Our souls return for the time it takes to fill in the holes our departure left, to help them survive until we see each other again."

I stopped walking, unable to move forward with the images in my head.

"Like spackle," Tank said and lightened my thoughts enough for me to move again.

"What if no one loves you? What if there's no one to fix?"

"Then your life begins again. You keep living lives until you do it right."

"What's right?"

"To live life right, you have to truly love someone." Tank's pace quickened so we could cross at the yellow light that was about to turn. Once safely on the sidewalk across the street, he returned to leading our stroll home.

Am I on my second trip through life? Is this my first time around? Did I love before?

"Tell me something about you, Nora."

"No." Tank stole me from the inside of his mind. "You already know too much."

Tank shook his head. "It's impossible to know too much about a person. Especially one you like."

"I'm done sharing. You tell me something about you."

"I talk all the time."

"But it's rarely about you. Tell me what's important."

We walked the next block in silence. My mind drifted to the hangover I was going to have tomorrow. I was already dreading my drive home.

"I can feel sound," Tank said and dragged me back from my thoughts.

I stopped walking again and let his words sink in. "What?"

"Sometimes I feel sounds. Like for days I'll stay awake and just feel them." Tank began walking again, taking me along with him.

"Tell me more about that," I said gingerly. I used my I-have-no-thoughts-on-this-subject tone, but I had lots of thoughts. Most of them included fear for my beautiful friend who seemed nothing but excited to share his gift.

"You know when your leg is resting against the speaker in the door of your car and you're playing music with tons of bass?"

"Okay."

"You feel it, right?"

"Yes. I feel the vibrations."

Tank stopped moving again and turned me toward him. "Well, when it happens I can feel every noise. They impact me physically, not just audibly."

"How often? Every day?"

"No. It comes and goes. When it's not happening, I forget about it, but then it'll start again and last a few days sometimes."

"Is it going on right now? Can you feel my words?"

"Yes." Tank started moving again.

"What do they feel like?"

"They feel like love." He smiled at me, but I couldn't tell if he was joking. I'd drunk too much to know if he was serious about any of it.

Rob came up behind us and jumped on Tank's back. Blaire was there, too. Always one step behind him. She was drunk. She'd answered the question of her pregnancy with the shots I'd watched her drink the whole night. I wondered if she was ever pregnant to begin with or just desperate for Rob to hear her. Rob climbed off Tank and rested his sweaty arm around Blaire's neck. Even her smile seemed sad as she leaned into him. My jealousy of Blaire had morphed into pity, and I wasn't sure which was worse.

The four of us walked the last block home together, but we couldn't have been further apart. The three of them opened beers. Rob sat in the living room, and Blaire climbed on his lap. Tank was tinkering with a sculpture he'd started earlier in the day using only straws and peanut butter as a medium.

"Good night," I said and disappeared into the night.

Jack was nowhere to be found. I dwelled on the disappointment his absence caused until sleep saved me from it.

I'D BEEN TO the Starboard for brunch twice since the summer had begun, but never without Mila. Tank couldn't wake Mila up, though. He dragged Stone and me out of bed twenty minutes ago, and then we found Jack asleep in the hammock in the backyard and brought him with us. He looked exactly like a guy who'd slept in a hammock the night before.

They took mercy on us and sat us at a table without a sliver of sun touching it. The weather was already stifling. The humidity of the day before remained throughout the night and now mixed with the bright sunshine of Sunday. My chest rose as I forced a deep breath into it. The air was thick. I closed my eyes and took a sip of my bloody Mary.

"What the fuck happened to your neck?" Jack asked Stone. I could only see half of him since he was next to me. Something was obvious to Jack across from him that wasn't in my vision.

Stone reached up and covered his neck with his hand. He

winced and closed his eyes. "Soul-sucking little whore. Toddlers and puppies you used to have to worry about biting you. Now you have to include drunk bitches."

"She bit you?" The words fell out of my mouth before I could hide their disturbed tone. I leaned forward, and Stone sat back in his chair and removed his hand. It wasn't just a bite. It was a perfectly formed row of teeth that was already scabbing over. My jaw fell open. The rest of me was paralyzed by the sight.

"Fucked up, right? She would have bitten my nipple off, but I pulled her off as soon as I saw the wicked look in her eyes. She was a demon."

Jack said, "Wow."

I stayed completely silent.

Stone shook his head. He appeared to be reviewing the events of the night before one by one, because he winced at a memory. "Why are you tapping your finger?" he asked, and I froze, realizing he was speaking to me. "You a biter, too?" I placed my hands in my lap. Stone turned his attention to Jack sitting across from him. "Where did you end up last night?"

"I'm not sure."

"Well, when I went into the bedroom with Dracula, you were underneath her friend with the tiger tattoo on her calf." I forced my expression to remain light. I wouldn't let Stone or anyone else know how little I could stomach to hear about Jack hooking up with someone.

"I'm sensing a theme here. Meat eaters," Tank said, and we all laughed as our food was delivered.

"Carnivores." I tried to help move the conversation along.

"So where the fuck were you?" Stone was not letting it go.

"She started crying." Jack shook his head. "I don't know what happened."

"Sounds like a virgin," Stone said. I secured my hands back in my lap.

"What's a virgin like?" I forced myself to ask, and Tank stared at me across the table. His eyes were kind. He almost seemed proud I'd asked.

"Timid, quiet, scared . . ." Stone began and shook his head, dismissing himself. "Don't listen to me. I haven't talked to a virgin since seventh grade probably. The last thing I want to run into is a virgin."

"Why?" Tank asked, and I hung on every word.

"Because it takes a perfectly good meaningless sexual encounter and makes it . . ."

"What?" I asked.

"Mean something," Stone answered as if the words tasted bad in his mouth.

"Did you like her chewing on you?" Tank returned again to the teeth marks on his neck.

"Fuck no. I couldn't relax. I'm all for creativity, but there should be some sense of safety when fucking. I was scared to death she'd bite my balls." Stone ate a fork full of his Famous Eggs Delmarva and surveyed the Starboard. He leaned into the table, and the three of us followed. "Then, right before she was about to come, she screamed at me to choke her." He shook his head. "Fucking. Freak."

"At least she wasn't crying," Jack said. His words were low. This was a private meeting.

"It's a goddamn freak show out there after midnight."

We ate the rest of our breakfasts in silence. There seemed to be nothing more to talk about. The world was full of freaks, more so when you took your clothes off with them. Finally full and after three pitchers of water and another round of Bloody Marys, we dragged ourselves back to the street. You couldn't force a beer down my throat Monday through Thursday. I saved all my alcohol consumption for the forty-eight hours I spent at the beach every weekend. It was the only way my liver survived.

Stone stopped on the corner and pointed down the street to the store with the overwhelming collection of rafts for sale. "I'm going in there to see if they have anything to cover this." He pointed to the bite marks.

Chairs the color of the sea lined the sidewalk with pinks and reds dotted in between them. There were blow-up pools leaning against the wall of the building and plastic torsos with T-shirts hanging from a sign behind the chairs. Even from two blocks away, we could see the second-floor balcony with rafts of all different sizes and varieties hanging from it. I'd had an American Flag raft when I was little. What hung from the sides of this building were giant, two-person happy faces, pretzels, ducks, swans, and Tabasco sauce rafts. It was difficult to take it all in, and almost impossible to imagine Stone as a part of it.

"You're going in there?" I pointed to Jeremiah's.

"Yeah." He, as usual, acted like I was stupid.

"Get us a raft," Tank said and then walked across the street without another word.

"Where the fuck is he going?" Stone asked. We all watched Tank stroll toward the beach, completely oblivious to the fact he'd just left us without saying good bye.

"I don't know," Jack said. He seemed scarred from the night before. "Get us a raft, though. Something fun more than one of us can float on."

"What am I? Your dad? Get your own fucking raft." Stone walked down the street and disappeared into the cloud of blow-up rafts, and Jack and I turned back toward our house in silence.

I wasn't sure what to say. It didn't appear Jack wanted to talk about last night, and I definitely didn't want to talk about any of it. Whether he liked her. If she was a virgin. What that meant to him. We stopped at the next block, and he smiled at me the way he always did. I forgot what I was worried about. It was Jack.

"Did you have fun last night?" he asked.

"Yeah." I sighed. "I drank too much, though." The heat was making me feel sick. The walk was too long. "I'm never going to feel hydrated again."

"You will. I'd stay out of the sun until you do, though."

I basked for a moment in Jack's concern. "Where do you think Tank went?"

"Something caught his attention. It happens with him."

We turned the corner onto our street. The rest of Dewey was rising from the dead and venturing out for breakfast.

"Jack?"

He stopped and turned to me without any recognition of the heat. He had plenty of time for me.

"Tank said some things to me last night that I'm not sure I understood."

He smiled and kept walking. He nodded for me to follow him inside. "You'll wilt out here." Once we reached the shade of our porch, he turned the box fan on high and pointed it toward my side of our porch. "Do you want water?"

I shook my head and collapsed onto my bed. "I have some."

Jack laid down next to me. "Was he cruel to you?"

"No." I wasn't sure if I'd heard him right. "What?"

"Sometimes Tank gets into a . . . a mood, and it can be a little scary."

I shook my head. "No. He's never scared me."

"Good. Tank's different. Not always in the most common ways."

"I know." I left it at that. I didn't want to speak negative-ly about Tank. He was the kindest person I'd ever met, but last night's conversation left me feeling responsible for something I didn't understand.

I rested my head on Jack's chest. He was warm, too. I closed my eyes and traced back over the memories of the last few days. Tank wasn't the only thing I didn't understand. I fell asleep on

Jack and didn't wake up until after lunch. He was the most comfortable place in the house.

I felt like a truck had hit me, but then I thought of Mr. Howe's claim, and I closed my eyes again. The depth of his loss stunned me in the afternoon light. What would fill the hole his son had left behind? I rolled over, away from Jack, and slowly my eyes focused on an enormous Popsicle raft covering Jack's entire bed. It was a rainbow pop, and I couldn't help but smile at the sight of it.

I sat up and shook Jack's arm. "Jack. Jack, wake up."

"What?" His voice was heavy, swarmed by exhaustion.

"It's time to go swimming." He pulled me back down next to him and spooned me. "Look at your bed."

He lifted his head above my shoulders and said through squinted eyes, "What the fuck?"

I laughed at the sight of it. "Stone's a good dad."

Sixteen

Stupid. Fucking. Virginity.

THE STREET IN front of the house was empty. The driveway was barren except for Jack's motorcycle. The entire town had fallen into quiet time at the preschool. The seagulls squawking in the air above the back bay were the only disturbance to the tranquility. It was the hangover of the beginning of the summer. It was the calm before the storm. It was Thursday night.

Rob and Blaire were at her roommate's wedding. Heather might never be back. Tank had said he had to work all weekend because his father was enduring the prep for a colonoscopy on Monday. Mila and Stone had offhandedly said they were coming down tonight, and there were always a handful of half shares I still hadn't made the effort to learn the names of who'd arrive tomorrow. It'd been nine weekends since Jack had appeared in my room, replacing the inevitable revolving door of half shares with his likeable self. I was thankful. I wondered if he felt the same.

The screen door screeched as I pulled it open. When I stepped inside, I was met with the sight of Jack asleep on the couch with a book on his chest. He was peaceful and beautiful, and I wanted to spend the rest of my days near him just like this.

"Hey," I said as he opened his eyes. "Sorry to bother you. Keep sleeping."

"No. What time is it?"

I checked my phone even though I'd just seen the clock in my car. The beach stole time from you. "It's five thirty." I wasn't sure if it was the silence of the house or the calm of the town, but I felt like curling up with Jack. He was as inviting when he was quietly reading as he was when he was flexing his muscles as he threw the football in the sand.

"I have to get up."

"Why? You're on vacation."

"Because I'm hungry and I want you to go out to dinner with me."

The concept was foreign. Breakfast? Yes. Dinner? "Huh?"

"We're never going to have this place to ourselves again. Let's play house."

I scanned the mud-colored room and listened to the deafening silence. "We're alone all night."

"Just until Mila and Stone get here. You seem excited. You are, right?"

"I'm fine." I straightened up.

"Oh, I know, Nora Hargrove." He stood up. He was shirtless and beautiful. When I looked up from his chest, he was grinning at me in the naughtiest way.

"The house I play in is abstinent."

He rolled his eyes. "Wow. Sounds like a fun house. Let's see where it goes."

"I'm just making sure we're properly managing your expectations."

"Or crushing my hopes?"

"Either way."

"Let's go to the Rudder."

I used the bathroom, left my bag on our porch, and met Jack out back. He was sitting on his motorcycle revving the engine. I stood still on the back concrete stairs as he checked the gauges in front of him, oblivious to my presence.

"Ready?" he said when he finally looked up.

"We're not riding that."

"Sure we are. I have a helmet for you."

"Do you know how many people die on motorcycles every year?"

"Do you know how hot you sound when you quote death rates?"

"I'm serious. Over four thousand people died in motorcycle accidents last year, most of which were single-vehicle accidents at night."

"Wow. You're a ray of sunshine. Can you be just 'fine' and get on the back, please? I think you're going to like it."

I took a deep breath. He handed me the helmet, and I put it on. Jack helped me straighten it and then put his own on.

"Watch your leg," he said. I was happy no one was around to see my less-than-graceful mounting of Jack's motorcycle.

"Please don't kill me." I tightened my arms around him.

"Lofty goals." He reached back to my thighs and pulled my body closer to his. "You're not going anywhere without me."

We took off out of the driveway of our shack. Jack made a right into the oncoming traffic on Route 1 and merged onto the road. We rode the few blocks to the Rudder slowly and cautiously. Jack maneuvered the motorcycle with the care reserved for eggs in a shopping cart.

He stopped near the entrance of the Rudder and lowered

the kickstand. I climbed off, happy to be safely standing on the ground.

"Why didn't we just walk?" I asked.

"After dinner I want to go ride some rides."

"Isn't this enough of a ride?"

"You're a thrill seeker. I can tell." He extended his arm, asking me to lead the way.

I'd never been to the Rudder before the band went on. The usually mobbed dance floor was filled with tables. There was a steel drum being played on the opposite stage, and an air of a tropical oasis pervaded the patio. It was serene, completely different than what I was used to, and the perfect complement to our empty beach house.

The hostess led us to a table in the middle of the floor. She pulled my chair out and handed me a menu as Jack sat in the seat next to me at our table set for four. "The specials tonight are mussels in a red diablo or white wine sauce and fish tacos."

"Thanks." This was a real dinner. Like, dangerously close to a date. There were napkins, and a waitress, music, and somewhat of a view, and about a hundred other couples to which this was definitely dinner. My attention wandered to the table next to us where a couple sat holding hands and sipping oversized tropical drinks. Their presence was disturbing.

"Hey," Jack said, drawing my attention back to him. "You okay?"

"Totally fine."

"Why do you lie so often?" His question threw me.

"I never lie about anything important."

"I think you lie about how you're feeling and what you think, and those are the *most* important."

"Can we talk about something else?"

Jack looked down at his menu, only slightly defeated. "Of course."

"So why did you become a teacher?" I'd played this get-to-know-you game before, and I always won.

Jack stared at me, making me fear I might not prevail this time. He leaned in, suggesting he was going to share an intimate detail with me. "I knew I had to work immediately after graduating, but I wasn't sure what I wanted to do, and my roommate was an education major."

"Oh," I said. Jack always seemed to know what to do. "So you didn't grow up wanting to teach? You weren't born to work with children?"

At this he laughed loudly. "No. I like it, though. But I like construction more."

"What are you going to do?"

"What do you mean?"

"Are you going to keep teaching even though you don't love it?"

Jack stared at me with a mix of confusion and disgust. I'd somehow insulted him, and it was the last thing I'd meant to do. "In my family, you work whether you like your job or not. I'm the first person to ever graduate from college. We *work*." I didn't move. He wasn't done. "You should hear my mother talk about how proud she is of me. It's never about teaching, it's about having benefits and a pension."

My mother and father both had degrees. My mother had her doctorate in psychology, and my father was an engineer. In my family, we talked about our passion.

"I'm going to keep contributing to my pension fund and after twenty-five years, I'll consider my passion." Jack's voice was light again. He wasn't offended. He was Jack.

"That seems like a long time."

"Mere minutes with the love of a good woman."

He had fully returned. We both ate fish tacos and talked about Jack's experiences at Bama. It sounded like he'd studied just enough to graduate and find a job. The rest of his time he'd wandered from bar to girl to the Alabama countryside on his motorcycle.

"Have you heard from Heather?" he asked.

"I haven't. Do people hear from people in rehab facilities?"

Jack took a sip of his beer. "Don't know. Heather's the first person I've ever known to go to one. In my family, we just keep drinking." His laugh was dark.

"Do you think she's an alcoholic?"

"I think she's rich," he said with such disdain that I put down my fork and stared at him. "What?"

"You seem like you hate her."

"I hate missed opportunities. You're new to this group. They're the kings and queens of those with enough money to find themselves, and they're bored to tears by it."

I didn't say a word. There was little to argue against his point. Mila was utilizing her Penn degree teaching yoga, Rob was an aspiring singer, Heather was on summer break from getting her Masters of Fine Arts to go to rehab, and Stone was studying for the CPA exam he didn't want to take.

"Tank's and my parents aren't sending us to rehab. They might put a foot up our asses, but there's no money for rehab."

I was stuck somewhere between the luxuries of money he described and respect for him. "You two are my favorites," I said to put him at ease.

"Funny. I thought Rob was your favorite." His stare bore down on me until I blushed.

I wanted to hide, but my years of practice kicked in. "Shows what you know."

We left the Rudder and rode south on Route 1. The heat hadn't dissipated since the afternoon, and the traffic was stacked on the only road that went across the Indian River Inlet. I held onto Jack and let his words roam around my head. He was always tolerant, always the one who calmed everyone else down, but his impatience with our roommates and our socioeconomic system as a whole had been pretty clear at dinner.

Just before Bethany, the traffic stopped. One road in. One road out. Jack made a right and took us off the highway and through farms unimaginably close to the masses of people at the beach only a few miles away. We veered west and tipped south, finally able to enjoy the breeze and the scenery. I tightened my arms around Jack and fell in love with the motorcycle as a mode of transportation.

We picked up Hudson Road and took it all the way to the Maryland state line where we turned east and rode through the Isle of Wight and over the Route 90 Bridge before rejoining the stopped vehicles in Ocean City, Maryland. The traffic was endless, but Jack weaved through it politely, and we kept moving until he parked near the Jolly Roger Amusement Park.

"Now you want to try to kill me on a roller coaster?"

"You're like a giant slice of birthday cake all the time, aren't you?"

"I'll try to be nice." We walked under the arch and into the outdoor carnival. The people from the lines of traffic were still trying to park and unpack for the weekend, so the rides were virtually empty. The sun dipped down in the sky. It wouldn't be long until the place was overrun with children. The ticket booth sat fifteen feet to our right. "I'll buy the tickets. What do you want to ride?"

Jack raised his eyebrows at me. "What do you want to ride?"

I took a deep breath. "The Ferris wheel."

"Is that your favorite?" Probing, always.

"Okay," I said and turned toward the ticket attendant. "Can I get twenty dollars' worth?" I exchanged the ticket book for my credit card and turned to Jack, who was watching the whole transaction with a forlorn look.

"You're charging ride tickets?"

"I have no money." I was almost stuttering. "Well, I have money, but no cash on me. I didn't know we were going out as soon as I got down here. I need to hit the ATM."

"And you're charging them on a gold card?"

"Okay, now you're just judging." I slid the card back in my wallet, ashamed of its existence. May he never discover my mother paid the balance every month. "How do you tolerate me? At least more than the others?"

"Oh, at times you're intolerable." His expression was relaxed. He was almost back to making fun of me. "You're clearly as damaged as the rest of them, but you're working. Except for the gold card, you live like a poor girl."

"Thanks. I think."

"I'm not sure that was a compliment."

"It didn't feel like one."

We waited in line. Actually we were second in line, but since the Ferris wheel was running, we waited. Jack stood behind me with his arms resting on my shoulders, and I let him. He pulled me against the front of his body at the exact moment the people in front of us boarded their car. I used their movement to take a step forward myself. One step was the equivalent of an ocean between us. I didn't turn around to see him. I questioned whether he was still okay with being just friends.

We boarded car number eleven. Jack sat across from me and as soon as we cleared the boarding platform, he began rocking our car back and forth. I didn't react.

"Ah, man. This reminds me of my childhood." He sat back and rested his arms on the back of the bench on each side of him.

Still no reaction.

"I miss it. What about you, Nora Hargrove?"

"Can't you ever just be near someone? Do you have to be *with* them?"

Jack leaned over toward me and very seriously asked, "Do you hear yourself?"

I lowered my eyes and hid from him, and with a finger to my chin he forced me to face him.

"Let's try this again." He was so incredibly kind. His eyes were a deep blue against the falling sun in the sky. I let myself unknot there. "What do you miss about your childhood?" He waited. I was sure he was preparing himself for my sarcasm.

"I miss having someone to respect." I didn't look away. I'd give him exactly what he asked for, and he'd probably regret it. "So, don't fuck this up. Okay?"

He ran his fingertips down the side of my face as my words sank between us.

AFTER A TRIP down the giant slide and once around the two-story merry-go-round, I rode home on the back of Jack's motorcycle, hugging him the entire time. I faked a necessary adjustment to excuse my hands moving across the muscles in his stomach. He was more than just physically strong. He was intelligent and playful, and I lost track of myself with him. I didn't let my guard down. He dismantled it by never being predictable or disappointing.

I was supposed to be out witnessing the drunken fiascos I roomed with. Jack was supposed to be across the bar, or on the couch, not nestled between my legs as we careened up Route 1 into Delaware. I hid from the wind between his shoulder blades and closed my eyes. I let my mind wander to every memory of him without his shirt on. I wallowed in the thought of his arms wrapped around me while we slept in the bed he'd made for us. I squeezed him tighter without wanting to. I couldn't not.

When we stopped at the first traffic light in Dewey, Jack sat up and reached back to rub my thigh. His hand roughly brushed across it and then he squeezed it, and I stopped breathing. I studied his hand, knowing I'd conveyed far too much on our ride home. I needed some distance from Jack. With only four blocks to go, I relaxed at the possibility of Stone and Mila joining us. It was hard to feel anything but anger if Stone was around, and Mila would chat and put us all at ease.

Jack pulled into the driveway. I exhaled at the sight of Mila's and Stone's cars, but the house was silent when we walked in. I checked the hallway and listened up the stairs. We were alone. Jack was in the kitchen opening two beers and setting them on the counter. The urge to run burst inside me.

"You're not going anywhere."

I turned back, my cheeks burning from embarrassment. I'd never been so transparent. Not even to my mother. It was an uneasiness that could only be quelled by flight.

"Come here." Jack obviously was thinking the opposite. He kept me right next to him to torture me as much as possible. There was nothing I could do. To leave would be absurd, even more so than staying, I thought.

It was stupid. I could have a beer with Jack. This was a beer with a guy I'd known a few weeks who'd never been anything but kind to me. No. Big. Deal.

"Where do you think they are?" I picked up the bottle and took a sip. The cold liquid slid down my dry throat. I took another gulp to soothe me.

Jack watched me as I leaned on the counter behind me. He was next to me. I could feel the heat from his tanned skin. It drew me to him. I pressed the beer against my arm and focused on the chill it sent through my body.

"I don't know," he said, but I didn't know what he was talking about. Jack stood in front of me. He leaned down and rested both hands behind me on the counter, trapping me between his arms. He was close. The heat coming off him was unbearable. My train of thought was lost, and I didn't care if it ever came back.

I wanted him to press himself against me—to let me feel the heat—but I knew I was getting too close to the fire. "Do you not want to be alone with me?"

I opened my mouth to say something. I had no idea what. When my lips parted, Jack's were upon them. I stood perfectly still until he pulled back and faced me. He was waiting for me, but I didn't know what to do. Jack inhaled and gently placed his lips on mine again, silencing my mind to anything but the sensation of his tongue, the pressure of his lips, and the tightening of every fiber inside me.

With our mouths still connected, I placed my beer on the counter and pulled him to me with both hands. I wrapped my arms around his neck, wanting him closer to me than myself. Jack lifted me onto the counter. I wrapped my legs around him, kissing him as if my life depended on it. I wasn't sure it didn't.

I was voracious in a way I'd never experienced before, and Jack responded with the strength I craved from him every minute I was in his presence. He pressed himself against me, his lips bore down on me until mine hurt from the force. I didn't relent for a second. I took everything from him.

A little voice inside my head broke free and said, "No."

"What?" Jack asked, and I winced, having realized I'd said it out loud.

The walls closed in around me. I dropped my arms from his neck to his stomach. I touched him one last time, knowing I was about to ruin everything. "I'm sorry."

"For what?"

"This is a bad idea." The words fell from my lips. I ran a finger across the bottom one to feel the pain of his kiss once again.

Jack leaned in, letting his lips drag across my neck. His hot breath followed to my ear. I tilted my head, trying to capture the longing it shot through my body. He whispered, "Why's that?"

I was on fire. My mind raced with need for him. I closed my

eyes, hiding from both of us. Jack's fingertips ran across my collar bone, and I shivered beneath them, telling him every truth I couldn't face.

I could have sex with him. If I'd had sex *ever* before in this *awful* life, I'd be naked right now, but this was my first time, and it couldn't be this.

Stupid. Fucking. Virginity.

It couldn't be with a guy who slept with Mila because she was lonely and had sex with a half share and didn't always come home because he was lying under a crier with a tiger tattoo. It couldn't be for just one night. Not with Jack. He already meant more to me than that.

"Talk to me, Nora. Tell me what you're thinking."

I kept my eyes closed. His lips touched my cheek, but he had no idea what we were up against. Twenty-three years of carrying it around with me, holding it so tight no one could pry it loose, had rendered me silent.

"Tell me."

With a hand on each of his shoulders, and the words that I knew would end this, I pushed him away. "I'm thinking he's right here." *The one.* " . . . and it's a mistake." I slid off the counter and walked to the other side of the kitchen. I still felt like running from the house, but this was Jack. It wasn't the first time a guy found out he wasn't having sex with me. It was just the first time I thought it would kill me.

"It's not a mistake," he said, and his stare bore into me, willing me to believe him, and I wanted to more than anything. He could be the one. I could do this, but I couldn't. Jack would never be mine, and *this* couldn't be my first time, and I didn't owe him the reason why.

I wished Tank were around to talk to about it. He'd know what to do.

"Talk to me," he pleaded.

I was silent. My lack of words was my only comfort. He had to stop looking at me. *Walk away, Jack.*

"I'm not going anywhere." He read my mind. I stared at the ceiling, wanting to hide more than ever before in my life. "I'm not leaving this room until you tell me what's going on." Jack stood in front of me. I let my gaze fall to his chest. I could almost touch it. I could lie down with him, rest my head against his chest, and forget anything bad ever happened in the world. In my world. "Nora." His chest expanded with frustrated breaths, and my eyes fixed on his muscular arms.

"You're strapping."

He lowered his chin and tried to decipher the words of idiocy flowing from my mouth. "Strapping?"

"I read it in a Nora Hargrove novel."

"Your words. Use your words, Nora," he snapped.

I hated him. I inhaled deeply, and he didn't flinch. Jack was as solid as they came. "You're beautiful." Relief flowed through me at the sound of the truth. "Absolutely incredible." Jack took a step toward me as I raised both hands in objection. "But it's July twenty-fifth. We have over a month left here together. This will only end badly."

"Who says it's going to end?"

"I'm . . ." I shook my head, searching for the words to properly replace the truth I wouldn't share with him, "not good at casual hookups. Especially when I share a bedroom with the guy." I looked Jack in the eye. "I'm not Mila, or whoever else. I'm not the type to be okay when you bring someone else home."

"What if there won't be anyone else?" He took two steps closer to me, and I didn't stop him. I was lost in the hope of his words. He towered over me in all his glory, and every girl's reaction to his presence ran through my mind.

"You're not the type for that," I said and insulted one of the best guys I'd ever known.

"Don't pretend to know me when you barely know yourself." It was a slap in the face. Jack had joked about my issues before, but now he was using them against me. "This is about him, isn't it?"

"Who?" There was no one else in my mind but Jack.

"Rob. You think I don't see the way you look at him?" He was disgusted. "You're practically a groupie."

"We're just friends."

"Oh yeah? What if Blaire weren't around?"

I stood there, unwilling to address Blaire's absence. I'd stopped hoping for it a year and a half ago. She wasn't going anywhere, and she had nothing to do with tonight.

Jack walked out of the kitchen. The screen door on the front of the house slammed shut behind him. I stayed silent and trapped and all by myself.

I was still standing in the same spot when the door opened again. Relief flowed through me. I had no idea what I'd say to him, but I wanted him near me. I didn't want him to hate me, and I was kind of hating myself. I stepped into the living room, waiting to face him, and was struck by the vision of Mila and Stone.

She was on top of him lying on the couch, writhing against him. Their mouths were locked together in a violent kiss as he yanked at the sides of her skirt. He raised it to her waist and reached down with both hands and squeezed her ass. They separated long enough for Mila to pull her shirt over her head. The neck opening caught on her hair, and I thought Stone would rip her head off as he threw it against the wall and kissed her again. They didn't see me. They didn't hear me.

"Fuck me, Stone," she said. She was clawing at the words and was barely audible she was so out of breath. I couldn't find a hole to crawl into. I tiptoed back into the kitchen and out to my porch, praying with each step that the old floor wouldn't creak. I picked up my bag and car keys and walked out the back door, guiding it back against the jamb.

My hands were shaking when I touched the steering wheel. They all just did whatever—*whoever*—they pleased. No one ever got hurt, and yet I was only a witness to all of it. *What the fuck is wrong with me?* I didn't cry until I was on the highway, back to where I could be alone, and Jack couldn't find me.

I LAID IN my bed in Wilmington and stared at the chalk-colored wall in front of me. Not one picture decorated it. It was the exact same as the day I'd moved in.

My phone dinged with a text. *Please let this be Jack.* It was from Tank, and all it said was *Fuck you.*

I assumed it was a joke. I sent back one of those cute smiley face emojis everyone likes. Tank would know what I should do about Jack. He'd understand.

Seventeen

It's Complicated

RICKY AND I stood facing the candy bar display in the commissary. Reese's always seemed to be a solid choice. I reached for one, and Ricky stopped my hand and shook his head.

"You don't really want that."

"No?"

"No. That's depression talking." He handed me a pack of Starbursts. "These will last longer and get you through the rest of this hellish day."

"It hasn't been that bad today."

"It's a prison. Impossible to escape."

"It's not a prison." I looked back at the Reese's, and my cell phone lit up with a text from Jack. It said, *Please tell me you're coming back this weekend.*

My breath caught at the sight of it. I ran my thumb over his name and let the frustration from the weekend before return.

"What is this area we're standing in right now?"

I pulled my attention away from my phone. "The commissary?"

"Do you know where they usually have commissaries?"

"Military bases?"

"And prisons. I snuck ten dollars up my butt this morning to come in and buy these Doritos. I'll probably be shanked on my way back to my desk."

I swiped the lock screen on my cell, and Jack's message came up.

I took a deep breath and read it again. I'd thought of nothing but him since I left last Thursday. I spent the weekend with Rufus. I told him all about Jack, and what happened to people who were unwilling to open up to others. How they spent their entire lives isolated and alone. By Sunday, Rufus met me at the edge of his cage when I sat down. He was coming around. I couldn't quite say the same for me.

"Do you want a dog?" I asked Ricky. He and Rufus would be perfect together.

"A what?"

"A dog." I spoke as if it was obvious. It should have sounded like a clear possibility. "Man's best friend."

"Does it seem like I've got the capacity to take care of another living being? Because I'm pretty overwhelmed just with myself."

"He'd end up taking care of you."

"That beach house is making you crazy. It's changing you."

"I know." Nothing was the way it had seemed before I'd met them. Rob, my father, my job . . . Rufus. "Everything . . . everyone seems different all of a sudden." I lingered on my phone. I read the text message again.

"What's that?" Ricky asked. He wasn't used to not having my full attention, or at least me only ignoring *him* when we were together.

"It's a text from my roommate at the beach."

"Is she hot?"

"He is."

Ricky examined me silently. He contemplated the phone in my hand and stared back at me. He was in shock. "You like him?"

I nodded. "It's complicated."

"It doesn't have to be." He rubbed my shoulders, and I stretched my neck back and forth between them. "You're both hot and you're sharing a room at the beach. What's so complicated?"

"Do you remember the first girl you had sex with?"

"Of course. I scribbled her name in a bible the Sunday after she fucked me, and my mother almost beat me to death." Ricky chuckled and looked up at the ceiling, probably still thanking God for the intercourse. "Why? Is this guy a virgin?" His expression twisted to repulsion.

I shook my head. "No. Far from it. I just think he means more to me than I mean to him, and no matter how many times I try to keep it casual, I can't stay grounded when I'm with him."

"It sounds like you love him."

My heart stopped beating, and a chill flew across my chest. *My God, I love Jack Randall.*

THE DRIVEWAY OF the beach house was full. The street was full. There were people everywhere, on the porches, walking the sidewalks, and spilling out of happy hour. It was exactly as I'd left it over a week ago.

I parked on the lawn. I didn't even pretend I was in the driveway. Just pulled right up and locked the car doors next to the front door of the house. I took a deep breath, not sure what I was going to say to Jack when I saw him. When my car was in PARK, I texted him, *I'm back.*

Even with me returning, nothing I was willing to tell him was going to explain why I was an idiot. Why I obviously wanted him and yet refused to have him. At the rate I was going, he probably already hated me.

I walked around to the backyard. Mila and Stone were lying together on the hammock. She was giggling at something he'd said, and he . . . was . . . smiling. I stopped, unable to move forward, and tried to digest the sight. She really could work miracles. Maybe she could work on me.

"What happened to you last weekend?" she asked and tried to climb out of the hammock, but Stone pulled her back down to him and kissed her.

I left them and their love and entered my porch. Jack had strung some of my shells along a string of white lights that hung from the walls of our bedroom. Like the beds, his thoughtfulness moved me. The direction was always closer to him.

"Where have you been?" Mila came in the screeching porch door and flopped on my bed.

"Sorry. I felt sick last weekend." It was kind of true. "How's this weekend so far?"

"It's a-ma-zing."

I started to say something, but the ecstasy on her face confused me. I shook my head. "What's going on with you and Stone?"

Mila rolled onto her back and let her arms hang off my bed above her head. "He made me want to be with him a second time." She was even shaking her head at the absurdity of it. "I couldn't wait to see him this weekend. We've been together every day since last Thursday night."

"Every day?"

"Every single minute of every day. I can't get enough of him."

I joined her on my bed and stared at the shell light strands. "These lights are awesome."

"They are." She took a deep breath. "Jack disappeared at the same time you did last weekend."

"He did?"

She nodded. "I thought you two were together, but then he came back pissed off late Thursday night. He wasn't himself the rest of the weekend."

"No one to hook up with?" I regretted it the minute the words flew out of my stupid, immature mouth.

"No one he wanted to hook up with." Mila's voice was soft and gentle like her. She was working on me the way she'd re-paired Stone.

I had to change the subject. I wasn't about to tell Mila or Jack that I was a virgin and the first person I'd seen have sex was my mother with my French teacher on my bed. I wasn't going to explain that I was completely fucked up, and that even though I fought the urge to rip Jack's clothes off every time he was near me, it wasn't enough for me to trust him. Nothing might ever be enough. I took a deep breath. "Why Stone?" I asked and rolled on my side to face her. "I mean, out of all the boys in Dewey, what did he do that made you want seconds?"

A peaceful grin settled on Mila's face. She was even more content than I'd known her to be. "He told me he loved me." A full smile took over as if she couldn't contain it with mere human strength. "And he told me if I let him love me, he'd never leave me." I got a little choked up hearing her. "It was the most beautiful thing I'd ever heard, and he knows, you know? He knows what that means to me and he said it, and I'm going to let him love me."

I swallowed hard. "Wow." I meant it. *Wow, Stone. You fucking good guy.*

He called her name from the backyard, and Mila left me alone to ponder her newfound love. Without her beautiful face pulling me toward the romance, it made me feel lonely.

I wandered the house until I found Rob in his room. It was so rare to find him alone.

"Blaire's got a bachelorette party this weekend." Rob said like it wasn't the best news ever. An entire weekend without Blaire looming over him. Rob could hang out the way he used to when he didn't live with his girlfriend. "I've missed you, Nora. Why don't you ever come down to see Heather?"

"Heather, our roommate who's now in rehab?"

"Yeah. Before she went off the rails? I haven't seen you since you graduated."

"I've been busy," I lied

"With what? Where are you working again?

"SafeOne Insurance."

"What do you do?" Rob lit the end of a joint, causing me to pause for a second and evaluate what was in it. I'd seen Rob roll all kinds of powders in joints before and forget to mention the exact drug combination.

"I adjust claims." He blew smoke rings into the air. "Auto claims."

"That sounds like it sucks."

"It's fine."

Rob took a drag, and another, and then finally handed it to me. "That's what I like about you, Nora. You're always fine." His phone tweeted with his obnoxious notification of a text. It continued for at least ten more times. "That's my girl. She's rarely fine."

I took a drag of the joint and closed my eyes as the thick smoke drifted down my throat. The notifications continued without him checking his phone. I couldn't dismiss them. They wouldn't be ignored, but Rob had no problem. He picked up his guitar and strummed it until I handed the joint back to him. "This is just weed, right?"

Rob's eyes were closing. He was fading into his own abyss.

"Oh, yeah. It's some seriously great shit, though. You're going to be completely fucked up."

"Great," I said and reclined on his bed.

"What's up?" Jack asked and leaned against Rob's bedroom door. His voice reached every corner of my interior. *I love him*, I thought. Panic struck me as I tried to ascertain whether I'd said it out loud.

"You wanna smoke?" Rob said. I closed my eyes and hid from Jack's scrutiny.

"Blaire's not coming down?"

"Nope."

I hadn't told him I loved him. I exhaled and relaxed. I laughed because my lips and mouth were forced into the expression. I had absolutely nothing to do with it or any other emotion I was feeling, but the disappointment in Jack's eyes forced me to own it. I hadn't wanted this to be the first time he saw me since last weekend. I'd hoped I'd have something poignant to say, but now that I was so high, I could barely come up with my name.

Jack turned around and walked out of the room, leaving me cold.

Rob and I didn't say another word.

THE BAR WAS darker. The music was louder. The harshness of the night continued to surround me wherever I went. It was the weed. I was high in a way I'd never been before, and it made me angry. I missed my non-high self. The Nora who knew what was going on. What was real, and who was fake. I didn't want to smoke that kind of pot ever again.

I tried to huddle near Rob, but instead of shelter he was an attraction to people. Strangers. He'd speak to anyone who would dote on him. Glasses crashed to the ground behind me, followed by bartenders cursing as they stared at the pile of broken glass at their feet. A bar back crawled under the bar and returned with a broom and dustpan, while the bartenders continued to take orders to the mob awaiting their light beers and vodka drinks. A round of shots was poured in front of me. I counted the nine tiny glasses lined up and watched the liquid drip out of the spout in slow motion. I was too high to be in here.

I walked onto the front porch, seeking some air and some grounding from the sensations of the night. Tank, hovering above the rest of the crowd, caught my eye. I took one step toward him and then froze in the hatred of his stare. He was glaring at me. Stone held an arm across his chest to hold him back . . . from me.

The absolute abhorrence in his eyes sent me home. I walked out of the bar and didn't look back until I opened the front door of our house. I'd led him on. This was why he hated me. He saw everything. The light, the sun, the sounds, how could he not have read my intentions correctly? We'd never kissed, never even crashed in the same bed, but Tank hated me, and I knew it was my fault. He was incapable of that horrid depth of emotion without being provoked, and yet I couldn't shake the deep understanding that he was *only* my friend and that he knew it, too.

I stayed silent in my bed, staring at the crumbling and stained ceiling of the porch, until I heard the first of my housemates return.

"What happened to her?" Mila asked in the kitchen. I could barely make out the words over the pounding of the box fan, but I knew she was talking about me.

"Rob gave her God knows what, and Tank scared her." It was Jack.

"He scared me, too."

"He's scared me a couple of times lately. He just gets so fucking angry, and I never understand at what."

The light turned off, and silence followed it. The party had mercifully moved from the kitchen to another part of the house, or perhaps another house all together. I stayed still, terrified that if I moved, my night would continue to propel me forward, and the unknown was worse than what it was right now.

Eventually, there was a banging on the house. Not on the door, on the actual side of the house. It might have been a fist hitting the siding.

"Who the fuck cares? Forget about her," Stone yelled. I wanted to disappear. "You've got to pull yourself out of this. She's no big deal." There was another bang on the side of the house. This one shook the wall of the porch next to my face. It might have been a foot hitting it. "You're so fucking dark."

"Shut up!" Tank yelled, and then there was silence. I leaned up in my bed to hear better, but there was nothing. I laid back down and was swallowed by everything I couldn't understand.

Jack walked into our room and startled me, but I didn't move. My gaze remained fixed on the ceiling, searching for answers to how I'd hurt Tank. I'd almost fully convinced myself it wasn't me. It was some other girl who was no big deal. I was being arrogant, thinking I'd had a thing to do with his anger. I meant nothing to him. We'd only known each other well in a prior life. My breath caught as a sob lodged in my throat. The abhorrence in Tank's eyes was seared into my memory.

Jack lifted my covers and climbed in bed next to me. I turned to him as he wrapped his arms around my shoulders. I buried my face in his chest and tears fell from my eyes.

"Don't take it personally," he said, confirming I was the target of Tank's rage.

"Hatred is a personal thing."

Jack's hand tangled in my hair, moving it away from my face. He brushed it to my back and away from my eyes. He was deliciously warm in the wake of Tank's coldness. "Tank can be unfathomably light. But lately, that light has come with some darkness. I doubt it has anything to do with you."

He hated me. I didn't imagine that.

I let myself forget it for a moment and fell asleep with Jack. I had nightmares I was drowning and no one came to save me. They just stared at me from the beach as I sank under water and was pulled out to sea.

When I woke up, my bed and our room were empty. I stayed still and listened for signs of life. The house was silent. A brushing sound repeated again and again. It was coming from the backyard, but I couldn't place it in my mind.

I sat up too quickly and felt dizzy. I leaned back on stiff arms before venturing farther into the daylight. The brushing sound continued. My gaze followed it to the backyard. Tank's leg and shoulder were sticking out of the shed.

As if he could feel me scrutinizing him, he stopped what he was doing and leaned out the door. The storm inside him was missing from the night before. It'd been replaced by someone searching through the damage for his lost self.

He stared lifelessly at the house. The anger was gone. He was wounded. I wasn't sure if I was ready to talk to him or not. I wasn't sure what to even say. I didn't understand most of what had happened last night, but none of my interactions with Tank made sense.

I lumbered to the bathroom and brushed my teeth. I splashed my face with water and downed drinks from my cupped hands. I actually felt pretty good, but I hadn't drunk much. I couldn't drink the night before. Thanks to Rob and his "seriously great shit."

I couldn't tell who was at breakfast and who was still asleep. Except for the half shares crashed on the couches still wearing their clothes from the night before. I tiptoed by them and back out to my porch. Tank had returned to whatever he was doing, and I missed him.

I left the house and approached the shed. My steps were small. My mind was foggy, but I tried to take in any signs of displeasure with my coming presence. I stopped for a moment, and Tank turned to me. He smiled. He was innocent and childlike. Just the way I loved him.

"Hey," I said as I approached his work bench. He had a large piece of furniture he was sanding. It was a worn black color except the spots he'd already lightened. The ground was covered with sand dust, and so was the middle of Tank. By the looks of the carnage, he'd been working for hours. Based on the top of the dresser, he'd only sanded a single spot. Over and over again. His eyes were dark. The circles around them deepened the darkness still lingering from last night. I feared he was deranged.

"Good morning." His words sounded like more of a question than a greeting.

"If I did something wrong last night, I'm sorry."

Tank kept sanding. My words flew by him. He leaned down and peered across the surface of the wood. "I found this dresser on the curb the next town over from my house. I'm going to restore it."

I looked at the dresser, but I didn't really see it. "That's great," I said and took a step back from Tank. We'd never spent a moment together before. We were no more than two human beings on the same planet. Our closeness was gone. I took a deep breath and smiled before turning to walk away.

"Nora?"

I turned back to my friend. "Yes, Tank?"

"Have you ever seen the Perseid Meteor Shower?" I could only stare at him. "It happens every year, and you can sometimes see fifty falling stars per hour." Tank's words rushed from his mouth like he was doing a radio spot and only had a few seconds to get every word in.

I slowed my response on purpose. "No. I haven't."

"It's next weekend. Let's plan on taking the kayak out Sunday night to watch it."

"Really?" My instinct was to hug him, but I was scarred from the night before. I didn't trust his kindness the way I used to. I left my confusion on full display for Tank to deal with.

"Yeah." He stopped sanding and faced me. "I want you to see it."

"Have you seen it before?"

"Every night inside my head, but you'll need to see it in the sky, and I want to be with you when you do."

He was breathing heavy. He was nervous about my reaction. Last night wasn't all in my mind. "I'd love that, Tank."

Eighteen

I Can't Wait Until We See Each Other Again

I NEEDED A break from the house. The weekend before with Tank had shaken me, or at least my confidence in the beach being an enjoyable distraction. Maybe just a distraction. I didn't know. What I did know was that I was in no hurry to get down there. Tank texted me to make sure I was coming for the meteor shower. His text was sent just after four in the morning Wednesday night. He ended it with, *I can't wait until we see each other again.* When I read it Thursday morning, I knew he couldn't sleep.

I stayed in Delaware Thursday night. I didn't get out of work until seven, and the thought of rushing anywhere exhausted me. After the endless day of fielding complaints, I wanted to lie on my bed in a dark room and forget the world around me. I could've had it worse. I could work with molested children or abused animals and be forced to feel something every single day of my life until my emotions dried up and I was swept away with them. At least the unending lack of satisfaction from everyone I came in contact with was merely mind-numbing and didn't impact my soul. It was only a nuisance.

I expected to hear from Tank several more times until I got to the shore. Usually his texts that began in the middle of the night were followed by several more that deteriorated in logic. Many times I assumed they were lyrics to a song I didn't know. I scrolled back through my texts from him. They ranged from sweet to obscure, to downright unintelligible. His depth was overwhelming to the shallowness I'd embraced in my life.

I drove to see my best friend. Our visits had switched from sad to friendly, and I was proud of him.

"I'm not going to lie," Janine said when I walked into the shelter. "I feared he was a total loss when they brought him in here."

"Me, too," I said and kept pace with her to his cage.

Rufus had heard my voice and was waiting for me when I reached him.

"Guess what I have?"

Rufus's tail wagged against the side of his cage.

"*Scooby Doo and the Creepy Chef.*"

He sat right next to me and listened to every word of the book and looked at every picture. When I was done, I gave him a treat and I told him I loved him.

I couldn't stop smiling my whole way to the beach. Rufus was going to do it. He was going to get adopted. I knew it.

The driveway to the beach house was empty except for Jack's motorcycle. It always surprised me the others didn't lounge here all week. They had no responsibilities of a nine-to-five nature, but they still adhered to the idea of only weekending at the beach because their weekly lives were demanding. What with yoga and music and reading and all. It was almost lunch time. Jack must've been on a job in Dewey or Rehoboth. Something close he could come home midday from.

The silent house didn't sound like a lunch was being eaten. I stepped onto the back porch, and the heat hit me first. Jack was asleep in my bed without the fan on.

I dropped my bag on the mattress next to him. He stirred and rolled over, facing me with a pleasant expression on his face.

"What are you doing in my bed?" I wasn't angry. I wasn't even surprised. The boundaries of my life had disappeared on this short block in this one-mile-long beach town.

"I was hoping you'd come down and climb in with me."

I tilted my head and pondered Jack. He was enormous. My boyfriend in high school had been a few inches taller than me, but we'd weighed about the same. Jack's arm might have weighed more than me, and when he spooned me and put one leg over my thighs, it felt like a tree was lying across my body. He was a man.

"Why are you even here? Don't you have to work?" My eyes rested on the arm he'd just put up behind his head. Even through my multi-year silent obsession with Rob, it was never about his body. Rob had that lanky, I-might-be-a-coke-addict look. He was always *maybe* dirty, but probably not, because his shoes cost more than most people's car payment. Every ounce of Jack was strong, and my admiration of his body threw me a little.

"No power. That's why I'm cooking myself out here. It's out on the whole island."

"Really?" I surveyed the room, but nothing was ever plugged in to note the absence of power except the shell lights, and we only turned them on at night.

"Really. How come you didn't come down last night?" Jack moved over until the back of his body rested against the wall.

I sat next to him, and he pulled me down to lie beside him. "I was tired. My job can be draining." He slid me closer to him. My back was resting on his chest. "And sometimes this house can be draining."

"Not on Thursday nights."

I pulled Jack's arm over my shoulders and closer to me. "No. Not on Thursdays."

"Any chance you can stay down on Sunday? There's a concert at the Bottle & Cork."

"I'm already staying down. It's the Perseids Meteor Shower."

"The what?"

"I know. I'd never heard of it either, but Tank says it's amazing, and I believe him."

"Did you guys make up from last weekend?"

I sighed. "I don't even know what happened last weekend."

"He probably doesn't either."

I sunk way into that. Tank scared me, and based on the way he'd spoken to me in the shed the next day, I thought it scared him, too. That combined with his ability to feel sounds had me worried there was something seriously wrong with him. Something amiss in his beautiful mind.

I searched for the words to ask Jack about Tank without being critical. Jack had never mouthed a criticism about him. I wasn't going to either.

"Let's go to the beach before everyone else gets here," Jack said and saved us from the conversation.

"Okay."

WE PASSED FOUR dogs with their owners on the short walk to the beach.

"Do you like dogs?" I asked.

"I love them."

I was relieved. I couldn't love a man who didn't love dogs.

"Just like cats, and birds, and lizards. I love them in someone else's house."

"They're nothing like those other animals."

"I know. I just love them all the same."

"Have you ever had a dog?" I asked, and he shook his head.

"That's why. Once you've felt the love of a dog, you'll have to have one the rest of your life. They're a gift."

Jack stopped walking and stared at me as if my romantic words had flown out of a second head attached to my body.

"What?"

"Nothing," he said, and we kept walking.

The beach was the most crowded I'd ever seen it. Even worse than the Saturday of Fourth of July weekend. No power had forced everyone from their houses to the sand. It was too hot to be inside, and the weather was absolute perfection. Bright blue sky, light breeze off the ocean—even the biting flies stayed away. The ocean was rough, though. Jack and I swam until I'd been beaten and crushed by the waves to the point of fatigue. Swimming was a constant battle of diving under the waves and fighting against the current to not be pulled away from our block.

"I need to get out."

"I know," he said before warning me of the approaching wave I had to dive into to avoid it breaking on my head.

"I hope the ocean calms," I said as I walked out of the sea. Jack held my hand, and me up a few times, as we dragged ourselves back to our towels. "Tank and I are supposed to go kayaking Sunday night." I turned back to the surf crashing on the beach. The lifeguards were blowing their whistles and trying to corral all the swimmers directly in front of them. "It's not going to work in this."

"Why do you guys have to go out in the middle of the night?" Jack dried his stomach, and I watched. "It's not safe."

"Tonight's a new moon, and a cloudless sky is forecast. There's no better place to watch the meteor shower than from the water."

"What about from the beach?" Jack and I were never going to agree about this.

"Did you have a swimming accident once? You seem overly cautious about it."

"It's called respecting it. Don't underestimate the sea, Nora."

His words were a demand. He was a teacher. "Yes, sir."

Jack laughed a little. "I'm serious."

I laughed, too. "I know."

I spread my towel out parallel to the ocean and laid on my stomach. Jack placed his at the end of mine so we were facing each other. I was leaning up on my elbows, and he took both my hands in his.

"I'm looking forward to the summer being over," he said, but his statement confused me. I was disoriented by his placement and my hands in his, and wondering why he'd ever want this summer to end. Jack had it better than the rest of us.

"Why?" finally came out of my mouth when I was able to draw my gaze away from our hands and look him in the eye.

"Because I'm going to take you out on a proper date."

I didn't say a word, but my heart raced near the surface of my chest.

"I want to take you out to dinner and then take you to bed."

My breath caught. I lingered on the possibility of both those things. "What if I'm not tired?"

Jack's smile was devious. "And it'll be so good, you'll beg me to be with you for the rest of our lives."

I loved him even more for not giving up on me weeks ago when anyone else would have. "Why do you keep trying?"

"Because you're worth it. I can feel it. We're going to be great together. You just have to let me in."

I started to pull my hands away, but Jack tightened his grip.

"Why does that scare you?"

"It doesn't." I was honest. His words didn't scare me. "It's just what I do."

He released my hands. "Pull away?"

"Pretty much." I kept my sight steady on him. The breeze blew around us, swirling our towels against our sides. "It's rarely necessary, though. No one usually gets as close as you have." I swallowed down the realization of how close he was.

"I'm special."

"You are." The words croaked out as if saying them was choking me. I was done lying to him.

I crossed my arms and lowered my head onto them. I didn't say another word until we had to meet everyone back at the house. I knew it was time, because Jack's phone blew up with notifications coming in every few minutes. Sometimes multiple messages dinged all at once.

"Our tribe has returned," he said.

"I can hear that."

"You ready?" He stood up and held out his hand for me.

"For what?"

"Whatever comes our way."

"In that case, I'll follow you." I took his hand and held it the entire walk back to our house.

The driveway was now full, and cars were parked on every inch of the roadside.

Stone was perched on top of the kitchen counter like a phoenix watching over his domain. "Nice picture of you on the fridge."

I turned to the refrigerator. "What picture?" The front of the freezer door was now practically filled with old photos. A new one of Tank and Jack looking like state champions in their football uniforms was in the top left corner, right above the picture of the eight of us out back. Stone in a wrestling singlet with some poor guy in an obviously painful headlock was taped almost on top of Heather and Mila at the senior prom

Heather got out of rehab this week.

"Did anyone hear from—" The picture of me and Heather in troll Halloween costumes complete with nude-colored skimpy dresses and crazy colorful, sticking-up hair stole my words. Heather's hair was royal blue. Mine was hot pink. Not pictured were the six other girls from our sophomore dorm who'd been trolls with us.

We were nineteen when the picture was taken. It felt like a lifetime ago, and it was hard to believe there was even a time Heather and I had coordinated a costume, or any other element of our lives.

Can I rub you for good luck? was the question I'd endured over and over that night. The six of us had been an incredible display on the dance floor.

Stone climbed down from the counter and studied the pictures with me.

"Is Heather here?" I asked.

"God no. Why?"

"Who put this picture up?"

"I did." I spun around, and Rob was standing in the doorway to the kitchen. He smugly stared at me, waiting for me to react to the picture. Why would he put it up? He'd walked me home the night it'd been taken. In my mind, it was the only time he'd ever chosen me over Blaire, but that was only ever in my mind. *She* was his girlfriend. I was her annoyance.

Jack walked into the kitchen. He looked from me to Rob and back at me again. The smile on his face was replaced by an annoyed glare as he brushed past me without a word and stepped out onto our porch. Rob's attention was becoming as much of a burden to me as it was to Blaire.

STONE HELD MILA'S hand the whole way to Northbeach. He kissed her neck while we waited for beers. I swore at one point I saw him dancing. Stone being sweet was as unnerving as him being angry. Rob and Blaire were getting along. It was as if the universe was listing, waiting to be righted before it capsized. I attributed it all to Tank's absence. Without him, nothing was the same.

I knew when we got home he'd be assembling a house obstacle course or cooking Thanksgiving dinner for us. Because, "Why not?" he'd say. His absence would be for some fantastical production I couldn't even imagine but that had just popped into his mind.

We stumbled home to an empty house, and Jack texted Tank again. They all did. I stayed quiet as they typed in their words, their questions of his whereabouts, and their jokes about what he was missing at the beach, and then I went to bed.

When I went to the bathroom in the middle of the night, Jack was asleep on the couch. I wondered if he'd been waiting up for Tank's arrival. His standing guard set a series of thoughts into motion about all the terrible things that could have happened to delay Tank's arrival. I couldn't sleep.

"Jack," I said as I shook his arm. He didn't move. "Jack."

"What?" He rolled over. "What is it?"

"I can't sleep. Come to bed with me."

He smiled and rested his hand on my face. "Are you begging me?"

"No. I just want to sleep with you. I'd carry you, but you're too heavy."

He stood up and without shoes on, I felt like I was half the size of him. He picked me up into his arms and carried me out to our porch. Jack laid me in bed and climbed in next to me.

"You're worried about him?" he asked and pulled me close to him.

"Are you?"

"A little. He's disappeared before, though. Go to sleep."

I closed my eyes. Nothing bad could happen to me in Jack's arms.

I HOPED IT was going to be like the first time Heather didn't come home. The time she separated from us on Friday night and reappeared at dinner on Saturday. No one was concerned. I'd wondered a few times throughout the day where she was, but the odds of her lying in a gutter off Route 1 in Dewey were slim. She was fine. We all knew it, and then she returned seeming tired and hungry, but no worse than she did on any other Saturday.

This was different, though. It was Tank, and no one had heard from him since Wednesday when he said he'd be down on Friday night. There were plenty of jokes about how whoever he'd met must have tied him up so well that he couldn't text back. Stone called him, which was unheard of. To actually dial a number and let it ring with the hope of speaking to someone on the other end was a reaction to something catastrophic.

I followed Jack's lead. He knew Tank the best and he always knew what to do. What to say. If he wasn't worried, then neither was I, but by Saturday afternoon I watched as he walked over the dune with his phone to his ear. I'd hoped it was Tank, but when Jack returned he didn't put me out of my misery. He didn't say a word.

We all showered. We drank beers while we ate pizza for dinner, and we skirted the subject of where Tank was, because we'd exhausted all the funny possibilities earlier in the day. Finally, Jack's phone rang with relief. It was Tank's number. The anticipation of his story bloomed the smile on my face. I couldn't wait until he came down. We'd spend the wee hours of tomorrow morning talking and watching the falling stars of the Perseids Meteor Shower, and I'd admit to him how worried I was when he was late.

"Where are you, man?" Jack spoke into the phone, and every person around him sat in silence.

Jack's expression twisted from relief to a deep hurt none of us had ever seen anywhere near him. Emptiness crawled up the back of my throat. It wouldn't be swallowed down.

"Yes," he said, and we hung on every breath from his body.

Jack's gaze dropped to the ground. His shoulders caved. He was breaking in front of me. "How?"

No one breathed.

Jack looked each one of us in the eye as he listened to the person on the other end of the line, and then said, "We're on our way."

There's been an accident. Tank's hurt and needs help. We need to go. The room swirled around Jack as every pair of eyes fixed on him and the words he'd utter that would forever change the make-up of our souls.

"Tank's dead. That was his brother." Jack stared at his phone in his hand, disgust covering his face. "I called his parents earlier, and they found his body in his apartment."

Mila was the only one who moved. She walked to Jack and pulled him into her arms. He leaned down and rested his head on her shoulder.

"No way," Rob said. "No fucking way!"

"Babe," Blaire said and approached him.

"Shut the fuck up!" he screamed, and Blaire retreated. She stared at him and burst into tears before running out of the room. "Fucking Tank," he said, but there was no one left to hear him. No one in the room who would ever hear anything again.

Stone's fist broke through the kitchen cabinet door that hid our unmatched dishes from the world on the rare occasion it was closed. He didn't shake out his fingers, he didn't look at his scraped knuckles, because he couldn't feel anything. Tank had taken the parts of us that felt things wherever he'd gone.

THERE WAS NO longer a reason to be there. The alcohol and the drugs had been forced out of our bloodstreams by a ringing phone in the center of our kitchen. It dulled our senses and delayed our reflexes while injecting a realization that we were small and temporary. None of us could endure the sight of one another.

"Are you okay?" Jack asked when he finished packing his duffel.

I was sitting on the edge of my bed. I couldn't move. If I stayed right here, this would end. Tank would come back. "What happened?"

Jack didn't answer. He stared through me. Tank had left Earth, and Jack had gone somewhere, too.

"Jack."

"I don't know." He shook his head and snapped out of his trance. "They don't know. He'd been dead a few days before they found him."

Claims, driving, Ricky, the red pepper soup I'd had for dinner Thursday, flew through my mind. The beach with Jack. Northbeach. The Starboard. Pizza . . . it had all occurred in this life while Tank was gone to another. I didn't even know he'd left, and he was alone.

"I'm so sorry, Jack." I thought he was going to cry. My head throbbed. Jack had to be in pain, too. Greater than I could comprehend. I'd only known Tank a few weeks. "Jack?"

He inhaled and exhaled. He peered at the ceiling and regrouped. When he faced me again, he asked, "Are you staying here?"

"No. I'm leaving."

Mila pulled her towel off the line out back.

"Text me when you get home."

I wasn't sure I was going home. I didn't know where I should be.

I did know. *I should be with Tank.* He should've been here talking too fast for me to keep up with him and preparing the kayaks for us to take them out later just before dawn. I'd be smiling just because he was near me.

"Nora."

"What?"

"Text me."

I nodded, and he picked up his bag and walked out the back door of our porch.

Jack talked to the others. No one could function without some direction, and he was the one they'd always depended on. He sent them home. Back to their families, and told them he was going to Tank's mom's. That he'd call when he knew something.

The engine of Rob's BMW was the only one recognizable. He revved it as he pulled onto Route 1. The rest were just a series of car doors being shut and engine rumbles, and then there was silence. The house was dim; the world was a flat beige. Air entered my body and pushed my chest out. I stood in the middle of the room and recognized I was a microscopic being in the middle of a shack off Route 1 in Dewey, Delaware. I was twirling around the sun in a universe that was miniscule in comparison to so many others, and I was devastated. If such a small being could feel this, how did the world go on?

I ran my hand across the kitchen counter but didn't turn on the lights. I let my fingers linger over the old boom box on the counter Tank would play the local radio station from and sing at the top of his lungs while he flipped pancakes. I stared back at the doorway he'd flown through and forced my eyes shut to hold back the tears.

When the others were there, when I wasn't alone, I didn't believe it, but now that I was by myself I knew he was gone. I couldn't feel the excitement anymore. I didn't hear the lightness of his words. I couldn't remember what his laughter sounded like.

I ran to the bedroom Tank had shared with Stone. His Thomas the Tank beach towel hung over the closet door. It had been left there to dry from his shower the weekend before. I pulled it off the door and held it to my face. I hugged it and tried to squeeze him from it, but it was only a towel, mere cotton. I laid down and curled my knees to my chest.

I didn't sob. There wasn't enough left of me to muster a sob. I cried with my eyes closed. I tried to hide from the reality of a world without him. It was absolutely impossible that he'd died. Except everyone had left. They'd packed their cars and one by one they'd gone home because he was no longer with us.

The depth of my sorrow hurt me physically. It tore through me. I'd felt empty for so long. I'd sealed off my interior so efficiently that no emotions could leak through, but now I was flooded with despair as if someone poured it down my throat. I was choking on it.

I wanted him to take me with him, out to the sea, and swim with me again. We could bring the kayaks. He could yell at me and punch the side of the house; I didn't care. *Why didn't he tell me he was leaving?* He had to have known. Tank knew everything. He listened and he thought. He was at one with the world. I was alone.

A touch startled me. I opened my eyes to Jack kneeling beside me. "Nora," he said, but I couldn't answer him. I couldn't stop crying. I gripped the towel harder between my fingers and closed my eyes again.

Jack laid down with me and let me cry until even sorrow abandoned me. I stayed on my side and stared past Jack to the outside. The hip-hop music our neighbors loved poured through the open windows and surrounded us. I didn't care about it. I didn't care about any of it. I started to cry again.

"Shh," he said and played with my hair.

It wasn't fair. I sat up and faced Jack. He was so good. How would he stay on this earth without Tank? How would any of us? Why would we even want to?

Jack sat up and faced me. He was some lost version of himself, no longer the same person without his best friend somewhere in the world. I searched his eyes for hurt or anger, but all I saw were questions.

He looked from my eyes to my mouth and back up again. "Were you in love with him, Nora?" My tears flowed again at his question, and I couldn't face them. I closed my eyes and lowered my head again. "It's okay. Tell me if you were."

I shook my head. "It's so much worse." Jack held my face in his hands, not letting me look away. "I was inspired by him." My head dropped to his shoulder, and Jack held me while I cried.

He pulled me on top of him and laid us back down. I held on to Jack, terrified he might disappear, too. He stayed with me until the house filled with darkness and my mind finally stopped thinking.

"Why did you come back?" I asked, tracing the seam of his T-shirt with my finger.

"He wouldn't want you to be alone."

"How did you know I was alone?"

"Because you're always alone. Except when you were with him."

I would have burst into tears, but there were none left.

Without a word, I shut my eyes.

Nineteen

Don't Break Me

"SAFEONE. THIS IS Sharon."

My eyes rolled so far back in my head I might have been permanently disabled. "Sharon. It's Nora."

"Why are you not here? Your shift starts in ten minutes."

"Sorry I didn't call sooner. One of my roommates died yesterday, and I'm not going to be able to make it in."

She was chewing something. It didn't sound like gum. My face scrunched up in disgust. "That's terrible. Who was it?"

"His name was Ta—Thomas Kragler." I assumed she was searching the internet as I spoke, because Sharon wasn't the type to believe a word her employees said. Perhaps a life spent in claims had dulled her to the possibility of honesty among humans. I didn't care what she looked up.

"When did he die?"

"I'm not sure. We found out about it last night." The words

sounded ridiculous leaving my mouth. How could I not know when exactly? There was a moment when people stopped being alive. When the truck hit them. When the water filled their lungs. When the blood poured out. But with Tank, I wasn't even sure what had happened, and no one seemed to know exactly when he'd left.

"Well, I'm sorry for your loss. Was he a relative?"

I now assumed she was searching the manager's toolbox to see if I was entitled to any time off. I fell back on my bed. She exhausted me, or maybe I was exhausted and she forced me to realize it because she was interacting with me.

"I can approve you for a half day off for the funeral."

A half day. I was going to need a year or two. "Well, then you'll just have to dock me or fire me, because I'm not coming back in for a few days."

"I'm not sure who you think you are." Sharon sounded truly confused. I'd never spoken to her with anything but respect before.

"Funny. I feel surer of it than I have in five years. I think that means something, don't you, Sharon?"

"I have to call HR. I'll get back to you."

"Great. Thanks." I hung up the phone and didn't care if I ever heard from her again. I texted Ricky that my roommate had died and I wasn't coming to work. He'd worry about me and he'd care that Tank had died. Ricky still felt everything. I was just starting to feel something when Tank had gone. Now I couldn't feel anything but pain.

I COULD SAY Mila's house was exactly as I'd imagined it, but the reality of her home was beyond my ability to dream. It was enormous, perched upon a pristine grassy lawn, and surrounded by other outstanding residences.

I rang the doorbell. My eyes followed the ornate iron knocker up the dark wood to the top of the door. I judged it against myself. It was at least ten feet tall, and there was a matching one next to it.

Mila swung it open without an ounce of exertion. It might as well have been the screen door on my porch bedroom. "Nora!" Her face lit up, and I was beckoned into Mila's world of light. She'd make this better. For all of us.

I followed her into the kitchen. The house was an endless stream of interesting walls doused in cool colors such as pale gray or white with a touch of rose quartz. Colors that reflected more light than I thought reached the earth. Walls of glass doors with windows above them drenched the room in daytime. It was the perfect mix of style and warmth. It was Mila.

The kitchen was surrounded by a counter top and six stools on the sides that bordered the great room. A table and six chairs sat off to the side, next to the first row of glass doors, and looked out onto the back terrace. An island in the middle of the kitchen sat three more.

"Just you and your dad live here?"

Mila stopped pouring water in our blue crystal glasses and considered the enormous room. My eyes rose to the exposed beams arched above us and the curved window at the end of the ceiling. They were all a bright white. "It's one of the big reasons I didn't go to the beach for the whole summer with Jack. I couldn't leave my dad here alone."

I nodded. I'd left mine alone with my mother. "Your house is beautiful." I took a sip of the perfectly crisp water. "It reminds me of you."

"It reminds me of my mother," she said, and I searched for a new subject to talk about.

"Thanks for letting me stay here for the funeral."

Mila stopped drinking and stared at me. How could I have not upset her about her mother, but stumbled with gratitude? Her story was as fucked up as my own, but Mila had somehow survived. "I should be thanking you. You're the only one who makes sense out of this group. Well, you and Jack, but now it's just you."

I shook my head. I was stunned. "What?"

"Nora, Tank loved you because you understood him, and somehow you could speak his language and still talk to the rest of us. You're good at it."

"I'm terrible at it. I never communicate with anyone."

"Well, then you're good at us. You're exactly what this group needs, and I'm thankful you're here with me."

We carried our glasses past the first laundry room and the library. We climbed the central staircase and walked by three other bedrooms before we arrived at Mila's suite. It was her in architectural form. The light poured into the room from her balcony. The walls were the same muted hue of a winter breeze, but her bedding exploded with color. It was Marrakesh, and the pillows piled high on it made me want to run from fifteen feet away and dive into it. Double doors opened to her closet, where beautiful things were housed. Over the door hung a purple dress with ruffles at the hem waiting to attend a ball that wasn't on the day's agenda. A special hanger peeked out with scarves of all different patterns and textures. The room was rich with color.

"I know there's going to be a lot of people you know. Don't feel like you have to take care of me. I'll be fine." *Fine.* The word even stung in my own mind. I might never be fine again.

Mila stopped searching her room for the black wedges she was looking for. "You stand by me. The whole day tomorrow."

"I feel strange even being here. You guys all knew each other for years. I barely knew him two months."

"Listen, Tank thought every person comes into our lives for a reason. That no interaction is insignificant. He was right. You're supposed to be here as much as the rest of us."

I let my gaze fall to the floor where Mila's weekend bag sat. It was still packed, not an item removed since she'd returned after hearing of Tank's death.

"Let's go," she said, and I forced my feet to move forward.

I drove, and Mila took me the long way to the bar where we were meeting everyone. We passed the Bethesda Chevy Chase High School they'd all attended. The home of the B-CC Barons, where you could try out for every team from football to bocce. The house Tank grew up in was quaint and on the corner of a busy street. It could probably fit inside Mila's bedroom. There was a candle lit in the window and soft light coming from the side of the modest two-story. Finally, she led me to Rob's house, which was almost as impressive as her own.

Mila walked in the front door as if she lived there. She breezed through the two-story foyer, not even looking up at the oval-shaped staircase with the iron banister. It didn't register in her mind; she'd been surrounded by beauty for so long.

Rob was pouring himself a glass of Scotch when we walked in. The way he steadied the bottle with two hands suggested it wasn't his first. "Hey," he said and barely pulled himself away from his current state to join us.

"When did you start drinking today?" Mila asked. I'd never have questioned him.

"Pretty much as soon as I woke up." He took a sip. Based on his lack of facial expression, the Scotch went down like water. "But I slept until three."

"Mila." Rob's father walked into the living room and pulled her into a hug. "Rob didn't tell me you were coming by." He loved her, too.

"Do you know Nora, Mr. Holloway?" Mila motioned to me. Recognition lit up Rob's dad's face.

"Well of course. From parents' weekend at the University of

Delaware. How are you?"

"I'm good." That was all I had. I was overwhelmed by the two-story stone fireplace and his perfectly matched tie and suit jacket.

He turned back to Mila. "Tragic about Thomas. What a shame."

"I know. It's devastating," Mila responded, and Rob took a sip of his Scotch behind them. His dismissal of his father hadn't subsided since college.

"Such a waste. That boy had such promise."

Mila nodded, and I followed her lead. I'd probably do well to mimic her the rest of my life, at the very least over the next twenty-four hours.

"We're heading out, Pops." Rob left his empty glass on the end table near the couch.

"Who's driving?" Rob's dad appeared equally impressed with him.

"I am," I said and took a step toward the door.

"Well, be careful. One tragedy is more than enough for this town."

We filed out. Me leading, Rob behind me, and Mila hugging Rob's dad again before climbing into the back of the car.

"What an asshole," Rob said as I pulled out of his driveway.

"He's trying," Mila said before turning to me. "Make a right at the stop sign."

"Trying my patience." Those were the last words Rob spoke. His silence the rest of the ride was an eerie reminder that the world was no longer the same.

We met Stone at the bar. No one had heard from Heather. I'd texted her to make sure she knew about Tank, but she didn't respond. I parked next to Stone's car. Jack's motorcycle was nowhere in sight.

"Where does Jack live?"

"He used to live two doors down from Tank, but his parents moved to Florida and he has an apartment in the city now."

"DC?"

"Yes. The school where he teaches is in the city."

The thought of Jack in a room full of seventh graders warmed me.

We occupied a corner of the bar everyone had to pass through to get to the bathrooms. We were a disgusting bunch. Fear and disappointment wrapped in anger and hidden behind dead eyes fixed on rounds of shots delivered too quickly to count. I stopped drinking after the second round. I was the one with car keys, and I was the one who knew Tank the shortest amount of time. I'd drive their drunk asses around.

"Doing shots?" Jack's voice was in my ear. He pressed against the back of me.

I sat up straight, my body immediately responding to his closeness. Even looking like he hadn't slept in a week, his presence was a relief. I didn't like anyone else missing, especially Jack. "This one's for you." I moved to get up, and Jack held me down.

"Stay there. I like you right next to me."

I stopped lingering on Tank's demise for a minute and focused on Jack in front of me. There was no place I'd rather be than right next to him. I just wished it were for any other occasion than this one. "How are you?"

He downed the shot and winced at the final drops. "Unbelievably shitty." He sounded drunk. He leaned back and stared down at the floor behind my stool. "I'm just thankful I'm not working. No child should be around this."

In many ways we were still children. It wasn't fair we were around it, either. There was an undertow of anger. It could be heard in the impact of the emptied glasses slammed on the bar and the way Stone glared at me. His disgust seemed reserved for me alone.

"You pissed him off," Stone said as I walked by him on my return from the bathroom.

"What?"

"*You* pissed him off. I could barely calm him down."

I still didn't understand the weekend Tank had been so angry. "I don't know what I did. He never told me."

Stone rolled his eyes, and I returned to my stool. "Whatever," I heard him mumble.

I couldn't get far enough away from him. I'd tortured myself that entire night until I'd seen Tank the next morning.

This wasn't my fault. We were going to watch the meteor shower together.

A guy bumped into Stone on his way by. Not really a bump, more of a shoulder rub. The guy didn't seem like an asshole. It was either an accident or he had a death wish, because people didn't look more murderous than Stone. He was in a constant aggressive stance. Except tonight. Except toward me.

To my utter shock, Stone shrugged the contact off and barely paid attention to the slight. Rob, however, did not.

"What the fuck, dude? Didn't you see him sitting there?" Rob was in the guy's face. They were about the same height, but everyone seemed to have a few pounds on Rob.

I'd never seen Rob get into a fight before. Besides Blaire, I'd never even heard him in an argument. He was dedicated to people liking him.

The guy stopped walking and scrutinized Rob. "You got a problem, crack head?"

Rob was a bit more disheveled than usual. Dark circles framed his eyes beneath hair that was long and unruly beyond trying too hard to seem carefree. "You're my fucking problem," Rob said, and the guy pulled back to throw a punch, but Stone cold-cocked him before he touched Rob. The guy didn't fall. It was impressive. His friends—as in six friends—were upon us before I knew what was happening.

It wasn't as much of a fight as it was a beating. Jack went down. Stone went down. I lost track of Rob, and for once I missed Heather. She was a bit of a street rat and not one to shy away from a bar fight. We could have used more people.

We survived because of the off-duty police officers drinking on the opposite corner of the bar the whole night. Mila explained to the cops about Tank, and Jack and Stone sat obediently with their faces bleeding and their mouths shut. Somehow Rob walked out of the chaos without a mark on him. He abandoned us and moseyed out the side door with a cigarette behind his ear. He was unbelievable, and I wasn't letting him leave Jack and Stone there. I stormed after him.

"What the fuck, Nora! How can he be gone? He was more alive than any of us." Rob leaned against the wall outside. He'd totally forgotten about the last ten minutes. Stone and Jack were inside with the others trying not to get arrested, and Rob was lighting a cigarette on the side of the building, completely oblivious to their situation.

"What are you doing?" He pulled me into a hug while I shook my head in disbelief. "You should be inside. Dealing with the fight *you* started."

The side door opened, and Blaire walked out. She stopped in front of us as I pushed Rob away in disgust. She stared straight into my eyes, willing her hatred to penetrate me, and I really didn't care. I no longer cared what Blaire thought. What anyone thought.

"Figures," she said and walked over and hit Rob on the shoulder.

The rest of our party followed Blaire into the parking lot. They split into cars to move to the next bar that we had no business being in. Jack's head was cut and already bruising. Stone's knuckles were all broken open.

"I'll drive you," I said to Jack as Mila, Blaire, and Rob climbed into Stone's car. I couldn't be near Rob and Blaire.

The tension subsided. I relaxed with Jack in my car.

"He liked you, you know?"

I took a deep breath and turned the car to follow Stone out of the parking lot. "Where's your motorcycle?"

"I took the Metro. For a while, I thought he was in love with you."

I always just felt loved by him. Except . . ."I wasn't sure he didn't hate me the past few weeks."

"No. He loved you. Deep down, Tank loved everyone. He always saw the good in people."

"Yes." The tears formed in my chest, crawling up and choking me. I swallowed back the sadness.

"But you, he loved more than most. The first day he saw you standing on the beach he stopped in his tracks and said, 'Thank God, she's here.'" Jack turned toward me in his seat, and I was grateful for Stone's car in front of me to force my eyes to the road. "I figured he was going after you, but you were different. He kind of adored you."

His words were hollowing me out. "Can we talk about something else?"

"Yeah." Jack fidgeted in his seat. I just wanted him to be comfortable.

"How's your head?"

"Hurts." He touched the cut above his eye again. "Dumbass."

"Rob started it," I said defending the guy who'd punched him.

"I was talking about me." He leaned his head back against the headrest. "I wish we were at the beach. I wish Tank was there singing opera or walking through the house naked. I wish I could crawl into your bed and sleep with you tonight."

The two feet between us in the car left me cold. I could feel him lying next to me in my bed. Even the thought of him getting out of my car terrified me. I needed him more than I realized on the drive to Mila's.

We drove past the Hyatt Regency, and I stared at it as we passed and then turned to Jack while we stopped at the light. "Just sleep?" I asked.

Recognition settled on his face. "I promise." He smiled for the first time today. "Unless you beg me."

I turned the car around and pulled into the parking garage attached to the Hyatt.

JACK HELD ME close in the elevator.

"I'm tired of crying," I said out of nowhere.

"Me, too."

He was sobering up a little and much steadier on his feet. I leaned into him. The key card to our standard room was in the palm of my hand. We walked the hall, and my exhaustion was replaced with the anticipation of being alone with him. It terrified me. Tonight couldn't be the night. Tank thought it was a big deal, and it was.

I paused just outside the room. Jack was unbearably close. His heat poured off him and warmed me beside him. "Just sleep." I was saying it more to myself than him. Why was I even here? *Why not tonight?*

His face was cut. He'd been punched. He'd lost his best friend forever and he was drunk. That was why not tonight.

Jack grabbed my hand as I slid the key card into the lock. "Wait." He leaned down until his lips were right next to my ear. "Kiss me now. Before we go in. If you don't, I'll drive myself crazy thinking of the way you taste." I turned to him, ready to go get back in the car, but then he added, "I promise," and I held still. "On my honor. Just sleep."

His lips slipped down to my mouth. His hands cupped my head. He waited there while the heat from his body melted me.

He licked my bottom lip, and I inhaled, fighting for air. I pressed my lips against his. He forced me to the wall behind us and pinned me there. I pulled him closer, knowing tonight was impossible. I didn't care. His tongue in my mouth made me forget every promise I'd made to myself. I pressed against him, quieting the waves of need flowing across my skin.

Maybe just a blowjob. We didn't have to have sex.

I reached down and rested my hand flat across the zipper of his shorts. He was hard as I stroked him through the fabric. Jack lowered his head and regarded my hand there as I fought to breathe.

He rested his hand on top of mine. "You're testing my honor."

Not tonight. I returned my hand to my side.

His chest heaved and he leaned against the wall next to me.

I faced him, still buried in sadness. "Are you okay?" I rested my hands safely on his stomach.

Jack nodded. "For the first time in six days, I thought of something other than him dying." My heart broke for him. "I thought of how your lip quivers right before I kiss you."

Jack followed me into the room. We didn't turn on the lights. He went to the bathroom, and I pulled the covers back on the bed and closed the curtains. I laid in our bed with the six white pillows and waited for him to come make me feel whole.

He took off his shorts and T-shirt and climbed in behind me. He slid his arm under the pillow beneath my head and wrapped his other arm and leg over the side of me. I was covered with Jack.

"You fit perfectly with me. You're so tiny."

"Don't break me."

"I won't, Nora Hargrove."

Twenty

And Then There Were Six

THE LINE WAS out the front door of the church and snaked around the side of the building. Funeral home employees came out and plucked the elderly from the line one by one so they wouldn't have to wait in the sweltering sun. They brought us water and apologies from the family, but none if it mattered.

When my spot in line reached the front door, Heather joined us. She stepped in front of me and I waited for the people behind me to say something, but unlike the bathroom line inside a bar, this was a somber event. I turned away when she spoke and hoped no one thought I was in some way connected to her.

"How are you?" Mila asked and pulled Heather into a hug.

"I'm fine," she said, and the words I'd utilized for years of camouflage seemed to fit as well on Heather as they had on me. There was nothing fine about her. I doubted there ever would be.

The line continued to move from the front door, through the

foyer, and finally down the center aisle of the grand cathedral. The closed casket stole the thoughts I'd filled my head with to avoid thinking of Tank. He laid between a woman older than my mother who smiled and hugged each person who presented themselves in front of her and a man who looked like he wanted to die, too.

I needed drugs. I wished I'd brought something. I searched the crowd for Rob. Surely he wasn't sober for this fiasco of an event.

Heather stopped and signed the guest book on the podium. She took the last prayer card lying next to it, and the sight of it in her hand paralyzed me.

"Are there any more prayer cards?" I asked the employee nearby.

"Sorry, that's the last one." He nodded toward the card in Heather's hand, and she and I both looked at it. "The turnout has been incredible."

I could have ripped it from her hand. I'd cherish it forever, and she'd drop it in the seat crack of her car while she lit a cigarette on her way home. She didn't deserve to have the last piece of paper with his name on it. She didn't deserve the prayer.

Jack was hugging Tank's mom. He leaned way down, and she rubbed the back of his head. She'd known him his whole life. I cowered at their loss and pushed the prayer card from my mind. It wasn't what mattered today, but even high-minded, I knew I'd hold it against Heather for all of eternity.

Tank's mother said something to Jack, and he said, "Of course. I'll be right here." He moved to stand behind her as the rest of the line continued its death march. I paid my respects with a useless sentiment of sorrow. It was so beneath Tank that I almost choked on it, but I couldn't speak. I'd written the only words I could find in a card I'd leave for Tank's mother, but nothing was going to be enough. Not a card. Not a sound.

I sat next to Mila in a pew toward the back. I searched the

cathedral for Stone. He'd be here soon, right next to Mila. Rob was nowhere to be found. My sight fixed on Tank's casket. He was in there. He was no longer a part of this world. He belonged to another. One that was better suited for the kind of extravagance that was simple to him.

And then there were six.

I lowered my head. I couldn't see the casket. I couldn't watch his mom, and I couldn't face Jack or his heartbreak.

"*Psst.*" Rob was leaning into the sanctuary. He pointed to me and waved me out to him.

What? I mouthed to him. The service would start any minute. Most people had already taken their seats. The last of the line were paying their respects to Tank's family, and Rob—of course—needed something.

"Come here," he demanded barely above a whisper. He wasn't going to stop.

I turned to see Jack staring at me. His sadness had been replaced with annoyance as he watched me stand up and walk away from my pew.

Rob grabbed my hand and pulled me outside as soon as I was close enough for him to reach me.

"Rob," I said. He yanked me down the block and behind the cars parked at the edge of the lot. "What are you doing?"

He lit a cigarette, aggressively inhaled, and blew the smoke out above my head. "I'm freaking out, Nora."

I exhaled and let my shoulders fall. I shook my head. "Rob, we need to get back in there. You're a pallbearer."

"I can't do it. I can't do anything. What the fuck!" he screamed up to the sky. "How can he be dead?"

Rob's reaction was delayed. "Here's how everyone works through grief. They freak out like this when they first hear of the death, and then they move into the numb stage, which carries them through the funeral." Having to explain this to him annoyed me. "Note Tank's comatose mother if you're still confused."

"Nora." He ignored me and pulled me into his arms. I think he was crying. He was making me soft. I was barely hanging on myself, and I was surely not solid enough to pull him through this.

The smell of something burning was followed by me screaming at Rob and pushing him away. "You're burning my fucking hair." I pulled it around to my face and sure enough, several strands were singed and kinky from where he'd rested his cigarette. I huffed and walked away.

"Nora. I'm sorry. Don't walk away."

I turned on him, ready to kill him, but the sight of him was too sad to hate. He was lost in a world without Tank. He was lost in a world he wasn't the center of. I pitied him. I let him catch up to me. I placed my hand gently on the side of his face and willed him to hear me the first time I spoke, because there wouldn't be a second. "I know you're hurting, but this isn't about you. It's Tank's day." I could have pierced him with my glare. "You can have tomorrow. He can't. You've got to get back in there."

I fought the urge to punch him in the face. Rob let his head hang low.

"What's going on?"

I rolled my eyes at the sound of Blaire behind us. "Nothing." I exaggerated as I spoke the word to her. "Nothing is ever going on. Nothing has ever gone on. We've never kissed. We've never done a thing."

Rob was grinning when I looked back at him. He was back at the center.

"Take care of your *fucking* girlfriend and get back inside." I'd had enough of both of them. They deserved each other, and Tank deserved better.

Twenty-One

My God, I was Full of Hate

I ABSOLUTELY HATED every single second I spent at my desk. It was a torture beyond my understanding. When I stopped talking into my headset and typing on my keyboard, I sat and wondered how I ever could have stood the prison in the first place.

Ricky hated being near me. He preferred me without any reaction. My utter despair was apparently a deterrent. He actually went to lunch with the new guy whose hair stuck up in the back, uncovering a premature bald spot. I couldn't even act like I cared. I couldn't care. I was dead inside because Tank was dead on the outside. I was a walking, oozing infection of hatred, and I couldn't stop feeling any of it.

I was wretched.

Rufus was the only one who could stand me. He was impossible to resist as he wagged his tail when I arrived. I didn't even have to read to him anymore. He was happy just with the sound of my voice, even if I was telling him about a horrific loss the world would now have to endure. Rufus loved me in spite of me.

"SafeOne Auto, this is Nora." God, I needed this shift to be over.

"This is Elizabeth Gorman."

I paused, preparing myself for whatever nonsense this call contained.

"I have a car insured with you that's being repaired." Elizabeth sounded about a hundred and six years old.

"Do you have a claim number, Mrs. Gorman?"

She did. She read it to me. Twice. I pulled up her claim after the first read-through and used the extra time to review the facts of the loss and the latest log entries. Her car was at the body shop, and the estimator had just approved a supplement for damage found after teardown.

"I just wanted to make sure everything's going to be paid for. The body shop said they found another eight hundred dollars in repairs."

I pulled up the estimate. "Yes, Mrs. Gorman. There's been a supplement approved for eight hundred and ninety-one dollars. We're going to send that amount directly to the shop unless you'd like us to mail it to you."

"No. That's fine. What a relief."

I couldn't believe she wasn't going to start complaining about a bumper or her rental car. It was completely improbable that she was actually satisfied with her policy benefits. I tilted my head to the screen. My eyes slit as I listened to Mrs. Gorman tell me about her accident.

"We were just sitting at the red light when the other car lost control and slid right into us."

"I see that," I said, hoping to move the conversation along.

"We were on our way home from the doctor's. My husband, he's also insured on the policy, had a heart attack in the spring, and now we go to the doctor's a lot."

I had no idea what to say. "I'm sure," was what came out.

"Then at the beginning of the summer, our car was totaled when a couch fell off the truck in front of the car next to us. That car swerved into our lane and trapped us against the guard rail." I scanned up the insured's information. Mrs. Gorman was eighty-nine. "Our car was totaled in that accident. So this is a new car."

"Oh my. You've had quite a year." I was astounded she was still alive and a little concerned she was still driving. Although neither of these losses appeared to be her fault.

"We've been very lucky."

I was speechless. Every other person who'd ever dialed this number should be forced to listen to this woman. "Yes. I guess that's the best way to look at it."

"There's really only one way to look at things. If you look at them the other way, you'll make yourself miserable."

In one sentence, she'd described the last five years of my life. "I know what you mean, Mrs. Gorman."

"Well, I guess that's all I need today. Thank you so much for all your help. You've been a lifesaver. I don't know what we'd do without all of you. Really, I'd be lost. Thank you."

"You're very welcome." I logged out and dropped my head to my arms on my desk. I rested there with my eyes shut. I missed Tank. He would have loved Mrs. Gorman, and she would have loved him. I thought maybe I just needed some time off. Maybe I could ask Sharon for some unpaid leave.

"Head up," she said and tapped her knuckles on my desktop.

Maybe not.

THE ONLY THING I was sure of was the fact that I didn't want to be at the beach house. The anger dulled to a comfortable numbness by the time I left work on Saturday afternoon. My bag was in the back of my car. I was supposed to hop on 95 South and exit the city before dinner, but I was just moving through the motions of traveling somewhere I wasn't even sure if I was wanted. Stone seemed to think Tank hated me enough to die. I'd pretty much made it clear to Rob and Blaire what I thought of them, and, in doing so, I had annoyed Jack. He'd been distant and quiet and absent throughout the luncheon in Tank's honor.

The beach house was fractured. It would never heal. Tank was gone forever. Never coming back. Blaire wasn't even there, according to Rob's endless texts. I hadn't heard from Jack. Mila could barely hold the rest of them up. She couldn't take me on, too. It wasn't fair to her. It wasn't fair to me.

I was less than ten miles from Dewey, and the tears welled up in my throat. I was in no condition to see anyone. I could have picked up Jack and taken him home with me. I texted him. I had no idea what to say, but if he'd just text back, I'd know it was going to be okay. I wrote, *How are you?*

The traffic lights on Route 1 were only slightly less brutal on Saturday night than on Saturday morning. The restaurants' and stores' parking lots were packed. All of Delaware and half of Maryland was spending the weekend at the beach.

I'm fine, was what Jack responded. It was worse than him not responding at all.

The sign for the Cape-May Lewis Ferry hung over the lane I was driving in, and I didn't move. I followed the road to the port terminal and parked in the lot. I didn't know why, but I needed to see my mother before there was nothing left of me.

The ferry was sold out for vehicles. I parked and locked my car. I walked through the parking lot like I'd taken the ferry a hundred times before, but this was a first. Onboard, I bought a soft pretzel and a bottle of water. I shouldn't see my mother on an empty stomach. I might disintegrate.

There were tables and chairs throughout the inside cabin of the ferry, but I wanted to feel the bay as we crossed it. I found an end of a bench on the upper deck as we disembarked from Delaware, headed straight for Cape May, New Jersey and my mother.

A couple sitting next to me debated the safety and comfort of their dog in their car below deck. The woman droned on and on until the man finally left us and went to sit in his car with the animal. I bet he preferred the dark silence to the bright sun and complaints of his significant other. Maybe the dog was his significant other, and the woman left next to me was just along for the ride.

The wake spread out behind the ferry, and I thought this was how it should be. It was my life. This Nora Hargrove's stories were tragic. There were no happy endings, just too many endings to count.

The shuttle was full. I was the last passenger to board. The other foot passengers and I rode to the transportation center in Cape May and then exited the shuttle without a word to each other. I walked down Lafayette Street toward the woman who'd raised me. The woman who'd ruined me.

At Congress Hall, I stopped and had a drink in the Blue Pig Tavern. I started to order the lemonade because it was the first thing on the menu, and the old Nora would have ordered it so she didn't have to think, but everything was different now. I got the Dogfish Head 60 Minute IPA and wished Tank were here to drink it with me.

As I sipped it, I realized I hate lemonade. I'd hated it my whole life. I surveyed the plates of the customers next to me. I also hated red meat. I hated arugula, pinot grigio, and mayonnaise. God help me, I was full of hate.

I paid for my drink—okay, I had two . . . three—and walked the five blocks to my parents' rented shore house.

I climbed the six steps of the front porch and rang the

doorbell. My mother answered the door. Her hair was pulled up into a loose bun with wooden sticks poking out of it, and she wore a tropical-colored kimono. She looked like she'd been raised on a Pacific Island rather than in Ringwood, New Jersey.

"I still hate you," I said and didn't smile. "But I miss you, too."

"Well, of course you do." She pulled me inside and hugged me. "I was horrendous. My behavior deplorable. But you can't give up on me. I'm your mother."

Her words echoed inside me. My reactions to her had been buried long ago. My arms remained at my sides. I didn't know what I needed from my mother, but a hug wasn't the solution. She released me, pushed the hair off my face, and kissed my forehead the way she had every night before putting me to bed when I was little.

"How are you, my sweet Nora?"

"I'm not sweet. Everything is fucked up."

Her expression was kind and generous. She was expecting me, but that was impossible. I hadn't expected myself. "Come in. I'll make us some tea."

I followed my mother into the most magnificent house overlooking the Atlantic Ocean I'd ever been to. Unlike the house I'd spent the summer in, there was nothing but room here. An enormous kitchen spilled into the great room that had windows on three sides with breathtaking views everywhere I looked. I turned around in it, knowing Jack and Rob and all the others were staring out at the same ocean today. Tank's parents should have scattered his ashes into the sea.

I shook my head to dislodge the thoughts of him.

"What's going on?" my mother asked as she placed the kettle on the back burner of the stove.

"I'm confused."

My mother fell into her kind I'm-listening stare that always made me want to hug her when I was a child. I knew she wouldn't say another word until I contributed more.

"A lot's happened this summer." Still no reaction. "I fell in love, and someone died."

"Oh my. The same person?"

I shook my head. "Not exactly. I fell in love with a lot of people." I stared out the window at the churning sea. It was rough today, and the lifeguards had yellow flags up on either side of their stands.

"Who are these people? Where are they from?"

"Outer space." I laughed a little, and my mother stayed still. I lowered my head, unable to face her judgment, but I needed to defend them. "They're the wealthy and the poor, the lost and the enlightened, and I love every one of them." I thought of Heather and Blaire, and sometimes Rob. "Some of them." My mother still didn't move. She was better at this than I was. I inhaled deeply. "But now one's gone, and nothing is how it should be." My mother poured hot water over the tea bag in the cup in front of me. "And I think I'm never going to see them again."

"If you love them, you can't throw them away."

I shouldn't have come here for advice. She was a horrible person. "That's rich, coming from you."

"I never threw you away. You or your father. I've loved you both every single day."

"Why then, Mom?" The last word was foreign leaving my mouth. She hadn't been a mom in years.

She sighed and put her teacup safely on the counter. "According to my therapist, I was professionally unfulfilled and resented your father and . . . my life."

"Your life? As in me?"

"I didn't say that."

"You know, it really pisses me off you've talked to a therapist about this."

"My God, why? You should see someone."

"Do you know how many people with *real* mental illness, not boredom, are suffering without the proper access to health care?"

She was regrouping, calming herself with one of her patented deep breaths. "You should talk to someone, Nora. You never do. You never *have*. Do you remember Joey Rivello?"

"Mom." I closed my eyes and shook my head. She was ridiculous. "Please." I didn't want to talk about Joey Rivello.

"You loved him. For years you loved him. If you could have seen how much work you put into his valentines every year." She shook her head reminiscing. "And then one day, in third grade, he pushed you down on the playground."

"Mom, I know."

"And you never spoke to him, or about him, again."

"I shouldn't have come here."

"Yes, you should have. I'm your mother, and just like Joey Rivello and these people from the summer, you cannot just throw me away because you've been hurt. Life is hard, Nora. You can't hide from it."

"You don't know what you're talking about." She'd hit a nerve, and I was going to slap her across the face with it. "You dragged Dad and me through the ringer! We're vegans. No. We're learning Greek this week. Remember the year of teeth whitening? My gums still hurt. Pilates, ceramics, meditation, essential oils, and dog walking. I didn't know if I was a Quaker or a witch's daughter from one day to the next. You can't stick with anything! You fall in love depending on the day of the week."

"And you love nothing!"

We stared at each other, hatred and love suspended between us. She was wrong about almost everything, but she was right about that. At least she was before this summer. Everything was different now.

"Do you remember how much you loved to read when you were little?" Her voice was gentle again. That of a mother parenting her daughter. "How you'd sit for hours and read all kinds of books? Mysteries, memoirs, those awful romances. You read *Gone with the Wind* in fourth grade. I'd never seen anything like it."

I thought back to the Nora Hargrove novels I'd snuck past her, knowing they'd only make her crazier. Stephen King, James Patterson, I'd torn through novels that adults were reading next to me on the beach. "What does that have to do with anything?"

"You preferred the make-believe to the real world and you were willing to hide inside those books to avoid it forever. You scared us. The only thing more terrifying than seeing your child struggle is watching her shut down all together."

I was losing this argument and losing my mind. If she were anywhere near right, what did that make me all these years? "I liked to read."

"You liked to hide. Your father and I did everything we could to pull you out of it. We signed you up for every club, sport, and activity. We were convinced that if you were busy and around everyone, you'd *be* with everyone else, and it was finally starting to work. Until . . ."

"I really do hate you."

"We're talking about you now." She raised her eyebrows. "You shut down completely. You didn't read. You broke up with your boyfriend, quit the play. I don't even think you'd have gone to college except it was your only way to move out."

I lowered my head, remembering the day they'd dropped me off at the University of Delaware. It could have been any school as long as I didn't have to watch them together every day. I'd stopped living my life because I didn't want to share it with her, but what I hadn't realized was it was a hard habit to break. Being alone.

"Nora, you've got to be willing to write your own story," she continued to say words. I raised my head and stared at her. I wanted to believe she knew what she was talking about. There was a time I would have taken every word from her mouth as fact. She was my mother. "And you've got to be brave enough to let someone else hear it."

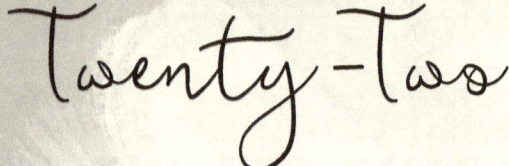

Twenty-Two

Life is Deep. Dive In.

I'D JUST TURNED my ringer on as I stepped out of my office when the bells went off. It startled me in my hand.

"Hello."

"Nora, it's Janine. From the shelter."

"Is Rufus okay?" I stopped walking and pressed the phone against my ear. He had to be all right.

"He's better than okay. He was adopted today." Tears overflowed from my eyes. "And he has you to thank for it. You did a great job with him."

I choked back the tears. "Oh, that's wonderful."

"The family's great. He totally won their twin girls over with his personality."

"He's such a sweetie. Thanks for letting me know."

"Thank you. I've got a new dog I need you to meet. When are you coming back in?"

"Soon. I need to get back there soon." I hung up and smiled through my tears the whole way to my car. He did it. He really did it.

I COULD HEAR the knocking on my apartment door from inside the shower. I'd just turned off the water, and the pounding on the door reverberated through the miniscule bathroom as I slipped into my robe. No one ever came to my apartment unless they were delivering food.

With the light step of a cat, I walked to the door and peered through the peephole without making a sound. Jack stood on the other side. His left hand rested on the doorjamb above it. His other held his motorcycle helmet, and he was gazing down at his feet. He was beautiful standing near the dust bunnies surrounding the staircase of my townhouse.

"I know you're in there," he said and banged again, making me jump from behind the door.

I reached forward and unlocked the two padlocks and the chain on the door. Jack turned the knob and opened it toward me. I was three feet inside the apartment with my wet hair dripping down my back. "It's Friday. Why are you not at the beach?" I asked.

"I'm here."

"I can see that." A lightness followed him into my apartment. The week of crying and hauling hatred with me everywhere I went was pushed to the past as Jack smiled at me.

"Why aren't you at the beach? I waited to see you all day."

"I have to work tomorrow." I paused, too tired of sharing grief with him. "And I don't really want to be there anymore."

Jack pulled me close to him. I rested my head against his chest and let his warmth engulf me. "You should have texted me."

"I didn't know what to say," I admitted and pulled myself closer to him.

"How about I miss you?" he said, and made me want to cry. I was tired of crying. My natural instincts were to pull away, but I stayed in his arms and let his warmth fill my wet body. I inhaled and exhaled with my eyes closed until we were no longer in mourning, until we weren't even here. We were someplace warm and sunny together, lying on the beach and laughing.

"I miss you," I said and I could have floated to the sky.

"That's better."

I laughed, but only a little, because anything really funny wouldn't register in my mind. I relocked the door behind him out of habit as Jack scrutinized my dismal abode.

"Nice place." I assumed he was joking. "How many apartments are in this building?"

I turned from Jack, who was running his hand over the navy corduroy couch that had been much cooler in my apartment at the University of Delaware. "Three. The whole first floor is mine. Two above me."

He looked from my kitchen counter to the family room with the ancient fireplace and into the dining "area" next to the large bay windows that I had to keep closed and covered at all times for fear of being watched or robbed, or worse. He was inspecting everything. It was the first source of information he'd ever had about me besides me. "This is nice," he said, but I couldn't tell if he meant it. My apartment was more of a cave than a residence, but I could pay for it myself.

The drip from my sink hit the pot waiting to be scrubbed in the sink. I vaguely remembered the eggs I'd boiled in it earlier in the week. The water droplet plopped down, followed by another one. The sound fell each time between us, and I locked eyes with Jack.

He walked past me to the sink. "Leaky faucet?"

"Wow. You are handy."

"And you are sarcastic."

Jack didn't need to put up with my shit.

"Mind if I take a look?"

"Whatever you want."

Jack removed the never-ending contents from under my sink. The cleaners I rarely used. The brushes and fire extinguisher. He raised his eyebrows at the collection of pillar candles that were covered in dust, and the bag of shells.

He worked in the kitchen while I sat silently on my couch and brushed my wet hair. What was he even doing here? Did fixing my faucet bring him some construction-based solace? I left him alone.

"Fixed," he said and dried his hands on the dishtowel from my counter. He was satisfied, and I was confused.

"I feel like I should make you dinner or something, but I don't cook."

"What do you do?"

I searched my mind for the answer he wanted to hear but forfeited from exhaustion. "I'm an excellent sleeper." Jack was close, unbearably so. The lack of distance robbed me of my sarcasm.

"Let's go out."

"Maybe we should just order a pizza?"

"Tank would want us to do a shot." Tank would want us to do a shot. He'd want us out raising hell through the streets of Wilmington. "And make love." My head lowered at his words. The heat welled up in my chest. He'd want me to make love, too. "What? What did I say?"

"Nothing." I shook my head and moved away from him. "I'll get dressed."

I climbed over my bed and reached for my wallet on my nightstand. It had thirteen dollars in it and my gold card. I rolled onto my back and stared at the ceiling of my apartment. "How could you leave me here alone?" I whispered to Tank.

"Let's go! I'm hungry," Jack yelled toward my bedroom, and pulled me from my depression. My closet was daunting. I didn't feel like picking something out. I didn't want to care about anything.

The off-white maxi dress with the spaghetti straps hung on the end of my closet. I hadn't worn it since last summer. "I'll be right out," I said as I threw the dress over my head and dabbed my lips with lip gloss. I was satisfied with my reflection in the mirror, and even that didn't feel right. Nothing was going to feel right ever again. Not until Tank came back. Not even to me. Just to Earth.

Jack was reviewing the pictures, magnets, and papers adorning my refrigerator door. He looked up and stared at me without a hint of a smile. He was devastated, too. That was why he wanted to come here. He knew I'd be in the same horrific state as he was. "Recyclables go out tomorrow."

I could have pulled him to me and held on to him until I'd aged enough to forget what the last eight days felt like. "Thanks."

"Who's the dog?" A picture of Rufus lying down in the back of his cage was on the freezer door.

"That's my friend, Rufus."

"He looks pretty sad."

"He was, but he's better now. He just got adopted from the animal shelter, so he's going to be fine."

Jack observed me as if he was filing that piece of information away, too.

We walked to Catherine Rooney's and ate at the bar. When the bartender took our empty plates away we ordered beers, and Jack turned me in my seat until my legs were straddled by his. I studied the side of my leg touching his. It was exactly where it should be. Jack was here for a reason, and the reason was to be with me. I touched his thigh and closed my eyes.

"Hey. You okay?" He pulled me from my trance, and I realized how loud the bar was and how many people were congregated around us.

"Fine—"

"Please." He shook his head with his eyes shut. "Don't say fine. Like, ever again."

I wouldn't. Tank would never say fine, and now neither would I. I was going to tell Jack everything, even if I choked on every word, because *I* deserved for him to hear it. "I think Stone hates me."

Jack shook his head before I got the last word out. "It wasn't your fault."

"I know." I stared down into my beer. I was sure I didn't mean as much to Tank as he did to me. I couldn't have impacted him in a way that would end his life. To think otherwise was ridiculous. "Stone seems to think so, though."

"Stone's an asshole." Jack ran his hand up the side of my thigh. His eyes followed his hand. He was lost in the sight of his hand on me. "And he doesn't really think that. We'd all seen Tank like that before, and there was never an easy answer as to why. Stone's just angry."

"He's always angry."

"Yes, but now the rest of us are, too. It's not his special thing. He's ramping it up a notch to stay relevant." Jack and I both laughed at his depiction. "Let's do a shot."

Tank would be sitting here with us. He'd be everywhere with everyone. He was the party within the party. Without question, shots would be done in the honor of a proper good bye.

Jack signaled the bartender and ordered shots as I heard my name being called from across the bar. I stiffened in my chair.

"Two things," I said. Jack turned to watch Ricky storming toward us. "Brace yourself." I tapped his hand on the bar. "And he's harmless."

"I thought you weren't going out tonight! What are you doing here, and why didn't you call me?" Ricky stopped to breathe and inspect every inch of Jack. "And who is this?"

"I was too sad to go out."

Jack regarded me with complete understanding in his eyes.

"Because of your friend who died?"

I nodded. "Jack just showed up. I didn't know I was coming out. I don't even want to be out. I just am." I let my stare linger on Jack. It was as if Ricky wasn't with us. We were completely alone. Tied by grief and exiled by pain.

"You know, when you look at him," Ricky began, and I braced myself. "It makes me think you're not really a lesbian." Jack dropped his head and laughed. "Or abstinent, or sick with mononucleosis." Jack was now laughing so hard his shoulders were shaking. "Or blind in one eye." Ricky huffed and leaned back. "In my country, we don't lie to the people we love."

I shook my head. Our shots came, and Jack ordered a third for Ricky as a peace offering.

"What country are you from?" Jack asked Ricky.

"You might have heard of it." I glared at Ricky. "It's called Pennsylvania."

"Oh," Jack said without blinking as he handed us our shots.

I took a deep breath. "To the greatest guy I ever knew."

We clinked glasses and downed our shots. Ricky bought us another round to help fill the holes Tank's death had left in us. He proceeded to tell Jack every detail of how he spent forty hours a week trying to get me to run away with him, or fall in love with him, or just have sex with him.

Jack hung on Ricky's words as if they were a detailed research paper on Nora Hargrove he had to memorize because he wouldn't be able to reference it later. Ricky stuck with us and kept our minds off Tank until his eye was caught by a blonde on the other side of the bar.

"I've got to go," he said and shook Jack's hand. "She's a liar, you know. Don't believe a word she says."

"I won't," Jack answered.

"She's devastated by the loss of your friend."

"We all are." Jack rubbed my thigh again.

"But she wouldn't let me comfort her." Ricky left us with our own thoughts and silence to deal with.

When I thought it might crush us beneath it, Jack asked, "Do you want to go home?" and I knew he was feeling the same way I was—claustrophobic.

Rain was trickling from the sky when we stepped out of the bar. I shielded my eyes and focused on the street light to gauge how hard it was falling. It was more than a mist, but not driving. I hadn't even checked the weather since I'd left the beach. What difference did the weather make in the city? Jack took my hand in his and began the uphill walk to my apartment.

After two blocks, the rain intensified. It drove down on us as our path stepped out from under a tree and retreated when we stepped underneath. We ran the last block. Jack didn't let go of my hand until we were safely under the roof of my front porch.

"You're soaked," he said and pushed my wet hair from my face. His hand on my skin set my senses on fire. The sound of the rain surrounded us. Cars drove by with their windshield wipers furiously switching sides. Everywhere his fingers touched felt hot, and the heat spread through me as I watched him.

I wanted him in a way I'd never wanted anyone before. Not even him the weekend he'd kissed me at the shore. Tonight I was desperate to feel something other than loss.

Life is deep, Nora. Dive in.

I stood on my tiptoes and kissed him. Gently. I placed my lips on his and tasted him. I felt his breath. I let my eyelashes brush against his cheek. I inhaled him, and the sensation of Jack replaced the rain around us.

"Give me your key."

I closed my eyes, wanting to touch him again.

"Nora."

I searched the bottom of my bag for my key ring. I pulled it out, and Jack took it from my hand. I followed him inside the vestibule and leaned against the wall as he unlocked the door to my apartment. Nothing about it seemed foreign. I hadn't had a guy in my apartment since Ricky had been too drunk to drive home months ago. He was so far gone he hadn't even tried to hit on me. Ricky had been an intruder; Jack's presence was as natural as being alone had become.

My heart beat raced in my chest. I closed the door behind us and locked it.

Jack pressed against the back of me. "Don't turn on the lights," he whispered near my ear.

The apartment was pitch black. His words rang through the darkness and sent a chill down my wet back. Jack took my wrists in his hands and raised my arms above my head. He held them there with one hand and moved my hair from the back of my neck with the other. I shivered at his touch.

"Don't run away." His words pounded through me.

"I won't," I said, breathless. I willed him to touch me again. I could no more leave him than I could imagine my life without him.

He turned me around and lifted me up. Jack held me against the wall, my legs wrapped around his waist. His hard-on pressed against me. I couldn't breathe. This was really going to happen.

Stop thinking, Nora.

Jack's lips trailed down my neck to my chest. He pushed my dress to the side and took my nipple in his mouth. I inhaled deeply and let my head fall back against the wall behind me. My starved body responded to his touch immediately. My nipples hardened; my muscles tightened around him. I needed him. Every inch of him.

He kissed me again, and I threaded my fingers in his hair. He was rough, forcing himself against me. I couldn't pull him close enough. I fisted my hands and fought his tongue with my own. My clothes needed to come off.

He carried me to my bedroom and fell on top of me on my bed. He spread my legs and laid between them. His lips found my neck, and I crossed my ankles behind his back.

Jack yanked his shirt over his head. His bare chest rested against mine as he kissed me again. The light from the street fought the rain to reach inside my window.

I lifted my hips and ground against him. He was everything I'd waited for. I wasn't going to wait one more minute. His lips trailed down the center of my chest, his hands moved behind my back so he could raise my stomach as his tongue traced my nipple. His touch sent tiny pulses across my electrified skin. My hips thrust against him. Every part of me wanted to touch him.

"I've wanted nothing but this since the first time you walked into our room," he whispered against my skin. "June and July were torture."

"Jack." I could barely think. He rose up and kissed my neck. His touch lit me on fire. I had to tell him. I needed him to know. "I've never done this before."

He paused. It was barely noticeable except I was glued to his every movement. "Done what?" His lips were near my ear again. He was lying on top of me, but the majority of his weight was supported by his flexed arms.

"This." The word was a bell ringing in the darkness. I felt his breathing stop. He lifted himself off me and looked me in the eye as a chill swept down my entire body. I didn't turn away. I'd let him have me in every way.

"Nora." He searched my eyes for some explanation, but he already knew. His head shook slightly. I waited as he put all the pieces of the summer together. All the information Ricky had shared. It answered the question of how I'd resisted him this long.

"Take it." My voice was low. I'd never been surer of anything in my life. "I want you to."

"Nora." Jack sat up next to me in bed. He ran his hands through his hair. I'd replaced my own frustration with his. "We can't do this."

"Yes, we can." I climbed off the bed and stood in front of him with my dress hanging from my waist.

"Is this what's been going on all summer?"

"Yes."

"Why didn't you tell me?"

"I've never told anyone. Except . . ." My gaze drifted away with the longing of our lost friend.

"We can't do this, Nora. It shouldn't happen tonight. Like this."

The rain beat on the only window in my room. It was a beautiful storm, and Jack was here with me in my bed. We were alone, and I needed him more than I needed air. "This is perfect."

"No."

"Jack—"

"You're drunk," he said and faced me.

I inhaled deeply and let the air out slowly, savoring every particle. I lifted my dress over my head and threw it on the floor next to us. Jack seemed like he was in pain. Before he could protest, I stepped out of my panties. "I'm not drunk." I willed him to hear me. Jack's gaze covered every inch of me until he faced me again. I blushed. There was nothing I had left to give him. "I'm begging you."

He left me standing there as he fought some mental debate. I was willing him to take me, sending every thought I'd ever had in his direction. He held out his hand, and I placed mine in it. Jack pulled me onto his lap, but as I sat down, I straddled him. Without any clothes on, I was sitting on Jack's lap. I twisted my legs behind his back and moved even closer to him.

He ran his hands up my bare back. He was gentle. My confession had turned this into something more than it had been ten minutes ago. For him.

It'd always been exactly what it was for me—perfect.

"Nora." His voice was thick and low. He swallowed hard and ran his lips across my bare shoulder. "You have to be with me every minute."

"I will. I promise."

"Promise me something else."

"What?"

"You have to talk to me. Tell me things."

I stayed silent. I couldn't speak.

"If you want me to stop, at any time. You have to tell me."

"I'm not going to want you to stop. Make love to me, Jack."

His lips crushed against mine, and he rolled me onto my back again. He kissed me until I couldn't breathe without him, until I'd never let him leave. I tightened my legs around him to quiet the pounding between them.

He shifted and laid beside me like I was a porcelain doll that he'd shatter with his weight. He brushed the hair off my face and kissed my cheek, but I wasn't going to have it. I didn't want him to be careful with me. I wanted him to take me.

I rolled on top of him and pinned him down. I forced my tongue into his mouth, and he responded instantly. I rubbed myself against him. Back and forth until I thought I might come just from that. I stopped and breathed heavily in his ear.

"I hear you," he said, and I knew he'd gotten the message.

He lifted me off him and stood next to the bed. I inhaled, and he yanked me to the edge. He placed each of my legs over his shoulders and dropped to his knees. His hungry stare caught me above my hip bones as both of his hands slipped under me and raised me to his mouth. He licked from the base of me to my clit, and my body convulsed into the air.

Jack stopped and waited for air to enter my chest, and for me to exhale. "You're delicious."

I couldn't look away. He pressed my legs wider with small kisses on each of my inner thighs, and then his lips found my clit again. He sucked it until it throbbed harder than my heart. Tiny moans slipped from my lips, and he stayed still until I was able to breathe again.

He rested me on the bed and slipped one finger into me. My legs closed around him, but he nudged them wide. I forced myself to concentrate on his finger inside me, and he moved it in and out. His tongue on me sent a pulsing to my core, which responded with a wetness everywhere he was. I was tightening around him.

"Jack." I could barely breathe. "I want to come with you inside me."

His movements were swift. He took off his jeans, reached in the pocket, and tore open a condom. I was chilled without him. He climbed between my legs and paused, waiting for my permission. I inhaled, nodded slightly, and without a word he pressed inside me. Jack stole the air from my chest and replaced it with his fullness as his warmth invaded me. He waited there.

"Keep going," I said.

He pulled out and thrust into me again.

My hands on his biceps, my hips writhing against him, Jack continued until the throbbing focused its pounding on my core. Every part of me was with Jack. I gasped for air and pulled him toward me as I came. I closed my eyes, unable to manage sight or sound, completely focused on whatever the fuck else was happening inside me.

I felt him come and pulled him to me. He rested on top of me, his heart beating against my chest.

"Thank you," I whispered.

"Open your eyes." He leaned up on his forearms behind my shoulders. "Look at me, Nora." I opened my eyes to his chin and let my sight wander up his beautiful lips to his endless blue eyes. "Thank you."

He kissed me, and I was ready to do it again. I let his tongue explore me without the urgency of before. I let him caress me with his fingertips over every inch of my body, and when he was hard again, we made love for the second time. It was different. I was no longer a virgin. There was nothing else to think about but the way Jack felt, hard in my hand, and in my mouth, and between my legs. He was mine.

MY AWARENESS CAME first, followed by my eyes flitting open. The rain from the night before had been replaced outside my window with bright sunshine. Jack's chest rose beneath my head. My hand rested on his pec. He was still here. I'd really done it. He'd really done it.

We'd done it.

I smiled as the memories of the night before flooded my mind. My lips found his skin, and I kissed him without considering if I should or not.

I was heavy with my wholeness. Jack had given more to me last night than he'd ever be able to comprehend. I wouldn't embarrass either of us by telling him I loved him, but I did. I didn't care if he knew it. I didn't care if everyone in our house knew it. Nothing seemed to be a secret anymore.

Jack stirred beneath me. He paused and kissed the top of my head. I was just about to roll on top of him when my phone rang. It was on the nightstand closest to Jack. He picked it up, looked at it, and handed it to me. Rob was calling, and the sight of his name terrified me. The last time a phone rang, Tank was dead.

"Hello?"

"Nora. Where are you?"

"I'm in my apartment. What's wrong?" I moved to sit up, but Jack held me tight against him.

"Nothing. Everything." Rob sounded a million miles away. "Blaire and I broke up."

I relaxed. Everyone was exactly as I'd left them. "I'm sure you guys will work it out. Tank's death has left us all in a strange place."

"It's not that, Nora."

Jack stiffened beneath me hearing the words through my phone.

"She broke up with me because she thinks I'm in love with you."

I stopped breathing. Rob was on the other end of the line, waiting to hear what I thought about him possibly loving me. Jack slid out from under me and walked around my room. He found his jeans and put them on. His anger flew from his eyes at me before he pulled his T-shirt over his head.

"Rob, I have to go."

"I want to see you."

"I'll call you back."

"Nora, I'm—"

I hung up on Rob and sat up in my bed.

Jack was completely dressed and staring at me.

"What are you doing?" I didn't hide the desperation in my voice. I wouldn't ever hide from him again.

"I'm leaving."

"Why?" He was hurting me, and I'd let him. He could do whatever he wanted.

"Because I've had to watch you love him the entire summer. Because he's nowhere near good enough for you, but for some insane reason you want him." His voice was raising; the blood was rushing to his head and turning his cheeks a deep red. "Because even after last night, I could feel your heart race when he just told you that."

"Jack—"

"Did you ever think you only want him because you've never been able to have him? He's the safest choice."

"Jack. It's not like—"

"Then why did you tell him you'd call him back?"

I didn't know why. It was what I'd always done.

Jack walked out of my bedroom and took a piece of me with him. The last physical piece of my soul and it walked out the door with him.

I raced from the bed and found the dress I'd worn last night. It was still wet. I threw on my robe and followed him out the door of my apartment.

"Wait!"

He stopped and turned to me on my front walk.

"Don't go." I was shaking my head, pleading with him to stay, and he was as hard as stone standing in front of me. "Not like this."

"Nora, I—"

Rob beeped his horn and pulled into a space on the street in front of my house and jumped from the car. He was halted by the vision of Jack at my house and me in my robe.

"What the fuck?" He turned to Jack. "What are you doing here?"

"Nothing," Jack said, breaking my heart.

My head shook and my eyes never left him as he climbed on his motorcycle and rode away.

"I need to talk to you." Rob didn't care if he'd interrupted something. He didn't care where Jack was going. Rob only cared about himself. I was exhausted just by the sight of him. He stood in the center of my front walk, waving his arms high above his head. I exasperated him. "Nora, please."

"What?"

He was back at the center of attention. He smiled at me the way he did with everyone else he'd ever met. I wasn't special to Rob, I was part of his entourage, and I was fine with him leaving me there. "Calm down. I need to talk to you." He pulled me into my apartment and onto my corduroy couch. Rob sat down next to me. "Blaire and I broke up."

"I know," I said without an ounce of care.

He was annoyed I wasn't giving him the proper response to his opening act. "I'm in love with you." He was willing to jump right to the climax to get this show moving.

I no longer resisted the urge to talk to him like the child he was. I would dummy this down as far as I had to to get it over with. "I don't think you are, but let's just say that's true. That you're even capable of loving someone else. Why now? We've known each other for five years. Why, all of a sudden, do you love me?"

"It's not all of a sudden." I raised my eyebrows at his lie. "I mean, it's different now. I always loved you, but now I want to be with you."

"Why . . . now . . ."

"You're different this summer." He stood up and took two steps from me before turning around. "You're open. You're alive. Something's changed in you. I can't resist it."

I shook my head. "This is stupid. You're not in love with me."

"Is this because of Jack?"

I inhaled sharply and tried to hide the pain his name inflicted from my face. "No."

"Why the hell was he even here?"

"Because I wanted him here."

"So it is about Jack?"

"No! You're not hearing me, Rob. You don't love me. You don't love Blaire. You can't love anyone else. There's not enough room for another person because you only love yourself." I stung him with my words. Rob was expecting me to fling myself into his arms. "And that's okay. Really. It's only a problem if you continue to date these girls who think they have a chance of being the center of your world. There's only one center, and you're occupying it." I stood up and walked into my bedroom.

"Where are you going?"

"I have to go to work and then I need to find Jack."

Rob wasn't defeated. He was planning what was next. Who was next.

Twenty-Three

Listen Up

"I LOVE HIM."

"You love him?" Ricky repeated in disbelief.

"Completely and totally."

"Did you tell him?"

I shook my head and lowered my eyes in shame.

"How come you can tell me, but not him?"

I faced Ricky with the sad truth of all my relationships. "Because you can't hurt me with it."

Ricky put his arm around my shoulders, and I leaned into him, facing the windows of the cafeteria. "Oh, Nora. You're so stupid." He laughed a little and turned to me. "I saw the way he looked at you. He's incapable of hurting you."

"Then why did he leave?"

"Because you hurt him."

I shook my head in denial. "You don't understand."

"Don't I?" he challenged. "You're the only one who thinks love is hard to understand. It's the purest of emotions. It'll fill your soul and rip your heart out, but it's not hard to figure out." He sounded like Tank. He had the same sensibility.

I sighed and stared at the soggy pizza on my tray. Visiting my mother had opened up old wounds that now festered next to the one Tank had left me with. Why had he died? I still didn't even know how he'd died. It was looking like I'd never know. Our entire relationship had been designed to haunt me. The lump rose up in my throat, and I swallowed hard to bury it.

I sniffed. "I think I'll be fine living the rest of my life like this."

Ricky stared at me. The discomfort of his glare made me squirm in my seat, and then my eyes filled with tears because I knew this wasn't the way I was supposed to live. It wasn't the way Tank would want me to live.

"Don't cry. Don't cry. What do I do? Hug you?" He reached for my hand, but it made me cry harder. "Seriously, what will make this stop, Nora?" Ricky stood up from his chair in the cafeteria. He loudly cleared his throat and fell over, mimicking a tree falling in the woods. The one-hundred-plus people around us all froze and stared at us. I stopped crying.

THE HOUSE WAS empty except a few half shares. They were last for the showers, the back of the line because they'd only paid for every other weekend and holidays. I looked around my porch. Three months ago it had been this tiny, dark space that was stifling hot and void of any privacy. Now I realized it was a doorway to my soul that opened the minute I walked through it.

Mila and Stone, Tank and Jack . . . they wouldn't let me hide here no matter how defiantly I tried. They were living, and they were determined to take me with them. I inhaled the salt air deeply and plugged in the shell lights Jack had strung for me. He was more than I deserved.

The half shares laughed hysterically at something in the backyard. I remembered the last time I'd laughed that way. I'd been watching Tank fly across the sky. How could they find anything funny without him here?

They were two years younger than Tank, and somehow didn't feel they knew him intimately. I found that impossible. Everyone he'd breathed near knew him, but I didn't begrudge them the ability to smile and laugh. In fact, I found myself listening to it as if they were speaking Italian outside my porch window.

They'd said the rest of the house was at the Bottle & Cork, and that was where I needed to be. Jack was at the bar. The bouncer handed me back my ID and waved me in. Jack was drinking his beer and talking to Mila. He didn't appear drunk, or happy, or angry. He was just there. The way I'd been when he'd found me. The depth of the summer's loss flowed through me until it grounded my feet into the floor.

Life is deep. Dive in.

The band had just taken a break. They were still shuffling around the stage, placing their instruments in safe places. I climbed up on top of it and waited for a bouncer to haul me down and throw me out of the bar. When he didn't, I walked over to the lead singer and smiled the way I'd seen Mila do a thousand times over the summer. She used it to get ahead in line, a free beer, a slice of pizza, or just some space. I used it because I had some things I needed to say.

"Oh hey," the lead singer said and admired me. "What's up?"

"I was wondering if the mic's still on. I wanted to make a toast to the end of summer. Would that be okay?"

He studied me for a minute, looking me up and down. I stayed steady on my feet. I wasn't drunk and I wasn't crazy. Yet. "Fine by me, darling." He picked up the mic and handed it to me. "Wait one second while we get it turned on." He motioned behind me. "What's your name?"

"Nora. Nora Hargrove."

"Well, Nora, when you're done, I'll buy you a beer." He faced the crowd below us and announced, "Hey everyone, Nora Hargrove here would like to lead us in a toast to the end of the summer. So grab your drinks and listen up."

I considered the microphone in my hand. This was insane. "Thanks," I said, and the entire band left me alone on the stage with the live mic. "Hi . . . Dewey." I swallowed hard and saw Jack staring at me from the bar at the back of the room. "I just wanted to say a few words before the summer ends and we go back to our real lives." I swallowed. "Bear with me. I'm not a big sharer."

Mila whistled and walked to the side of the stage. She willed me to keep speaking just by the look of love in her eyes.

"It's been a summer of firsts for me, and maybe for some of you. This was my first time in Dewey, Delaware." The crowd erupted at the mention of our beloved town. I waited for them to quiet down. "I've never had a beach house before.

"Parts of this summer can be forgotten." I inhaled and reminded myself to exhale. "I fought the traffic on Route 1. I neglected to use the proper amount of sunscreen. I dialed 911, and declined my first offer of a ball gag . . . not on the same night." My new drunk friends liked this, too.

"There were moments though, that have changed me forever." I stared right at Jack. He wasn't moving, just watching me from the back of the crowd in utter shock. His T-shirt was tight on his shoulders. I closed my eyes and could see his naked chest beneath my face. "I learned the healing power of a good Bloody Mary and a dip in the Atlantic. I kayaked in the dead of night and witnessed the only shooting star I've ever seen."

I took a deep breath. "I fell in love on a bed made of pallets."

Someone in the crowd yelled, "Woo!" and I remembered

where I was.

"This summer I learned to fly . . . and to live . . . and to exist among the stars. Every day I spent in Dewey was the universe forcing me not to just witness life, but to revel in it." Mila's hands were clasped at her chest. "And I felt tremendous, heart-wrenching, life-altering loss that will forever leave a hole in my soul no one and nothing will ever fill."

Stone and Rob came up behind Mila. Stone put his arms around her shoulders, and she held him close behind her. I considered getting down, but it all needed to be said.

Jack pushed his way through the confused crowd and stood alone in front of the stage. I could have floated from it and landed at his feet, but I kept going.

"And in the midst of all that I found someone. Someone I could believe in. I trusted him more than I trust myself, and I gave to him something I've never shared with anyone before. Something I'd locked away because with each day I kept it, it became too inconceivable that I'd ever let it go." I stared at Jack. "I gave him my heart."

I watched as he exhaled. He calmed me with his presence. I was lost in Jack's eyes. I could have stayed there forever. The microphone in my hand was heavy. The bouncer moving beside me reminded me we weren't alone; we weren't locked away on our porch or in my apartment in Wilmington.

"And there's no better man to have it."

The guy behind Stone whistled, and Stone didn't punch him.

I reached down and took the beer from Stone's hand and held it high in the air. "So please join me and raise your glasses to the summer, to my summer as a full share."

Jack reached out his hand, but I couldn't move. Stone took his beer back, and my eyes never left Jack. When he smiled at me, I placed the mic on the floor and jumped into his arms. I straddled him and kissed him right in the middle of the dance floor at the

Bottle & Cork. I squeezed my arms around his neck and buried my face near his ear. I was done facing people.

Jack carried me through the cheering crowd and out the door.

I didn't move. I didn't say another word.

Strangers whistled and yelled as Jack walked down Route 1 with me hanging on the front of him. We stopped at a red light, and I still didn't move.

"What's up?" the guy waiting for traffic with us asked. I felt Jack shrug. He was maybe sixty years old and carrying a twelve pack of light beer. "Have a good one," he said when the light changed and we crossed the road.

Jack carried me to our house. He opened the door to the porch and climbed the steps inside without ever saying a word to me. He sat on my bed with me still clinging to the front of him.

"Nora." His voice was home, and sitting on top of him was the most wonderful place I'd ever been. "Nora." He ran his hands through my hair. I knew I had to speak. I wouldn't hide from him. Not anymore.

I lifted my head off his shoulder and faced him. "I love you," I said, and the confession left me naked on top of him.

"Nora—"

"Let me finish."

Jack half laughed, the way I loved it when he did. "Of course."

"I love you and no one else. I've loved you since the first day you walked in here. I trusted you and I wanted you." I choked up a little, but I wouldn't cry. "And I never told you, but I'm telling you now. You have to believe me, even if you don't want me."

"Nora—"

"I'm not done." He nodded in his cute way. I took a deep breath. "I know you didn't want to be my first because of exactly this, the dramatic clingy horror show of virgins, but even if I never see you again after today, I'm the luckiest person alive because it was you."

He kissed me. I let myself disappear inside him.

Well before I'd had enough, he pulled back. "Can I speak now?"

I nodded because I had no words left in me.

"I didn't think that *night* should have been your first, but there wasn't a second of doubt that I wanted it to be me."

I let myself believe every word he said. I somehow moved even closer to him, and I kissed him. It was a desperate need for him that wouldn't be satisfied. In my apartment, I'd believed in him. In this beach house, I believed in us. The memories of the rainy night in Wilmington overwhelmed me as I leaned him back on the bed he'd made for me.

Jack rolled us over and laid on top of me. "Only me. Forever."

Twenty-Four

May Peace Find You

JACK RANDALL

TANK WAS MY best friend. Since I could walk, he had my back, and now he was gone. He'd left me here with Nora. I felt like he'd picked her for me, or maybe he'd picked me for her. I only knew that it was right, and the two of us together had made perfect sense to him.

I'd tried to sound nonchalant when I'd first asked Tank about her. "Hey, what's up with you and Nora?" If he even so much as liked her, I'd have stayed away.

"She's looking for something very specific."

I laughed at him. Only Tank would describe her this way. Every other guy we knew would place her in a bangable/non-bangable category, but Tank never reduced anything to the basic level. "Did she tell you what specifically?"

Tank finished assembling the lasagna that I'd already told him was a bad dinner idea. It was too hot outside to turn on the oven. "She's the second strongest person I've ever met," he announced, and I was confused. She barely weighed a hundred pounds. "Nora carries a tremendous burden, and she does it completely alone. She's going to need someone even stronger than she is." He opened the oven and slid the pan in.

"I have no idea what you're talking about."

Tank stood up and faced me. "Have I told you you're the strongest person I've ever met?"

Tank's riddles only added to my growing obsession with her. After watching her moon over Rob for a few weeks, I'd sat next to him on the beach and asked him, "What the fuck is up with Nora and Rob?"

"They went to school together for four years." He was dismissive.

"She stares at him like he's God."

"He's a child and probably always will be. Strong women need stronger men."

"That's great. You should start a blog. Maybe something on YouTube."

"I don't get what the problem is." Tank stopped building the drip castle by my feet and looked at me like I was supposed to be doing something weeks ago that I'd neglected. "You've gotten every single girl you've ever wanted."

"I've never wanted one this much."

His expression changed from annoyance to fear. "Don't fuck her over." He pointed his finger at me. "Don't just want her because you haven't had her. She's been through a lot."

"Like what?"

"No idea, but you can hear it every time she stays silent."

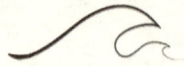

NORA WAS LYING on her bed, reading the Cromwells' novel, when I walked in. It was our bedroom. We'd shared it the last fifteen weekends. Two nights ago, I'd fallen asleep with her naked in my arms, and I didn't want to sleep a night without her ever again. I was dreading the thought of school starting. She'd have to quit her job and live with me, or we were both going to have to quit and live somewhere else, because I wasn't going to spend every weekday without her. Too much had already been lost.

Nora wiped her face with the back of her hand.

"Are you crying?" I could handle anything but her crying. It shredded me.

She sat up and placed the book in her lap. "The girlfriend did it. He was right. Tank was right." She stared sadly at the Cromwell Clan's book in her lap. "Do you mind if I take this with me?" As long as she took me, too, I didn't mind at all. "It's just I have nothing of him. My time was so short." I nodded, and she slipped the picture of the eight of us from the refrigerator inside the pages of the book. "I'm sorry for crying."

"Don't be sorry, but he'd say you were wasting time."

I'd imagined what I was going to do to her a thousand times. I pulled her hair into my fist and imagined her beneath me and on top of me. Nora being a virgin was never a part of the fantasy, and it had thrown me. Almost as much as losing Tank.

"How was Tank's mom?"

I'd asked her to come with me today. Mrs. Kragler should know the girl I was in love with, but Nora had thought this first visit I should go alone.

"I mean, how is she even surviving? Is she able to walk and talk? How could she have had him as her son and then lost him?" Nora began to cry again.

I laid down on the bed next to her and pulled her toward me. The seagulls squawked outside our window as if they had something that needed to be said. Some message they were delivering.

The complete despair in Mrs. Kragler's voice rang in my ears. At the funeral, she'd been stoic, but today, without the crowd surrounding her or the acts of the funeral, she'd been heartbroken. She was traumatized by Tank's death. From the minute I'd entered her kitchen, she'd stayed in motion. She'd fixed me a glass of iced tea and cut me a slice of cake she'd just baked. The house was full of food. She must not have stopped cooking since the day he'd left us. The only time she'd sat down was to show me the letter Nora had written her.

"Read this," she'd said and handed me the card. There was a single blue bird soaring above the gray ocean on the front. I had no idea what it was. There was a stack of cards next to an endless line of drooping flowers on her kitchen counter. I'd have thrown them all away, but Mrs. Kragler could never waste a thing, including flowers.

"What is it?" I took the card and ran my hand over the raised bird.

"A girl Thomas knew gave me a bag at the luncheon. This"—she grabbed Tank's Thomas the Tank beach towel from off the couch and carried it to the kitchen table—"was in the bag with the card." Mrs. Kragler wrapped her arms around the towel and held it close to her face the same way Nora had done the day we'd heard Tank died.

I forced myself to open the card.

Dear Mrs. Kragler,

I spent exactly twenty-four days with your son. Not even the time it takes to exhale in the course of an entire life, even one as tragically short as his. He's gone, and I have this undeniable urge to say something. If you knew me, you'd know that's an uncommon inclination. I rarely say a thing. I've spent the last few years observing life, rather than living it.

To Tank, this was a tremendous waste. He lived fully. Every second he was on this earth, he was present. He forced me to speak, and I told him things I'd never told anyone. He did it just by being himself. He taught me to laugh, to explore, and to believe in the world. With only a few words, he made me understand what I have and what others live without. He forced me to feel things, but now he's gone, and all I feel is empty. It's as if he taught me to love the ocean just in time to drown in it.

Your world without him is unfathomable. If in twenty-four days, he changed my entire life, yours must have been permanently swirling around the amazing aura of your son. His absence, I'm sure, is a thousand times harder to bear than what I'm feeling now. I can't imagine how you'll go on.

Tank had his own notion of the afterlife. It was insightful, and merciful, and full of wonder—like his ideas on most subjects. He believed that when we die, our soul returns to those who loved us while we were alive. That it fills in the holes left by our departure and heals our loved ones enough to survive until we see each other again.

Tank also believed that every person we meet is for a reason. I think he met me so I'd send this letter to you. I loved him very much, and I can't wait until I see him again. My heart goes out to you and your family.

May peace find you.

Nora Hargrove

Tears blurred my vision. I took a deep breath and tried to steady myself next to Tank's mom.

"At first I thought it was a joke. After all, I've read every Nora Hargrove novel ever written," Mrs. Kragler said. I couldn't help but laugh. Nora would have laughed, too. "But after I read the letter, I knew this was a different Nora. Do you know her?" I could only nod. "Well, she's lovely."

"She is," I said and finished my iced tea.

Nora turned in my arms and pulled my attention back from my visit with Tank's mom. "She's doing okay. She showed me the letter you wrote her."

Nora stiffened and sat up to face me. "Was she angry? Did I overstep?"

I shook my head. "No. No. I think it helped. She really appreciated it. It was kind."

"I just felt like she should know what he thought on some of those things. Life things, you know?"

"I do."

"Hey," Mila said and waltzed onto the porch like it was her room. "I want to do . . . something." Mila paused, and my mind flew from a cruise in Tank's honor to a poetry reading on the beach tonight. Mila's ideas could be anywhere and everywhere at the same time. She was torn apart by her own thoughts. "I feel like we need to do *something*. We can't just let him go."

"I know what you mean," Nora sat up and said. I stared at her, wondering if the words had come from someone else. I was used to her quietly letting everyone else speak, not contributing. Especially on a matter as sensitive as Tank. "I do. I feel like we should erect a statute in his honor or start a religion with the teachings of Tank. He can't be lost to the entire world." She really did love him as much as I did.

Mila reached over and pulled her into a hug. I wanted to hold her. I needed her to make me whole again, because Tank's soul had apparently not made its way back to me yet. All I wanted was Nora. Mila caressed Nora's hair, and I realized she loved her, too.

"I was thinking about a scholarship fund in his honor. Maybe something to do with science," Mila said causing me to shut down.

Who the fuck wants a scholarship set up in their honor?

I wasn't even sure Tank thought college was a worthwhile experience for people. He was so much more about learning from others as we *floated* through our existence. Mila should know that. I hid my disdain from my face. She was only trying to help.

"Maybe funding for children to receive swim lessons who

otherwise cannot access them."

Mila and I turned to Nora. It was perfect. Tank would have taken each and every person in the ocean one by one if he could. He'd spent the summer forcing us all to go in. He'd taken Nora in the middle of the night. Tank had some connection to it that was different than the rest of us, but that was true about everything with Tank. Not just the ocean.

"Tank equated swimming to flying for humans," Nora continued. "He said, 'It's the only time you can soar through time suspended above the earth.' He felt it was a tragedy some children would never get to feel what diving through the water is like." Nora took a deep breath and exhaled. She was taking my breath away.

"That's beautiful," Mila said, never taking her eyes off Nora.

"That was Tank. The only other idea I have is . . ." Her words trailed off. I couldn't imagine what she could possibly say that she feared might offend us. "Maybe something to do with mental illness." "Illness" was barely audible. She was the only person to ever suggest there was something wrong with Tank. Something more wrong with him than the rest of us. She was brave. She was as strong as Tank thought she was.

The shame washed over me. I could have done something different to make sure he was still with us, but no one had dismissed normal faster than Tank. I thought he was just different, and troubled, and brilliant, and *not* normal.

"But I think Tank's mom would find the most comfort in the swim lessons, and it's a great way to honor his teachings."

"It's brilliant," Mila said and hugged her again. Nora relaxed in her arms. Her expression turned from fear to acceptance as she closed her eyes. "Don't you think, Jack?" She released Nora and turned to me for my approval. It wasn't mine that mattered, though.

I nodded. "Tank would love it."

Mila left us alone on our porch, and I pulled Nora back down to me.

"I need you to quit your job and move to DC with me." I waited for a shocked expression, but Nora barely blinked.

"Done." She kissed me. I forgot it was broad daylight and we were lying together in a room of windows. "I need you to adopt a dog from the animal shelter."

She waited for my refusal, but all I wanted was her. If she came with three dogs, a cat, and a lion, that was how I'd take her. "Done."

"I love you," she said. The words fell from her lips without hesitation. She didn't pull away or stumble over the expression. She was mine. Forever.

Epilogue

IT WAS AS if Tank had given his life for mine. That he'd sacrificed whatever time he'd had left on the earth to force me to participate in the time I was here. Such an arrogant thought. That someone's death was to benefit another. That Tank could even impact the universe in such a way, but I blamed him for that, too. He'd made every person he'd laid eyes on the center of his world. The captain of their existence. He'd forced me to accept I had a place here the day he'd given up his, and I wasn't going to waste it.

MY SWEET ANGEL walked over and plopped down next to me. He ran his hand across the sand. I knew from every other thing he'd ever touched that he loved the way the granules felt on his fingertips. He was this tiny bit of joy the world had bestowed upon me. He was a part of me. In my mind every second of the day, stealing my heart from his father who I thought could never be displaced. Unbelievably, there was room for this little being, too.

He watched me as he stood and toddled across the sand in front of me, completely unaware that it was the middle of the night and not the height of the day. He reminded me of the other person I'd loved who'd had such an intense light within, but that light had been accompanied by darkness. This little one only knew peace. He was enamored with the world around him and truly kind. He was a gift.

"Mommy," he said and handed me the remnants of a broken shell he thought were still beautiful. He never differentiated the broken ones from the whole ones. They were all perfect in his mind, and he'd leave piles of them next to the leg of my beach chair every day we brought him here.

I'd been to the shore every summer since I'd met his father. I found myself among the crashing waves and scorching sunshine. For fifteen weeks, I'd been trapped in a too-small cottage with housemates who were larger than life. It saved me.

"Thank you," I said. My voice overflowed with love. I put the shell next to me on the blanket.

Jack laid on his back, staring at the black sky, believing the answers to all his questions resided there. "It's good there's no moon tonight," he said and kept looking up.

"It's going to be spectacular. I wish we could be out on the water, but I don't want to take him out until he's bigger."

"He shouldn't be in the ocean without a lifeguard." He raised his eyebrows at me. "And neither should you."

I rolled over and kissed the man who'd found me, lost and alone, some five years ago. "I love you for being here."

"I know." His words gave me a chill. He knew everything. I'd stopped wondering if he'd helped me find myself or just happened to be standing next to me when I'd made the discovery.

Jack was the foundation I'd built my life upon. He was more than I'd ever thought was possible, and now I had him and our son. "You're going to be amazed." He pointed to the sky. I looked up in time to see the last bits of a shooting star. "Ahh. It's starting."

"Come here," I said to my little shell hunter. "Come watch the falling stars."

Without any understanding of what I was talking about, he came over and snuggled between us. He cuddled close to me. I put my arm across him and touched Jack's stomach. I was a million miles away and right there all at the same time. I was a girl who knew no one, including herself, and found her voice in a chaotic mix of words spoken by strangers she'd come to love. I was a mother and a wife.

I was the luckiest girl in the world.

We waited in silence. My eyes searched the endless night, and I remembered the first shooting star I'd ever seen. At the time, I'd dulled myself down to no longer wanting a thing but to be left alone. Now, I wished for those in heaven to be patient and give us time together here on Earth and for the two guys lying next to me to stay with me forever. However long forever turned out to be.

"Ahh," I breathed as another star shot across the sky. "Aren't they pretty?"

They were both silent. I leaned up to see if they'd fallen asleep, but they were staring at the night sky, waiting for the show to continue.

I laid back down as three more stars shot across the night. The light met the darkness in the summer sky. It was a flash, and it was beautiful.

"I love you, Mommy."

I kissed his sweet little cheek. "I love you, too, Thomas."

Also by

Eliza Freed

The Devil's Playground
(Book One in the Faraway Series)

Former U.S. Attorney, Meredith Walsh, took some time off to raise her children. But the time took away everything she once trusted about herself. She's lost within the mundane confines of her children's schedules of lacrosse, soccer, Cub Scouts, and math facts. Desperate for a sliver of her former passion, and isolated in the small town her corporate husband relocated her to, she counsels herself on risking her family for the rush of a fling.

But Vincent Pratt, the local chief of police, weakens Meredith's abhorrence of affairs and her dedication to her family. With him, she finds a new version of herself, one capable of contributing in her new world, and thriving in her lonely home. In spite of the fact, she's not the kind of woman who has an affair.

Please see the next page for an excerpt of the stunning first installment of The Lost Souls Series.

Forgive Me

one

"My soul is forgotten, veiled by a boring complication"

MY FOOT WILL bleed soon. Judging by the familiar curve in the road, I'm still at least two miles from home. Of course I end up walking home the night I'm wearing great shoes. The pain shoots through my heel as the clouds flash with lightning in the dark sky.

Maybe I'm bleeding already. I mentally review the last few hours. Anything to distract me from the agony of each step. The texts, the endless stream of drunken texts, run through my mind.

We're soul mates. I roll my eyes. Brian deserves a nicer girl-friend; someone sweet like him. Someone who doesn't roll their eyes at this statement.

We belong together. Bleh.

What does it say about my relationship when the only thing I ever tell people about my boyfriend is, "He's a really nice guy"? And how, after two years of being apart, did I ever take him back? The last three weeks have felt like years, years I was asleep.

We're perfect together. My mother thought we were perfect. Hell, this whole town thought it.

No one is ever going to know you the way I do. He was watching me as I read this one and I had to work hard to keep a straight face. At the time I wasn't sure why, but here on this deserted road, in the middle of a thunderstorm Brian would never walk through, I know it's because he never knew me at all. Or my soul. It's not his fault. I'd nearly forgotten it myself.

I stop to adjust the strap on my sandals and two sets of eyes peer out from the ditch next to the road. They're low to the ground, watching me. I've always hated nocturnal animals.

"Anyone else come out to play in the storm?" I say to the other hidden night life. I move to the edge of the shoulder, facing the nonexistent traffic, and give my new friends some room. I wince as I step forward, and watch as a set of headlights shines on the road in front of me and the scene around me turns mystical. The steam rises off the pavement at least five feet high before disappearing into the blue tinted night. The rain only lasted twenty spectacular minutes, not long enough to cool the scorched earth.

I'm lost in it as the truck pulls up beside me, now driving on the wrong side of the road, and Jason Leer rolls down his window. I glance at him and turn to stare straight ahead, trying not to let the excruciating torture of each step show on my face.

"Hi, Annie," he says, and immediately pisses me off. I might look sweet in my new rose-colored shorts romper, but these wedges have me ready to commit murder.

"My name is Charlotte," I say without looking at him, and keep walking. The strap is an ax cutting my heel from my foot. *Why won't he call me Charlotte?* Of course the cowboy would show up. What this night needs is a steer wrestler to confound me further. The same two desires he always evokes in me surface now. Wanting to punch him, and wanting to climb on top of him.

"What the hell are you doing out here? Alone—" A guttural moan of thunder interrupts him, and I tilt my head to determine the origin, but it surrounds us. The clouds circle, blanketing us with darkness, but when the moon is visible it's bright enough to see in this blue-gray night. We're in the eye of the storm and there will never be a night like this again. *God I love a storm.* The crackling of the truck's tires on the road reminds me of my cohort.

"I'm not alone. You're here, irritating me as usual." I will not look at him. I can feel his smartass grin without even seeing him, the same way I can feel a chill slip across my skin. It's hot as hell out and Jason Leer is giving me the chills.

Lightning strikes, reaching the ground in the field just to our left, and I stop walking to watch it. Every minute of today brought me here. The mind-numbing dinner date with Brian Matlin, the conversation on the way to Michelle's party about how we should see other people, the repeated and *annoying* texts declaring his love, and the eleven beers and four shots I watched Brian pour down his throat, all brought me here.

"If you're trying to kill yourself by being struck by lightning, I could just hit you with my truck. It'll be faster," he says, stealing my eyes from the field. His arm rests out his truck window and it's enormous. He tilts his body toward the door and the width of his chest holds my gaze for a moment too long.

"Annie!"

I shake my head, freeing myself from him. "What? What do you want? I'm not afraid of a storm." I am, however, exhausted by this conversation.

I finally allow myself to look him in the eyes. They are dark tonight, like the slick, steamy road before me, and I shouldn't have looked.

"I want you." His voice is tranquil, as if he's talking the suicide jumper off the bridge. "I want you to get in the truck and I'll drive you home." Thunder growls in the distance and the lightning strikes to the left and right of the road at the same time. The storm surrounds us, but the rain was gone too soon. Leaving us with the suffocating heat that set the road on fire.

I close my eyes as my sandal cuts deeper into my foot, and Jason finally pulls away. My grandmother always said the heat brings out the crazy in people. It was ninety-seven degrees at 7 p.m. The humidity was unbearable. Too hot to eat. Too hot to laugh. The only thing you could do was talk about how miserably hot it was outside. By the time Brian and I arrived, most of the party had already been in the lake at some point. Even that didn't look refreshing. The sky unleashed, and Michelle kicked everyone out rather than let them destroy her house.

I stop walking, and shift my foot in the shoe. The strap is now sticking; I've probably already shed blood. Jason drives onto the right side of the road and stops the truck on the tiny shoulder. He turns on his hazard lights and gets out of the truck. *He's a hazard.* I plaster a smile on my face and begin walking again. As soon as he leaves I'm taking off these shoes and throwing them in the pepper field next to me.

Before I endure two steps, he's in front of me. He's as fast as I remember. Like lightning: always picked first for kickball in elementary school. His hair is the same thick, jet black as back then, too. The moonlight shines off it and I wonder where his cowboy hat is. He's too beautiful to piss me off as much as he does. He blocks my path, a concrete wall, and I stop just inches from him.

"I'm going to ask you one more time to get in the truck." A lightning strike hits the road near his truck and without flinching he looks back at me, waiting for my answer.

"Or what?" I challenge him with my words and my "I dare you" look on my face. He hoists me over his shoulder and walks back to the truck as if I'm a sweatshirt he grabbed as an afterthought before walking out the door.

"Put me down! I'm not some steer you can toss around," I yell, as I fist my hands and pound on his back. He's laughing and pissing me off even more. I pull his shirt up and start to reach for his underwear and Jason runs the last few steps to the truck.

"Do you ever behave?" he asks, and swings the truck door open. He drops me on the seat and leans in the truck between my legs. I push my hair out of my face, my chest still heaving with anger. "Why the hell are you walking alone on a country road, in a goddamned storm, this late at night?"

My stomach knots at his closeness and this angers me, too. Why can't Jason Leer bore me the way Brian Matlin does? Jason raises his eyebrows and tilts his head at the perfect angle to send a chill down my spine.

"Brian and I broke up tonight."

"And he made you walk home?" Shock is written all over his face. Brian would never make me walk home. He is the nicest of guys. Not great at holding his liquor, but nice.

"No." I roll my eyes, calling him an idiot, and he somehow leans in closer, making my stomach flip. "He proceeded to get drunk at Michelle Farrell's party and I drove him home so he didn't die." I think back to all the parties of the last six years, since Jason and I entered high school. Besides graduation, we were rarely in the same place. I've barely hung out with Jason Leer since eighth grade. At the start of high school everyone broke into groups, and this cowboy wasn't in mine.

"Why didn't you call someone for a ride?" He breaks my revelry.

"Because apparently when Brian gets drunk he texts a lot. My battery died after the fiftieth message professing his love for me."

"Poor guy."

"Poor guy? What about me? I'm the one who had to delete them, and drive him home. I thought he'd never pass out." I'm still mourning the time I lost with Brian's drunken mess.

"Why didn't you just take his car?"

"Because I left him passed out in it in his parents' driveway. I got him home safe, but I'm not going to carry him to bed."

At this Jason lowers his head and laughs. My irritation with him twists into annoyance at myself for telling him anything. For telling him everything. I want to punch him in his laughing mouth. His lips are perfect, though.

"It's not easy to love you, Annie."

"Yeah, well I've got fifty texts that claim otherwise. Judging from the fact you can't even get my name right, everything's probably hard for you." Jason leans on the dash and his jeans scrape against my maimed foot, causing my face to twist in pain. Before I can regain my composure, his eyes are on me. He moves back and holds my foot up near his face. He slips the strap off my heel and runs his thumb across the now broken and purple blister. I close my eyes, the sight of the wound amplifying the pain.

"My God, you are stubborn," he says, his eyes still on my foot. Thunder groans behind us and he straightens my leg, examining it in the glimmer of moonlight. I'm not angry anymore. One urge has silenced another, and awakened me in the process. He pulls my foot to him and kisses the inside of my ankle, and a chill runs from my leg to both breasts and settles in the back of my throat, stealing my breath.

I swallow hard. "Are all your first kisses on the inside of the ankle?" I ask. His hands grip my ankle harshly, but he's careful with my heel.

His eyes find mine as he drags his lips up my calf and kisses the inside of my knee. I shut up and shudder from a chill. There are no words. Only the beginning of a thought. *What if,* arises in my mind against the sound of the clicking of the hazard lights.

The lightning strikes again and unveils the darkness in his eyes. He lowers my leg and backs up, but I'm not ready to let him go. I grab his belt buckle and pull him toward me. Jason doesn't budge. He is an ox. His eyes bore into me and for a moment I think he hates me. He's holding a raging river behind a dam, and I'm recklessly breeching it.

With a hand gripping each shoulder he forces me back to the seat and hovers over me. Even in the darkness I can see the emptiness in his eyes and I can't leave it alone. He kisses me. He kisses me as if he's done it a hundred times before, and when his lips touch mine some animalistic need growls inside of me. He's like nothing I've ever known, and my body craves a hundred things all at once, every one of them him. With his tongue in my mouth, I tighten my arms around his thick neck and pull him closer, wanting to climb inside of him.

Jason pulls away, devastating me, until I realize there are flashing lights behind us. His eyes fixed on mine, he takes my hands from behind his head and pulls me upright before the state trooper steps out of his car and walks to our side of the truck.

"CHARLOTTE, HONEY, ARE you going to get up? I heard you come in late last night."

I roll over and put my head under the pillow. I don't want to get up. I don't want to tell my mom that I broke up with Brian . . . again.

"Is everything okay?" She's worried. I take a deep breath and sit up in bed. The sheet rubs against my heel and the pain reminds me of Jason Leer.

"I broke up with Brian last night."

"Oh no. I have to see his mother at Book Club on Wednesday."

"I can't marry him because you can't face his mother at Book Club."

"I'm not suggesting you marry him, just that you stop dating him if you're going to keep breaking his heart." My mom leaves my room. Her face is plagued with frustration mixed with disappointment. I climb out of bed and lumber to the bathroom. My green eyes sparkle in the mirror, hinting at our indelicate secret from last night. I wink at myself as if something exciting is about to happen. My long blond hair barely looks slept on. I think breaking up with Brian was good for me.

"JACK, SHE BROKE up with Brian again." I catch, as I enter the kitchen.

"Through with him, huh?" My father never seems to have an opinion on who I date as long as they treat me well. Brian certainly did that.

"Dad, he just didn't do it for me." Jason's eyes pierce my thoughts again, haunting me. The trooper sent us home and I left him in his truck without a word. There wasn't one to say.

"Do what? What did you expect him to do for you?" my mother spouts. She's not taking the news well.

"When he looks at me a certain way, I want to get chills," I start, surprised by how easily my needs are verbalized. "When he leans into me, I want my stomach to flip, and when he walks away I want to care if he comes back." My parents both watch me silently as if I'm reciting a poem at the second-grade music program. They are pondering me.

"What? Don't your stomachs flip when you're together? Ever?"

"Does your stomach flip when you look at me, Jack?" she asks.

"Only if I eat chili the same day," my dad says, and they both start laughing.

"Charlotte, I remember what it was like to be young. And your father did make my stomach flip, but I think you're too hard on Brian. He's a nice boy."

"Yeah yeah. He's nice." I butter my toast and move to sit next to my father at the table. *He is nice.* For some reason Brian's kindness frustrates me. He's a boring complication. "I ran into Jason Leer last night." *And he kissed the inside of my leg.* I smile ruefully.

My mother's eyebrows raise and I fear I've divulged too much. My father never looks up from the newspaper.

"Butch and Joanie's son?"

"That's the one." I try to sound nonchalant as a tiny chill runs down my neck.

"I haven't seen him since Joanie's funeral. Poor boy. She was lovely. Do you remember her?"

I nod my head and take a bite of the toast. "From Sunday school."

"Jack, do you remember Joanie Leer? Died of cancer about a year ago."

"I remember," my dad says, and appears to be ignoring us, but I know he's not. He always hears everything.

"If you don't want to be with Brian, that's fine, but please not a rodeo cowboy," my mother pleads, not missing a thing.

"I only said I saw him. What's wrong with a rodeo cowboy?"

"Nothing. For someone else's daughter. I really want you to marry someone with a job. Someone that can take care of you."

"Can't a cowboy do that?" *From what I've seen, he can take very good care of me.*

"Charlotte, please tell me you're not serious. They're always on the road. Their income's not steady. It's a very difficult life." My mother's stern warning is delivered while she fills the dishwasher, as if we're discussing a fairytale, a situation so absurd it barely warrants a discussion. She's still beautiful, even when she's lecturing me. "I know safe choices aren't attractive to the young, but believe me you do not belong in that world and he'd wither up and die in yours. Do not underestimate the power of safety in this crazy life."

"How do you know so much about rodeo cowboys?" I ask.

"Yeah, how do you know so much?" My dad asks. He stares at her over the newspaper.

"Is your stomach flipping?" She asks, and gives him her beautiful smile she's flashed to quell him my entire life.

"Yes," he says, and winks at her.

Forgive Me
Available Now

ELIZA FREED

ELIZA FREED GRADUATED from Rutgers University and returned to her hometown in rural South Jersey. Her mother encouraged her to take some time and find herself. After three months of searching, she began to bounce checks, her neighbors began to talk, and her mother told her to find a job.

She settled into corporate America, learning systems and practices and the bureaucracy that slows them. Eliza quickly discovered her creativity and gift for story telling as a corporate trainer and spent years perfecting her presentation skills and studying diversity. It was during this time she became an avid observer of the characters she met and the heartaches they endured. Her years of study taught her that laughter, even the completely inappropriate kind, was the key to survival.

She currently lives in New Jersey with her family and a misbehaving beagle named Odin. As an avid swimmer, if Eliza is not with her family and friends, she'd rather be underwater. While she enjoys many genres, she is, and always has been, a sucker for a love story . . . the more screwed up the better.

To keep up with all of Eliza's new releases and giveaways, sign up for her newsletter on her website.

www.elizafreed.com

ACKNOWLEDGMENTS

THE MORE BOOKS I write, the more people there are to thank. I consider myself lucky to acknowledge everyone below.

Thank you to the people of Dumont who shared their shore house with me. Don't look for yourselves in these pages. You're not in here, but you'll be in my heart forever. Party on, sweet friends.

To those who braved my first job with me. We drank our way through it. You had me at my best. I really did know it all back then. Now, I know very little.

A very special thank you to the group of friends who let me bounce ideas off them and send them early drafts. Marcia Carter, Michelle Mann, Maryann Morris, Michelle Ottaviano, and Tricia Steiner—this book would not exist without you. In some situations it's nice to be first, but instead of this beautiful package, they saw the homegrown cover concepts and poorly written paragraphs. They stopped their lives to help me figure out Nora's. It's not easy to receive random texts like, "Did you tell the first person you had sex with that you were a virgin?" If I were the captain of the team, I'd pick all of you first.

To Regina Holloway, who not only survived being my boss for a while, but is also a great friend.

To my editor Rhonda Helms, I'd like you to adopt me.

To my copyeditor Ashley, you are smarter than everyone else in the world.

To Christine and Nichole at Perfectly Publishable, thank you for making me look this good. And not dropping me as a client when I torture you with, "just one more change."

To Regina Wamba who created this incredible cover that I looked at every night before I went to sleep and every morning when I woke up for over a month because it absolutely enchants me.

To Theresa Heitter for taking me to Dewey in the first place. That town is almost as fun as you are.

And thank you to the readers and reviewers who take time to send me a message, write a review, and tell a friend. If it weren't for you, I'd be talking to myself. (more)

www.ingramcontent.com/pod-product-compliance
Lightning Source LLC
Chambersburg PA
CBHW021222250626
47155CB00008B/2901